ADVANCE PRAISE FOR
PHILIPPINE FEVER

"Filled with suspense, intrigue, humor and a dash of romance...will appeal to lovers of international espionage."
—Shirley Roe, *Allbooks Reviews*

"Enough mystery, sex, and violence for three novels...put me in mind of Barry Eisler's *Hard Rain*."
—Robert Fate, *Baby Shark*, Academy Award winner for *Dune* and *2010*.

"Characters so vivid and clearly drawn I could swear I'd met them."
—Toni Ann Johnson, Humanitas Prizes for *Crown Heights* and *Ruby Bridges*

"Complex, topical, and scarily believable."
—Sheila Lowe, *Handwriting of the Famous and Infamous*

"Well paced storytelling..."
—Norm Goldman, reviewer *BookPleasures*

"In Philippine Fever, Bruce Cook tells a riveting tale as contemporary as tomorrow's breaking dawn. Philippine Fever stands out as being among the most auspicious debuts in recent years. Bruce Cook is a major talent with whom the crime fiction world will soon need to reckon. Set against the often gritty backdrop of the modern day Philippines, Cook's novel deals with international smuggling, worldwide terrorism, homeland security, murder, intrigue, espionage, and more than a dash of romance. His Sam Haine creation is truly a winner. Philippine Fever is an action-packed story, and Sam Haine is the perfect mystery lead for our new millennium."
 —Kent Braithwaite, *The Wonderland Murders*

"Violence, and weapons, and sex...oh my!"
 —Dorothy

"Bruce Cook has written a wild, yet convincing ride of a crime novel set in the underbelly of modern day Manila, and peopled it with characters who stick long after the story ends. Cook needs to write another one—this cast should return. "
 —Kirk Russell, *Deadgame*

"We eagerly look forward to more in this series."
 —Kim Reis, *ArmchairInterviews.com*

PHILIPPINE FEVER

Bruce R. Cook

CAPITAL CRIME PRESS
FORT COLLINS, COLORADO

FIRST EDITION

Published in the United States by Capital Crime Press, Fort Collins, Colorado.

Library of Congress Catalog Card Number: 2005938851
ISBN-13: 9780977627677
ISBN-10: 0977627675

FIrst edition published August 2006
10 09 08 07 06   10 9 8 7 6 5 4 3 2 1

www.capitalcrimepress.com

DEDICATION

This book is for my family—
first for my wife Robin, who is always my earliest and most supportive reader, but especially for my son Troy for the books he is writing, and my son Erin-Bruce for the stories he would have told.

ACKNOWLEDGMENTS

I have had the tremendous good fortune to be part of the Santa Clarita Valley Mystery Writers. I especially want to thank Sheila Lowe, Robert Bealmear, Gwen Freeman, and Bobbie Cimo for their constant criticism—and I mean that in the best possible way. They have made me a much better writer.

one--

Harvey Tucker, 59, had died with his boots on—but nothing else. Two hundred and twenty-three out-of-shape pounds had twitched for about thirty seconds before coming to rest.

Dr. Chin, M.E., took another look at the visa photo. Harv's face, never much to look at, was now unrecognizable.

From the abrasions on his legs and chest, it appeared that he had been dragged by his ankles down a flight of stairs, face thumping on each tread. The broken nose and jaw, the fractures to the cranium, had all occurred post mortem.

None of them had done anything to improve his appearance.

Lying in a dumpster in ninety-degree heat for three days had caused the body to plump up like a ballpark frank. Visits by curious dogs, peckish rats, and an uncountable number of insect friends had left him almost unidentifiable.

Chin found the task of positive identification unpleasant, but rewarding; not every day yields a white male corpse in Manila. Even rarer was one with Taser prongs tangled in his pubic thatch.

The good doctor knew he would get a lot of mileage from this one at cocktail parties. Because he was ethnic Chinese, he was disliked by most of the Filipino doctors who worked for him, but they would all laugh dutifully as he related his findings. After all, he was the chief coroner.

He'd have to make as much of it as he could before Ol' Harv's peccadilloes surfaced in the papers.

two--

Sam leaned across the counter and pointed out the purchaser code to the very pretty Filipina clerk. "That stands for Bureau of Alcohol, Tobacco, Firearms, and Explosives, Homeland Security."

"Is this official business, sir?"

Sam wondered where this might be going. "Yes, I have an investigation in Manila."

The clerk looked at him for a long moment. "Let me make a call and see if I can upgrade your ticket for you. I don't think the flight would be—comfortable—for you in economy. And there are still a few seats open in business class."

She picked up a phone, half-turned away from Sam, and spoke in Tagalog.

The passengers behind Sam seemed resigned to the wait and offered no complaint. In fact, the elderly Filipina woman behind him offered a toothless grin and said, "All lines are the same—endless. But we will get to where we should be, by the grace of God."

Sam wasn't sure what to make of this, so he just smiled. She smiled back, revealing a furrowed tongue darting around her spotted gums.

He didn't like international travel all that much, but all the other agents working out of Los Angeles had families, so he was getting the short end again. Still, he thought it was better to be busy in the field, rather than be stuck behind an analyst's desk.

"Mr. Haine? I received clearance to upgrade your ticket—as a courtesy from Philippine Airlines to your government."

Sam teased out the meaning. "I'm sorry, miss. I can't accept favors or gifts from companies. You can see how that would compromise my ability to do my job. Let me pay the difference in ticket price myself. Perhaps I'll get reimbursed, if I'm lucky."

The clerk nodded, as if not sure she understood. She punched in the new ticket info, took two hundred dollars from Sam, and issued him a boarding pass.

During the three-and-a-half hour wait before departure, Sam scanned the Filipinos who were flying economy class on his flight. That line stretched across the lobby until it hit another airline counter, where it doubled back on itself.

Each passenger was taking a golf cart-sized load of assorted goods to the family back home. The luggage of choice was a large cardboard box, tied with string, which was opened for search, retied, and loaded on the luggage conveyor belt.

First-class passengers had a separate, considerably shorter, check-in line. They awaited boarding in a private club where the airline staff treated them with a degree of deference most often accorded rock stars. Sam viewed it all through the club door's porthole window while he stood outside nursing a beer.

Boarding the plane, Sam passed through the first-class cabin, where the seats reclined into beds, amid an air of calm. Situated between the haves and the have-nots was business class. He slid his six-foot frame into a seat of reasonable size.

He was in the last row of business class. Just beyond the partition a chorus of infants began their pre-flight howl as the cabin was pressurized for take off. Sam looked back, noting that seats in economy didn't recline more than two inches, engineered to squeeze the maximum number of Filipinos into an aircraft fuselage. Average-size Americans need not apply.

He checked his watch—five hours since he had left his house and the plane hadn't even started to taxi. Flight time plus a refueling stop in Hawaii would make it twenty-one hours before he could retrieve his luggage.

"Would you like a pillow and blanket, sir?"

"Thank you," said Sam, noting that the woman now serving him was the same one who had earlier upgraded his ticket. "Must make a long shift for you—first ticket collector, now flight attendant."

"Have a good flight." She flashed him a bright smile and moved on. Four hundred passengers didn't leave time for chitchat.

Glancing about, Sam realized his was the sole white face on the plane. In the row ahead, two Japanese businessmen wearing identical charcoal suits murmured together. He pulled a file folder from his briefcase and reviewed the case notes on Harvey Tucker and his Tasered testicles.

He needed to synchronize with the local homicide investigation as soon as possible. If suspects weren't found in the first three days, the search tended to drag on for weeks, losing momentum as new cases demanded the attention of a detective force spread too thin.

Branch Supervisor Ricci had given him a contact number for the lead detective handling the case: Raymond "Bogie" Lorenzano, Philippine National Bureau of Investigation. Sam wondered what kind of guy chose to call himself "Bogie."

three--

For the second time in the interrogation, Detective Bogie Lorenzano motioned for Detective Garcia to back off. He placed a stack of Polaroid photos on the table.

"Nothing you haven't seen before," Bogie said to the young Filipino seated there.

"I don't want to look at these!" said Chito, pushing away the Polaroids. The deal table was stained by the "accidental" nosebleeds of a thousand earlier interrogations.

Chito sat with his back straight against the chair, and Bogie thought he appeared prissy, almost girl-pretty in that way many slim, athletic, eighteen-year-old Filipinos can look. The heavy gold chain on his neck and multiple jeweled rings on his fingers revealed that he wasn't your average citizen of the republic.

Detective Garcia grabbed the back of Chito's neck and turned his boyish face toward the photos. "No one cares what you want. We found these a block from the club where you work."

Bogie touched Garcia's arm, motioning his partner to move away from Chito. He realized how tired he was of the way Garcia always tried to impress the higher-ups, making every move at high velocity.

Not for the first time, he thought Garcia might be doing speed. Bogie had never moved that fast, not even when he was twenty. And that was nineteen years ago. He reflected—again— that it was a long time until his pension kicked in.

Garcia, feathers ruffled, was smoothing the lines of his suit. Bogie noted the preening, as well as the hint of makeup.

Though Bogie's suits were well tailored, chain smoking left them with a stale scent and smudged by ash. He accessorized the ensemble with three days' worth of stubble and pouches under the eyes. Bogie reached over and picked up the top photo.

The picture showed a willowy, well-built Filipina wearing a sheer peignoir over a leather bustier. Bogie thought it could have been some boyfriend's keepsake photo— except the woman in the photo was also wearing a pig mask.

Bogie observed that Chito sucked back a small gasp. Garcia snorted his derision at Chito's reaction. Bogie put down the first Polaroid and picked up another.

"You take these pictures, Chito?"

The photo he was now holding showed the woman taking off the bustier, exposing her breasts. Obscuring the foreground was a man's arm covered with reddish-gold hair.

Bogie saw that even with the fan blowing on Chito, he was sweating profusely. Half moons of perspiration darkened the armpits of his spandex wife-beater.

"She doesn't do the kinky stuff any more!" Chito blurted.

"Looks like she still does, when the price is right," Garcia said, flipping over a picture showing part of a man's tattooed torso, his hand holding a whip. The woman was now nude except for the mask.

Bogie stared at Chito as he smoked his cigarette. He took a deep drag and let the smoke trickle from his mouth, never taking his eyes from the nervous boy.

"What's making you so unhappy, Chito? Could it be that you didn't see any of the money from this john?"

He turned over the next photo, making sure that Chito saw it. There were stripes of blood on the woman's back, and her arms were manacled above her head. The john was revealed to be a sixty-ish redneck wearing a cowboy hat.

Bogie watched Chito bite his own hand to keep from crying out. There was real pain in the young man's eyes— and that bothered Bogie. Pimps made a point of not being emotionally involved with their stable. He wondered what was going on.

"Where can we find her?" His voice was all business.

Chito fought back tears, tried to speak, but it was garbled.

Garcia lashed out, slapped him across the cheek. "Don't wanna hear 'I don't know'," said Garcia. Bogie gave Garcia a hard look, but Garcia smirked, and added, "A pimp always knows where his top whore is."

Chito tried to push away from the table, but Bogie blocked the chair with his foot. "Even a stupid pimp like you," said Bogie.

"I'm not her pimp! She's my sister!"

Garcia held up the photo and pointed to the porcine mask. "So? You and Miss Piggy are relatives?"

"She's an entertainer, not a whore!" said Chito. "I'm her manager."

"If you're her manager, I think your client has a problem," said Garcia. Bogie saw that Garcia was on a roll and let him carry on.

"Your Miss Piggy hooked a Taser to this fella's pee-pee. Not only did this cause premature ejaculation—which I suppose saved everybody a lot of valuable time—but it also triggered a premature coronary." Garcia smacked Chito again. This time harder. "You're *gonna* tell us where the suspect is."

Bogie thought that Chito's confusion was genuine when he stammered, "Suspect? What do you mean?"

Garcia drew his arm back to belt Chito again, but Bogie stopped him with a look and stubbed out his cigarette. He lit another before breaking the long moment of silence that he'd created. He spoke slowly, patiently to the boy.

"The *kano* in the picture ended up assuming room temperature, Chito. In a dumpster behind a certain night spot—Club de Sex. And since that club is owned by your 'sister,' you can see how she might be considered a suspect."

Chito processed that for several moments, and took a new tack.

"You can't charge Olivia with murder," he said. "You can't tell for *sure* who the woman is in that picture. I made a mistake. It's just someone wearing a mask."

Garcia leaned in close, ready to deliver another smack. Again, Bogie caught his eye and stopped him.

Chito saw Bogie's signal, and it gave him enough juice to take the offensive. "And if *I'm* not a suspect, you don't even have the right to be questioning me!"

"Since you are also part owner of the club where the body was found, it just makes us wonder," said Bogie. To himself he thought, *How similar all these interrogations have become.*

"Wonder what?" said Chito. "About who?"

The detectives exchanged a look.

"All right," said Bogie, "since this *mystery* lady—the one with lash marks all over her back—is unknown to you, we'll leak these pictures to one of the tabloids. Maybe some public-minded citizen will be able to identify her."

Chito shrank in on himself.

Bogie gestured for Garcia to take Chito back to the holding tank. "Meanwhile, we'll detain you for another seventy-two hours," said Bogie. "Just in case your memory improves."

Garcia levered Chito out of the chair, jacking his arm high up behind his back. "Hey Chito," Garcia whispered from behind Chito's head, "I hear romance blossoms overnight in these tiny cells. Yeah, good-looking kid like you oughta make some close friends."

As Chito was frog-marched from the room, he looked back over his shoulder, his face distorted by rage and fear. "Don't put those pictures in the paper!" he screamed at Bogie, saliva spraying.

After they left, Bogie sorted through the photos and pocketed the most salacious for himself. He picked out two others, inspecting the background in one of them, rather than the people. The second one he held close as he examined the woman's back with care, spotting a small mole among the weals.

These should do.

four--

PHILIPPINE INSTITUTE OF VOLCANOLOGY AND SEISMOL-OGY—Part of the Pacific "ring of fire," the Philippines has fifteen active volcanoes. The volcanoes are the underlying reason for the large number of seismic events throughout the islands. There are 453 quakes of magnitude 3.5 or higher per annum, i.e., more than one per day.

With the exception of the immediate vicinity of Pinatubo, the likelihood of being affected by seismic activity is quite small in any particular location.

MNL AIRPORT TERMINAL—6:40 A.M. SUNDAY

Fifteen hours of flight, five movies, three meals, and about forty minutes of fitful sleep later, the wheels hit the tarmac in Manila. The in-flight personnel looked considerably less perky now.

As Sam deplaned, the temperature was already seventy-five outside, humidity hovering between ninety-nine and one hundred. Through the thick airport windows he saw that a July monsoon was about to deluge the streets.

As he pushed his way through the muggy heat, making his way toward Customs, he noticed a lone white woman. She seemed to float across the lobby, her complexion stark against the sea of brown skin.

The image made him think of Christy, and he remembered how she had liked to quote a favorite poet: "The apparition of these faces in the crowd—petals on a wet black bough." *How did she always remember just the right phrase?*

Flashes of a dream he had on the plane came back to him, glimpses of Christy, her features hollowed out by pain. *What brought that back?* He suppressed those memories and focused on the task ahead.

Sam expected someone to meet him and help him clear Customs, but no one showed. During the next half hour, he watched the hash of broken cardboard boxes, clothing, food, and bric-a-brac as it tumbled from the cargo chute in Manila, promising hours of entertainment for all concerned.

After forty-five minutes, he made his way to Immigration Control, wondering whom he could pay to stamp his paperwork before he fell asleep on his feet.

An impossibly thin man with bad teeth scooped Sam's luggage into his cab. "Where are you going, sir?"

"Makati. Galleria Suites," said Sam. "The sooner the better." It had taken him close to two hours to retrieve his luggage and clear Customs. His service weapon had been the cause of much discussion and numerous phone calls to the US Embassy, even though his paperwork was in order.

The car pulled away from the curb, traveled a few blocks, and came to a halt. Traffic was already gridlocked on Epifania de los Santos Avenue. The driver edged over a couple of lanes by means of vigorous hand gestures, steering the taxi into crevices between the vehicles.

They crept along, the air conditioner doing its best. Ragged children came to tap on the windows of the car, offering small bouquets or packs of gum for sale. Sam waved them off, but the promise implicit in a white face kept bringing fresh kids to the window.

The driver snarled at the kids through the closed window. "Get away from the car!" He cleared his expression and smiled at Sam in the mirror. "Just ignore them, sir. They will get tired soon."

Sam nodded and stared ahead at the endless stream of cars. "How long till we get to the hotel?"

"Perhaps one and a half or two hours, sir. It is rush hour, as you can see."

"How far is it?"

"About six kilometers, sir."

"That's less than four miles. I could walk there faster."

The taxi driver gave a polite laugh. "But it is so hot outside, sir. And it will rain soon." He paused to suck on a decaying front tooth. "If everyone just walked, there would be no need for a taxi service, and so how would the families of taxi drivers eat?" He gave Sam a discolored grin.

Sam decided to make better use of his time. He pulled the contact numbers from his briefcase and tried calling on his cell phone. After a long hissy wait, a pre-recorded voice told him that service was not available in this area.

Next he dialed his supervisor at ATF in Los Angeles, but international dialing didn't work, either. He checked the battery level. OK.

"I was told in the US that my cell phone would be compatible with the system here," said Sam to the cabby. "Are we in a dead spot, just bad reception?"

"No, the reception is quite good along this avenue. Many visitors from around the world have made that same complaint, sir," said the cabby. "I am thinking your phone company has deceived you." He glanced out the side window. "Wait one moment, sir."

The driver had spotted a break in the traffic on the other side of the boulevard. He zipped across the median, narrowly avoiding a legless mendicant. As the oncoming traffic neared, he nudged up onto the divider and motioned for another driver to let him back onto the correct side.

The taxi had gained five car lengths.

Using the rearview mirror, the driver gave Sam a snaggle-toothed smile of victory. "I am doing my best to get you there as soon as possible, sir."

Sam gave him a thumbs up, and settled back in his seat. They moved into a shaded stretch of the street, and he saw a narrow storefront bar, with an animated neon sculpture of a topless dancer sliding up and down a pole. He checked the name of the club, but it was something he couldn't pronounce.

"Do you know the Club de Sex?" said Sam.

"Of course, sir. It is bodacious popular. Do you want to go there now, instead of your hotel?"

"No, I need to check in, and after that I have an appointment. I just wondered if it was in this part of town."

"It is back near Pasay, sir. But don't worry, there are other gentlemen's clubs and karaoke bars near your hotel."

"So the gentlemen's clubs are not together in the same area?"

"There are many such areas all around Manila and Quezon City. Wherever there used to be US military buildings."

Sam thought perhaps he could catch a nap. As he rolled his neck he saw a beggar family on the divider. Two small naked children played with some road litter while the mother watched. A limp infant lay across the lap of the father. It looked dead to Sam.

"Look at that baby," he told the driver.

"It's nothing, sir. They are here every day, begging." The driver put a twist on the last word to indicate that he was far above such things. "We are a poor country, sir. But growing fast. Some of the peasants cannot keep up."

Sam reached for his wallet, feeling that a dollar might reduce their misery, at least for the morning. As he moved to roll down the window, the driver looked at him with reproach in the rearview mirror.

"It will just encourage them, sir," said the driver. "They should leave the city, go back to their village."

Sam hesitated, leaned back again, and closed his eyes. The car moved by fits and starts, but not too roughly. He lapsed into a semi-conscious state—twenty-six hours of travel, a fifteen-hour time difference, and lack of breakfast were taking their toll.

The car made an awkward lurch, and the jolt wakened Sam. Rain drummed on the roof of the cab as he struggled back toward awareness.

"Did we hit a pothole?" Sam pawed at his eyes with the back of his hand. *How long have I been out?*

The driver shrugged his shoulders.

"No. I think it was just a small earth tremble, sir." In the mirror the driver smiled and gestured out the window. "We are in Makati now. Almost there."

High-rise office towers surrounded them. Several new buildings were under construction. A crane moved steel girders into place at one site.

Across the street, a twenty-story scaffold made of bamboo rose from street level to the top of a steel structure. Like a line of ants, workmen climbed the stairs of the scaffolding, each with a concrete block in either hand.

On the street itself a group of laborers sat on the curb hunched over their morning bowls of rice, trying to keep the rain off their meals, while crowds of office workers scurried around them, the men wearing suits or white shirts with ties, the women in dresses.

Sam noted the contrast between the laborers and the office workers, the latter being well-groomed, well-fed, and healthy, moving purposefully toward their respective offices. The laborers moved just fast enough not to be fired.

The cab pulled into the semicircular drive of the Makati Galleria Hotel. A dozen uniformed doormen, valets, and bellhops waited beneath the entry awning. A doorman assisted Sam from the car, and retrieved his luggage from the trunk. While Sam paid the driver (and over-tipped him), the bellhop moved his luggage to the front desk.

As Sam checked in he asked, "I'd like a wake-up call in two hours, please."

"Of course, sir."

The small army of uniformed hotel workers reminded him of a Hollywood musical in the thirties. Maybe he was being cynical, but a nice thing about third world countries was the availability of cheap labor to provide superb levels of service. As long as there were five-star hotels, the international traveler could find a haven.

An attendant ushered Sam into the elevator. Two more attendants greeted him warmly when he got off at the twenty-fifth floor. His bellhop followed with the luggage and unlocked his suite for him. Sam tipped him to get rid of him and collapsed on the bed.

He noted, before falling asleep, that the TV was on—a view of a small aquarium, tropical fish milling about. It reminded him of the crowds of Filipinos thronging the streets.

He wondered vaguely about the quality of cable television programming in Manila. Very vaguely.

five--

CIA *Factbook—Republic of the Philippines (RP)*
Population 85 million; 85% Catholic, 9% Protestant, 6% Muslim. More than eighty dialects in five major language groups, several of which are spoken on each of the larger islands.
Situated near China, Indonesia, Malaysia, and mainland Southeast Asia. Capital city of Quezon has merged into Metro Manila, population 8 million.
Largest export is Filipinos, who work as servants throughout the world. Filipino émigrés provide the largest source of foreign currency trade balance.

NATIONAL BUREAU OF INVESTIGATION (NBI)—NOON SUNDAY

Bogie hunched over an ancient manual typewriter, pecked out "Interrogation Report" in Tagalog, and obscured it with a cloud of smoke. He thought a bit, hit the carriage return and typed rapidly.

He was a skilled typist and knew what he wanted to say. There were infrequent momentary pauses as he worked, most often to tap his cigarette into the overflowing ashtray.

The office door burst open and Garcia hustled inside. Bogie looked up in annoyance, but didn't get time to complain.

"Captain's on his way to see you," said Garcia. "I always knew you'd piss him off sooner or later." He cut his eyes away from Bogie. "Mind if I ask for your office?"

Before Bogie had a chance to answer, Captain Velasquez pushed through the doorway, using his well-developed gut as a battering ram to sweep Garcia aside. Bogie knew Velasquez expected things to be done his way and that he didn't suffer fools or smartasses.

He also knew that in Velasquez's book he qualified as at least one of the above. The captain glared at the report still in Bogie's typewriter.

"That was supposed to be on my desk at eight this morning," said Velasquez.

"So get me something newer than this steam-powered typewriter and—" said Bogie.

Velasquez cut him off. "It can wait. This *kano* investigation is more important than we thought," said Velasquez. "You're getting some extra help."

"I already have Garcia," said Bogie without enthusiasm. "And he's plenty."

Velasquez covertly motioned him to silence and removed his bulk from the doorway, letting Sam squeeze inside.

Sam stopped and regarded Bogie through fatigue-fogged eyes, as if looking down from some great distance. The cramped office and decrepit typewriter appeared to confirm his worst prejudices about the Republic's police.

Velasquez made the introduction. "Detective Bogie, this is ATF agent Sam Haine from Los Angeles. You'll be working together on this case."

Bogie controlled his exasperation with difficulty. He ignored the American, glaring at the captain. "I don't need help."

"I'm also pairing Saddul with Garcia, under your lead." Velasquez ignored Bogie's attitude. "There's new info, so it's a new deal. The *kano* didn't get killed because he got his rocks off in the wrong place. Turns out he was here buying AK-47s for the—" He paused to look at Sam. "What is it? The Freemen's Militia?"

Sam took over. "Paramilitary group in Texas. I've been tracking Tucker's buys for eighteen months. I thought this Manila trip of his was going to break the case."

Bogie continued to show no enthusiasm.

Sam made the first move, reaching across Bogie's desk,

proffering his hand. "Pleased to meet you—" He glanced at the nameplate on the desk. "Mr. Lorenzano."

Though Bogie couldn't refuse the handshake being offered, he replied stiffly, "Detective Lorenzano."

In the background, Garcia snickered. "But his friends call him Bogie."

Velasquez scorched Garcia with a look that indicated he should have kept his mouth shut. The captain ripped the unfinished report from Bogie's typewriter and handed it to Garcia, motioning him to follow.

"I'll let you finish this report—since you seem to be at leisure."

A reluctant Garcia followed Velasquez from the room.

Sam and Bogie stared, sizing each other up.

"You just made detective?" asked Sam.

Bogie shook his head in the negative. "In this country it's considered polite to address someone by his title." Bogie could see the American was too tired to care.

Sam dismissed his gaffe with a shrug as if to say *I must have missed that at the political correctness seminar.* He looked around for a chair, saw there wasn't one, and settled on a two-drawer file cabinet instead.

"Tucker was here to pay for a cargo container full of weapons—automatic rifles, rocket-propelled grenades, maybe some satchel mines. We wanted to track him to the pick-up point in the US and see how he was getting them past Customs. We figured we could squeeze the ship's captain to trace back to the point of origination—threaten him with the loss of his license. But with Harvey dead, we need to follow those guns from the point of payment here in Manila."

Sam opened a sleek black briefcase and pulled out the files on Tucker.

"I brought all my background info on Tucker. It includes records of phone calls made to the Philippines over the last three months, plus all his calls in the week before he flew here."

Bogie sighed and held out his hand.

"Let me see the phone records. Maybe we can catch a break."

Sam watched for a quarter of an hour as Bogie sorted all the Philippine numbers into regions. The bulk of them were in Metro Manila, a few in Subic, and one number that had been called several times was in Pampanga. Meanwhile he sifted through Tucker's US calls.

Sam was sick of the stale air in Bogie's windowless cubicle. He wanted to get outside, be in motion, make things happen. He chewed on the edge of the cardboard coffee cup while going through Tucker's phone bill, putting names to the numbers he recognized, checking others against a list of known associates, until just two remained unidentified. He looked over at Bogie.

"I know it's Sunday, but do you think we can call these Philippine numbers, find out what they know about Tucker?"

Bogie looked at the lists.

"I'll give this batch of Metro Manila numbers to Saddul and Garcia. I'll take the Subic and Pampanga bunch." He glanced over at Sam's annotations on the US call log. "Anything of interest there?"

Sam pointed to half a dozen items.

"These numbers are in Texas, where the Freemen's Militia is based. The ones I checked off are all hard-core survivalists, and they definitely won't say anything over the phone that will be helpful." He pointed to the two starred numbers. "If it's all right, I'd like to try these two from your phone. My cell doesn't seem to be compatible with the system here."

Bogie punched a button on the phone base. "This connects to an outside line." He pushed the handset toward Sam. "While you call those two, I'll check on my guys, and call the Pampanga number."

Sam dialed the first number, watching Bogie head for the

office next door. A few moments later a recording came on to tell him that the number was no longer in service. He notated his log and dialed the remaining number.

After the eighth ring an angry, quavering voice answered.

"Do you know what time it is?" Apparently this was a rhetorical question. "I'll tell you what time it is. It's nine-thirty in the pee em and decent folk don't call a good Christian widda at that hour. It sets people to talkin'..."

"I'm sorry; I'm calling from the Philippines—"

"The Philistines?! Is this about my boy Harvey? What else did that jackass do? If my Cornelius was still alive he'd have whupped that boy's butt to Abilene and back again. Damn Philistines! I'm not surprised God told Moses to smite 'em. I don't want no Philistino grandkids."

Sam tried to stem the flow. He surmised that he had reached the dead man's mother, and wished he were better at speaking to someone who had just lost her child.

"Mrs. Tucker, I'm Sam Haine from Homeland Security—"

"So how in Sam Hill'd you get this number? I ain't listed on purpose, so's I won't have no salesman calling me at all hours, just when I had my hair up in rollers—"

"I'm not a salesman—"

"You got that right. I don't need no ee-lec-tronical security dee-vice. I got me a German shepherd name of Chief and he's one hunnerd and seventeen pounds of mean, take a bite outta your backside so fast—"

"Mrs. Tucker, I am so sorry to intrude on you. I know this has to be a difficult time for you. I'm investigating your son's death."

Sam heard the woman begin to cry, and he waited for her to pause, remembering all the stupid, empty things people had said to him about Christy. With an effort he jerked himself back to the present.

"We're trying to find out what happened to your son during the last few days."

"I never thought I'd live to see my baby boy burr-ied. I'm eighty-two years old and now all I got left is my little girl." She made gulping noises.

Sam knew she would hear nothing else he had to say. She was lost in her memories.

"Sone-ja's flying halfway round the world to pick up his body, bring Harvey back home, and lay him to rest next to my Cornelius—"

Her voice dissolved into muffled sobs and the line disconnected.

Sam hung up, wishing he could take back the last five minutes. A moment later it came to him: *Why is the sister coming to pick up the body? Why not just arrange for it to be shipped?*

Bogie came back in the office.

"Bull's-eye on that number in Pampanga. Turns out Tucker had a Filipina wife. She didn't answer, but we pulled the address from the phone company." He looked at Sam. "Get anything helpful from Texas?"

"That was his mother's number. Sounds like she's in her eighties, and starting to lose it. Although it could just be the reaction to news of her son's death." Sam replayed the conversation in his mind. "From something she said, I think we might find that Mr. Tucker had not only a wife, but children as well. Any word about how his family in the US reacted when they first heard about it?"

"Garcia called the US Embassy," said Bogie. "They told him Tucker had a sister, mother, and an ex-wife. The assistant ambassador made the next-of-kin call, said the sister seemed disturbed, the ex-wife just sounded relieved. The mother was distraught, but that's what you'd expect."

"The mother said something a bit strange. She told me the sister is coming to claim the body."

"That's a long trip to make, with nothing good at the end of it," said Bogie.

"Yeah."

"We'll grab a snack, get a van from the motor pool, and head out to Pampanga. You and I can interview the wife, Saddul and Garcia will canvass the neighborhood for impressions about Harvey."

DIRTY HARRY'S BAR AND GRILL—2:00 P.M. SUNDAY

The cop's hangout was smoky, humid, and dim. The large paddle-bladed fan sluggishly turned the air over, but it didn't smell any better on the other side. In one corner, several off-duty uniformed cops played foozball. A ghetto blaster blared forth a distorted version of "Magic Carpet Ride" while two busboys cleared a table.

A flamingly gay bartender poured four beers into glasses with a flamboyant flourish. A sleek waitress, who looked about fourteen, hoisted the tray of drinks and brought it to the table where Bogie, Sam, Garcia, and the cop named Saddul sat eating *meryenda*.

Sam noted that both the bartender and the waitress gave Bogie appraising glances. Bogie seemed unaware of the attention.

A stifled sneeze turned Sam's attention to Saddul, who appeared to be suffering from a terminal cold, coughing and honking with clocklike regularity. He kept stuffing the used tissues into his coat pocket.

Sam watched the other three while he worked on his bag of chips. Shop talk was on hold, even though large photos of the crime scene covered the table. There was a full-face photo of Harv Tucker, the Polaroids from Chito's interrogation, a blow-up of some betting stubs, and a posed portrait of Harv in full camouflage gear standing beneath an entry sign to a ranch named "Freemen's Fortress."

Garcia ignored the pictures and addressed his Filipino colleagues. "So we just got this new maid from the provinces, and my uncle is having a big dinner party and he asks her to bring him a glass of water."

The waitress put the beers on the table, smiling briefly in response to Sam's "Thanks."

Garcia took a gulp from his glass and continued his story. "Fifteen minutes goes by and no sign of the maid, and I can tell Tito's getting thirstier and angrier by the second. Finally he sends another maid to find out what happened to the first maid. And she comes back and tells him that the new girl's still at the gate, waiting to let in his father."

The other two Filipino detectives burst out laughing. Sam stared at them in puzzlement. He sipped his beer thoughtfully.

"I've got another one," said Saddul. He paused to wipe his nose on a tissue. "My parents' new maid is from—"

Sam broke in. "Guys, I don't mean to be rude, but I don't get it. That's the fifth 'new maid' joke, and I didn't laugh at a single one of them."

The Filipinos looked at him blankly. After a pause Bogie replied, "These aren't jokes. They really happened."

"Really happened?"

Garcia appeared to be offended, perhaps thinking that Sam was putting them down. "I suppose you just get a better quality of maid in America," he said, with some sarcasm.

Sam sat back against the booth. "I've never had a maid in my life. Not me, not my parents. In fact, no one I know personally."

The Filipinos looked at him warily. "Are you putting us on?" asked Saddul. "With the amount of money that ATF agents make?"

"Yeah, with all that money," said Sam. "I'll be lucky to retire and not be someone else's maid."

The Filipinos didn't look as if they believed him. They busied themselves with their food to cover the awkward moment. Sam watched them eating, decided to change the subject to something neutral.

"I thought this *meryenda* stuff was just a snack," he said.

Saddul finished a mound of rice. "This is just a snack." He coughed wetly behind his hand.

Sam let that sink in. *These guys really put away the carbs. Why don't they all look like sumo wrestlers?* He shook himself mentally, realized he was losing focus. He wanted to get back on task so he could finish and get some sleep.

"Maybe you guys do things differently here from the US," he said. "Seems like we ought to be looking for the woman."

Clearly Garcia didn't like rushing his food. He grumpily downed the rest of his plate, and fastidiously cleaned his face and hands with a moist towelette.

"We've got her pimp."

Sam flipped through the interrogation report. "I thought you had her brother."

Bogie lit a new cigarette off the half-inch stub hanging from his lip. "Brother as in 'Hey Joe, you wanna meet my sister'."

"And you arrested the pimp?"

"Of course not." Saddul waved off Sam's surprise. "We're only detaining him. She'll show up trying to post his bail and we'll tag her."

Sam looked at them quizzically and decided to ask the obvious. "Presumably Chito's got an alibi." Bogie nodded assent, and Sam continued. "Seems unlikely that the woman's the one who overpowered a man six feet two who weighed—" He stopped for moment to do some mental math. "A hundred eighty-five centimeter man who weighed a hundred kilos."

"Damn! Did you swallow a calculator?" said Saddul.

Sam looked at them all, holding for dramatic effect. "So who took the Polaroid pictures? Maybe the murderer?"

Though Bogie and Saddul remained still, Garcia couldn't hold his temper.

"Thank you, sir. We poor aborigines hadn't thought of that, sir."

Sam realized he needed to back off. "I'm sorry if that sounded condescending. We're all on the same side here." It looked like his apology had been accepted. "I know your focus has to be on the homicide, but for me that's just the means to find the arms dealer behind this."

Saddul and Garcia exchanged a glance, then both looked

at Bogie, so Sam directed his next question to the lead detective.

"You have any idea how we could track that?" said Sam.

Bogie gave his Filipino cohorts a look that Sam couldn't interpret.

"Why don't we ask your father?" Saddul said to Bogie. Sam thought he heard some hesitation in Saddul's voice.

Bogie shook his head.

"Is he in law enforcement, too?" said Sam.

Garcia snorted, quickly stifled it. "His father builds armored vehicles for private armies."

Bogie glared at Garcia and said, "Let me clarify that. He provides secure transport for wealthy families that need more protection than the government can provide."

"Let's give him a call," said Sam. "He might have heard something that closely related to his business."

"I don't think so," said Bogie. He pointedly glanced at his watch and signaled for the tab. The waiter handed the bill to Sam.

Sam looked at the check. "You want to know what each person's total is?"

The others stared at him blankly, so he just pulled out his wallet. They split the check four ways, without discussion of who had what.

On the way to the van, Garcia dropped back to speak to Sam on the side.

"Just a word for you," said Garcia. "Bogie's father usually won't take his phone calls. They haven't seen each other in a couple of years. Last time they talked I was there and it wasn't a happy reunion. Bogie thinks his dad sometimes crosses the line with the weaponry he provides his clients. And Mr. Lorenzano thinks the government has no right to hamper a citizen's ability to defend himself."

"But he still might know something about—" began Sam.

"And he also thinks most cops are corrupt—part of what citizens need protection from."

Sam looked hard at Garcia, trying to ascertain if he was being given some message.

"I see," he said.

But he didn't.

six--

MacArthur Highway, Northbound to Pampanga
—2:45 p.m. Sunday

Sam looked at his watch, still set to LA time, and realized he
was no longer capable of computing how many hours it had
been since he had slept. The highway was congested, the van's
AC had long ago lost its battle with the tropics, and *meryenda*
sat in his stomach like a year-old fruitcake.

He slumped down in his seat, put his head back, and let
the conversation of the detectives wash over him. He didn't
sleep exactly, but neither was he functionally conscious. He
saw nothing of the countryside that passed by the window,
understood nothing of the others' discussion.

When the van pulled to a stop outside a barrio of shanties,
most of them roofed with corrugated steel, Sam struggled
upright. He looked blearily to Bogie for instructions.

"Sam and I'll go talk to Tucker's widow," said Bogie to Saddul and Garcia. "Let's meet back here in an hour and a half."

Saddul pulled a handful of tissues from the box on the
dashboard and stuffed them into his pants pocket before

exiting the van. Garcia checked his appearance in the rearview mirror. Apparently refreshed by the view in the looking glass, Garcia got out and joined Saddul a few yards up the road. The two men sauntered into the maze of narrow passages between the shacks.

Bogie looked at Sam, who yawned and pinched the bridge of his nose.

"You going to be OK, Agent Haine? Do you want to just nap here in the van? I'll fill you in on whatever turns up."

Sam opened the sliding door and got out. "No. I'm game for it. I just need to get moving."

Bogie led the way, stopping to inquire several times, as he tried to locate the house of Tucker's wife. Sam followed woodenly, reviving as he walked. He looked around as they searched, marveling at the poverty of a city only fifty miles from the capital.

The lanes between homes were unpaved. Clearly the residents had neither electricity nor indoor plumbing, as evidenced by the occasional public hose pipe where children stood in line with motley assortments of containers to collect water.

Eventually they came to a wider lane, and on the other side of that Sam could see the houses were more substantial, some with electrical wires snaking over to their roofs. On the near side stood a small hut about fifteen feet by twenty, constructed of ridged fiberglass sheets for the walls, and palm frond thatching for the roof.

A naked, light-skinned toddler played in the dirt by the entry, sticking a twig into an anthill, drawing out the creatures, and inspecting them closely. A little girl of about six stood behind the child she was minding, glancing shyly at the two strangers who had come to her neighborhood.

Just inside the doorway stood a woman in her twenties, wearing a thin cotton housedress, washed to the point of colorlessness and shapelessness.

Suddenly it hit Sam. He touched Bogie's arm and stopped. Bogie turned to look at him inquiringly.

"This woman doesn't know Tucker's dead, does she?"

"No. We'll question her first, inform her after."

"I don't work homicide cases in the States, Detective. I've never had to deliver any news worse than to tell someone their brother or son or husband has been arrested."

Sam ran out of steam, not sure what else he wanted to say to Bogie.

Bogie looked in Sam's eyes. "This is the worst part of my job. Usually they already know. But if they don't, we need to find out what we can before the shock sets in." He paused. "Listen, if you don't want to do this, there's a bar across the street over there."

"No, this is my responsibility, too. Let's go."

They discovered that the woman spoke only the most rudimentary English, and Bogie switched to Tagalog. It turned out that wasn't her language either; she spoke Ilocano.

"I'm going to find a neighbor that can translate for us," said Bogie, and he headed for the next hut.

The woman gestured that Sam should come in out of the sun and he followed her, ducking through the low door into the dim interior. Once his eyes adjusted, he saw a small open cupboard where two pots and a small skillet sat next to a single knife and fork. The floor was hard-packed dirt.

A wall woven of grass divided off a section where the children slept. Incongruously, a nearly new Sealy Posture-Pedic mattress leaned against the wall, next to a meager sleeping pallet.

In an elevated niche was a small statue of the Virgin Mary. Next to it was an eight by ten photo of Harvey Tucker. The votive candle burning there could have been for either of them. Next to the candle, seeming like another religious icon, was a small cell phone.

Lucinda—they had been able to discern that was her name—followed Sam's gaze to Harvey's picture. She gave him a worried look, and tried to piece together a question.

"Harvey—trouble?"

"No, not exactly."

Clearly he had exceeded her vocabulary after "no."

"Harvey come—Pampanga—soonest."

"No, he won't," said Sam uncomfortably.

"Yes—soonest." She gazed reverently at Tucker's picture, and murmured to herself, "Soonest."

Bogie came into the house with three women entrained behind him. It looked to Sam that they might be Lucinda's cousins.

The youngest of the three had a newborn slung in a shawl across her chest. She immediately sat down on the edge of the bed, opened her blouse, and put the baby to her breast, where it suckled noisily, with an occasional pause to belch at a volume level entirely disproportionate to its size.

Once the adults were inside, several children gathered in the open doorway and peered curiously into the gloomy interior. Sam wasn't normally bothered by crowded conditions, but the air soon became stifling, and he felt the sweat trickling between his shoulder blades.

Bogie took in the shrine-like display of Tucker's picture and spotted the cell phone, just as Sam had. He turned to one of the women and spoke to her in Tagalog, asking about the phone.

The woman translated to Lucinda, who answered. Next the process reversed. Sam settled in for what looked to be a long afternoon.

After a few minutes the naked toddler from the doorway made his way into the room and came over to Sam. He grabbed Sam's leg with one hand, sucking his thumb reflectively, and staring at Sam, unblinking.

Sam looked back and thought he could see some of Tucker's features reflected there. Finally the little guy pulled his thumb from his mouth and said one word: "Papa?"

This brought gales of laughter from the assembled group, and Sam felt himself blushing. Bogie used the interruption to fill Sam in.

"Our guy would call her on this cell phone, give her a number, and she would dial that number to create a conference call," said Bogie. "Since the conversations were conducted in English, she says she doesn't know what they talked about."

Sam added, "And that way there's no record of who Harvey called—at least not on his US phone bill. I assume we can get the Philippine cellular company to give us past records of calls made from this phone."

Bogie nodded assent. Sam looked at the phone next to the candle.

"Does that make sense to you? How did the phone get charged when the battery went down?"

Bogie snapped a question to one of the women. She didn't bother to relay it to Lucinda. Just pointed to the bar across the street, and said something to Bogie.

"She recharges it every couple of days over there for five pesos," said Bogie.

Lucinda spoke and the room went quiet. The friend translated to Bogie, but Sam already knew she had figured it out. All eyes in the room focused on Bogie, and Sam could see his body tense up. He said one word in Tagalog: *"Patay."*

It needed no translation. Lucinda fell to her knees, her mouth wide open, but no sound came out. All the other women shrieked, crossed themselves, and knelt beside their friend. The immediate sense of loss and desolation swept the children into its vortex and they began to cry as well.

Sam thought he was going to suffocate. He pried the fingers of the bawling little boy from his pant leg, and moved to the door of the hut.

At the last moment he turned back to Lucinda and bent down to look her in the face.

"I'm sorry. For your loss."

He walked out, crossed the street, went into the bar, and ordered a whisky, hoping to blot out the hopeless look on Lucinda's face. Whatever crimes Harvey Tucker had committed, he had been the center of her world, the support of their little family.

She'll be lost without him.

He wondered if that same look was still in his own eyes.

seven--

It was nearing nine p.m. and Garcia drew the short straw, having to stay behind and collect whatever crumbs of evidence might be in Lucinda's *nipa* hut. Bogie, Saddul, and Sam began their weary nighttime drive back to Manila. Traffic crawled along the highway, so Saddul turned off and drove along a one-lane road toward a small village.

"I know a shortcut, guys."

"I've heard that before," said Bogie. "Just don't get us lost."

About a mile on the far side of the village the road appeared to dead end against a cement levee. Saddul set the hand brake, got out, and went to talk to an old man by the side of the road.

Sam wondered what anyone was doing by the roadside at this time of night, but figured it was just another mystery of the Philippines he'd never understand. Bogie was trying to get some sleep in the front seat and doing a grumpy job of it.

Saddul got back in and put the van in gear. He pulled into a narrow track and drove up the side of the levee.

"What are you up to?" said Sam.

"This levee is made out of the lahar that came from the Pinatubo volcano. It flowed down the valley, covered up some villages. The Philippine Army Engineers bulldozed it into a forty-foot-tall levee to divert any more of the stuff away from population centers. Turns out lahar makes a pretty good highway. Once we get on top, it's like a paved road. It'll cut off twenty miles of traffic."

Sam was a little anxious as the van chugged up the steep grade, but once they made the peak, the levee ran straight as an arrow, moonlight gleaming on its crest.

It was about as wide as a three-lane road, and Sam saw that enterprising villagers had set up small snack stands along the improvised highway. Sam was glad they had all closed for the night. He was sure that otherwise they would be stopping for midnight *meryenda*. They drove along for half an hour at about forty miles an hour.

"It's lucky the moon's so bright tonight," said Saddul.

"Makes it easy to drive fast," said Sam. He settled back, hoping to catch a nap.

At that moment the van lurched, and Sam sat up straight. He looked behind them, but didn't see any potholes.

"What was that?" asked Sam. The van lurched twice more.

"Earthquake," said Saddul.

Sam rolled down his window and looked over the edge of the levee. "How far to the highway?"

Saddul's voice had a worried edge to it. "I can see it just ahead."

Sam looked at the jungle forty feet below and found it uninviting. "We better get off before we're shaken off. It's either that or drive over the edge and down into the jungle."

Saddul stomped the accelerator and the van leapt forward.

"Hey! What's up?" said Bogie, coming to from a fitful doze.

The van pitched again before he got an answer, and a large crevasse opened along the right edge of the levee. Sam jabbed a finger to make sure Saddul saw it.

Saddul yelled something back, but his voice was lost in the roar of the lahar as it liquefied under the seismic action.

Sam saw the right edge of the makeshift road slide away into the jungle, leaving a narrowing strip on which, so far, they could still drive. Another lurch and new cracks appeared everywhere in the lahar surface.

Sam looked at the speedometer—a hundred and twenty kilometers per hour. But the surface was turning to mush, slowing them. The edge of the paved highway proper was no more than a hundred yards away, but the lahar road was slumping lower as the base of the levee vibrated to the frequency of the temblor, losing cohesion.

The next three seconds stretched interminably as Saddul fought to get the van to the firm foundation of the national highway. Sam shot a terrified glance behind and saw the entire road disappear in a dusty cloud.

Even after they made it onto the edge of the engineered roadway, Saddul drove the van screaming along the shoulder, trying to outrun the cloud of sand and ash. The drivers that were idling along in the traffic on the highway found themselves blind and immobile. Sam saw car after car's windshield wipers come on as the drivers struggled to regain sight of the road.

None of the three spoke for a good ten minutes as they sped along the shoulder. The adrenaline rush had cleared Saddul's sinuses, because he no longer was honking his nose every two minutes.

Sam said, "It's lucky I'm from California. If I weren't already used to earthquakes, I might have been frightened back there."

Bogie looked at Sam over the back of the seat. "You're telling me that you weren't scared?"

"Scared?" Sam gave a wan smile. "I hope you can get the stain out of the seat covers."

Sam sat back in his seat, still sweating, heart pounding. He wondered if the island itself were trying to tell him to back away from the Tucker case.

An hour later Saddul dropped Bogie and Sam at NBI and left to return the van to the motor pool. Bogie hailed a cab and Sam climbed in with him.

"The club where they found the body is open now," said Bogie. "We'll wrap up today's tasks there."

Sam wondered if the day would ever end. This time of night

traffic wasn't gridlocked, but it was still slow. Bogie and Sam sat sweating in the back seat of the taxi. Bogie lit up and Sam rolled down the window, hoping to let the smoke out.

Three beggar children saw the open window and worked their way toward the car. Sam quickly raised the window and turned to Bogie.

"Your desk nameplate says your first name's Raymond," said Sam. "Why Bogie?"

"I love American detective movies, especially those with Bogart."

"Got something in common," said Sam. "Not Bogart so much for me, though. I like my movies in color."

Bogie looked at him askance, and blew a stream of smoke. "Real detective films are in black and white."

Sam pointed out the window at the brilliantly lit hotels, restaurants, and nightclubs. "Yeah, but you're a real detective, and the real world you work in is in color."

"Didn't you see Bogart in *The Big Sleep*?"

"*The Big Sleep*?" said Sam. "That was Robert Mitchum."

"Not the remake. The original with Bogart. A film noir classic," said Bogie.

"Film noir?" Sam snorted. "They teach film criticism at the NBI academy?"

As the taxi came to a stop, an almost naked girl, no more than eight, tapped on the window, holding up a pack of gum. She looked wet, hungry, and tired.

Bogie waved her away, avoiding Sam's eyes.

"The real world's not color. It's all shades of gray. Wait till you see this club."

> *CIA FACTBOOK—RP POLITICAL SITUATION:* Communist insurgents on Luzon. Separatist Muslim movements on Mindoro and Mindanao, allied with radical Muslim movements throughout Asia, Middle East, and Africa. 99% of population landless, living in poverty.

KEY INSURGENT GROUPS

ABU SAYEF—founded by Osama bin Laden and still allied with Al Qaeda. Principal activity is kidnapping businessmen for ransom, putatively to fund a Muslim revolution.

MILF—Mindoro Independence Liberation Front. Mindoro is a local name for Filipino Muslims. Wants a separate country and a clerical state. Already has an autonomous region.

NPA—New Peoples Army. 8,000 troops act as the military wing of the National Democratic Front (NDF), a Maoist movement seeking to establish a socialist state. The political party has 80,000 members.

CLUB DE SEX—10:48 P.M. SUNDAY

A short line of club-goers waited behind a rope at the entry. Mega bass dance music assaulted Sam's eardrums as they neared the doorway. A video monitor over the entry showed an extreme close-up of the tip of a bright pink tongue. Rhythmically the tongue emerged from, then retracted into the puckered mouth.

It looked like a snail in orgasm trying to get out of its shell. It struck Sam that he had seen porno movies less erotic than the image of just that tongue.

Bogie was stopped by the doorman, who looked like doormen the world over—big, steroidal, bald, short on IQ. Even so, Bogie had a good four inches on the doorman, and Sam realized that Bogie had to be five ten, tall for a Filipino.

"Members only, sir," said the doorman. He caught sight of Sam. "Or foreign guests."

Bogie pulled out his badge. "You must be new here."

The doorman opened the door with reluctance, though he gave Bogie a worried look. He rubbed his fingers together at Bogie, who shook his head.

Sam noted the exchange without comment, but made a

mental note to see if Bogie had an ethics rap sheet. At the moment it was just curiosity. He hoped it wouldn't become a concern.

Inside the club the music was not just loud, it realigned Sam's skeleton. Multiple screens over the bar repeated the image of the tongue, which seemed to throb to the beat.

Sam and Bogie moved clockwise around the perimeter of the dance floor. The walls of the club were matte black. Mounted on the walls were huge monochrome photo blowups of lips, nipples, labia, mouths, nostrils, and one-eyed snakes.

The dance floor was translucent white plastic, lit from beneath. Miniscule tables of smoky acrylic bordered the dance floor. Small chrome picture frame lights provided six or seven watts per table, just enough to see the drink glasses.

Bogie seemed to be known here. Patrons moved aside to let him pass and the women gave him inviting glances. Sam realized that his partner had some sort of animal magnetism, some pheromone that got female noses open. He noted that Bogie seemed oblivious to his impact on women.

A few of the men gave Sam hard looks as if to ask what a *kano* was doing in their club. Sam shrugged it off, motioning that he was with Bogie.

Most of the men smirked at that, others looked a little jealous, leaving Sam puzzled. He let his face go stony and stared back at them.

Strobe lights and a certain spasticity of choreographic style made Sam think the entire room was suffering a simultaneous grand mal seizure. The patrons and the club's paid dancers wore black and white clothing, with spandex and chiffon predominating. The only color came from the flesh tones of the crowd.

Sam caught a glimpse of the nightclub act on the low stage. Two Filipinas wore blood-red patent leather bondage costumes, fishnet stockings, six-inch stiletto heels, and printed circuit board earrings. Gleaming raven hair was pulled back into severe buns. Licorice lipstick set off the perfection of their complexions. Handcuffed together, they pranced to the driving bass.

A slender young man groveled at their feet, clad in pink faux fur and feathers, writhing like a frou-frou serpent. He raised his face from the floor, weaving back and forth as he got to his knees. He faced the first dominatrix, miming supplication.

She stroked his cheek, while he jerked his head about, his Adam's apple bobbing frantically. A few moments later he disgorged an entire chicken egg and offered it to her on his tongue.

Sam saw that video cameras were transmitting the act to the screens. The audience had stopped their dancing and turned to watch the dominatrix.

She took the egg and cracked the shell, letting the raw white and yolk slide into her open mouth. She pulled his face to hers and dripped the raw egg into Pink Boy's mouth. Sam thought he might hurl as he watched it all in extreme close shots on the TVs.

The man/boy turned to the second dominatrix and unsnapped her patent leather bra. He let the raw egg dribble from his lips into the hollow of her throat. As the egg trickled between her breasts, he and the other woman slurped it up.

The bartender cracked eggs into a row of tall glasses and mixed them with rum and coconut milk. Bogie bought two drinks and handed one to Sam.

"Bottoms up. It's a house specialty. Supposed to increase potency."

Sam watched Bogie slug down his drink. He looked into his glass and felt ill. The yolk was sitting on top and seemed to be staring at him. "There's a spot of blood in this."

"Lucky you," said Bogie. "Shows the egg was fertile."

On stage the three performers took their bows, albumen dripping from their lips.

Upstairs in the club's surveillance room, Juan Samoa handed Olivia a packet of information, waiting as she read. Juan was the son of a Samoan-American sailor, and had the heft to prove it. He weighed a little over two seventy and stood six foot three, which made him a giant in the Philippines. He was forty-five years old, tough and hardened, a Subic Bay Naval Base bastard. If he could have gotten his old man to acknowledge him legally, he would have been an American citizen.

Juan liked watching Olivia when she was concentrating. He had taken the shots of Olivia with Tucker, and he thought that she was even more sultry than the Polaroids had captured.

He loved that she could still manage to look like an innocent schoolgirl when the occasion demanded. Visiting businessmen from Catholic countries regularly asked for her parochial school routine, with the plaid jumper and braids.

Juan owned one quarter of Club de Sex, but he made most of his income selling things from one person to another, sometimes things they didn't even know they wanted until they saw them. Like pictures of a man's mistress with her new boyfriend. He watched Olivia, trying to judge her reaction to the packet, when something caught his eye on the monitor.

"Olivia. Cops."

Olivia glanced at the video feed from the bar where Sam and Bogie were showing a photo to a bouncer. Juan saw Olivia's eyes narrow when she recognized Bogie. He made a note to find out who the white guy was and why he was with the Filipino detective.

He didn't think Olivia knew the *kano*, and hoped she wasn't going to get acquainted. They'd each had their fill of them for a while. He followed her through a doorway covered by strings of beads.

Sam and Bogie made their way toward the staircase leading to the private section of the club. They were intercepted by the floor manager, an ethnic Chinese with silver-capped teeth, a polyester suit, and a fake Rolex watch. The manager eyed Bogie with unhappiness and pointed to Sam with his eyebrow. Sam pulled out his ID.

"Alcohol, Tobacco, and Firearms? From the USA?" He

switched to rapid-fire Tagalog, addressing Bogie. *"What does he want? I'm not going to pay 'insurance' to fucking foreigners."*

Sam watched Bogie stare the Chinese down. He knew something was wrong, but it wasn't clear what.

"Speak English, please," said Bogie. "This 'fucking foreigner' doesn't speak Tagalog."

The Chinese pulled out his wallet and searched for small bills. "I don't need any insurance," he muttered.

Bogie reached over and smashed the man's hand and wallet against the countertop. He grabbed the manager's blazer and pulled him close.

"This isn't about insurance. You remember me from the last time I was here, right?" Bogie waited until he nodded yes. "Well this is still about the body in the dumpster—the one behind this club." Bogie let go of his blazer.

Sam could read the manager's confusion as he tried to figure out what was going on. It was clear what the guy was thinking: if this wasn't a shakedown, then what was it?

Bogie pulled a stack of pictures from his coat. He first showed Harvey Tucker's passport photo to the manager. "Seen this guy before? The truth this time."

The manager nodded yes with some reluctance. "He was here maybe three nights last week."

"Did he meet anyone here?"

The manager pointed to the crowded room, and just shrugged. "Hard to say."

An older Japanese man in an expensive suit walked up and tapped the floor manager on the arm, holding Bogie's gaze as he did so.

The manager saw who it was and flinched slightly. "Mr. Nosaka. I didn't realize you were in the club tonight, sir."

"Are these gentlemen causing trouble?"

Bogie pulled out his badge and held it in front of Nosaka.

"I'm Detective Lorenzano. This is Agent Haine. We're investigating a homicide."

Nosaka had curiously narrow shoulders, so Sam wasn't sure whether the man actually shrugged or not. He looked dismissively at Bogie's badge, turned his attention to the floor manager.

"See to the needs of our other patrons. I'll deal with these gentlemen."

"And how are you involved in this?" said Bogie.

"Let's just say I'm a sleeping partner in this business," said Nosaka. "I don't like complications where my investments might be affected."

Bogie showed the photo of the woman in the pig mask to Nosaka. "Where can I find this woman?"

Nosaka didn't even glance at the picture. "We don't let such women in here. Never. This is a respectable club."

Bogie pointed a finger at a detail in the Polaroid. "See that wallpaper behind her? Looks just like the wallpaper in your VIP lounge."

Sam looked at it too, pretended to recognize something, and nodded agreement. "I guess we'll have to take a look for ourselves."

"Sorry I couldn't help you gentlemen."

The two policemen turned from the bar and pushed through the crowd. Nosaka stared after them.

Sam spoke to Bogie as they walked. "Insurance?"

Bogie lit a fresh cigarette before answering. "A beat cop here makes about five hundred US a month. 'Insurance' premiums for special services can supplement their income."

"So why not bust the guy on the beat?" asked Sam. "He's giving the rest of you a bad name."

"I'm homicide, not internal affairs." He looked at Sam, a stream of smoke drifting from his nostrils. "You should know how this story goes. Your file said you worked New Orleans for two years."

That shut Sam up. He followed Bogie upstairs to the VIP room, though by now Olivia was long gone.

eight--

CIA NOMENCLATURE—*Agents* are foreign nationals in the employ of the CIA. Agents report to *operatives*, who are US nationals on active duty in a foreign locale, most often under cover of a civilian employer, who may or may not be aware of his employee's covert activities. *Officers* and *analysts* work inside the US, providing supervision of operatives and interpretation of intelligence collected.

MAKATI GALLERIA HOTEL—11:53 P.M. SUNDAY

Some endless time later, a weary Sam asked for his key at the hotel desk. "Room 2512." Sam took in the clerk's cheerful smile, brand new gold blazer, and fresh haircut. He figured the guy had finished a hotel management course and must have been promoted as well. No more elevator attendant duty for Mr. Perky.

"I need a six a.m. wake-up call."

"Of course, sir," chirped the clerk. "And here are the messages that came while you were out."

Sam took an envelope and the stack of forms, neat notations filled in by a series of desk clerks as they changed shifts throughout the day. He thought the hotel school ought to let its students know that constant chirpiness was an irritant to guests suffering from jet lag.

Sam glared at the fistful of paper, bleary-eyed and sour-faced. Without a thank you he headed for the elevator. Alone in the lift, fatigue slowing every move, he went through the message forms.

He wasn't sure if they were meant for him. They seemed to be a series of non sequiturs. Return flight confirmations. Per diem clarification. He stuffed them in his pocket with frustration.

The elevator door opened at the mezzanine and a massive Polynesian man got on, half filling the elevator all by himself. Sam thought he had seen smaller linemen playing in the NFL. The man tried to catch his eye, but Sam didn't feel like elevator chit chat.

Once the door closed, the man touched Sam's arm.

"You are putting a CIA operation in serious jeopardy. Drop the Tucker case." All business, speaking at high speed. "You should have picked up your messages hours ago. If you had returned the call to ATF in Los Angeles, you'd know—"

"Know what?" The unexpectedness of the encounter brought Sam fully awake. "Who the heck are you?"

"Agent Juan Samoa." He looked irritated at Sam's interruption. "Look, I don't have much time. We can't be seen together."

"I don't follow," said Sam, wary. "LA will have to confirm before I suspend an investigation."

Juan was impatient. "There was an interagency snafu. Just back off till you hear from headquarters. Check with Brent Treznor."

Sam glanced at the floor indicator, saw his floor was coming up soon. "What's CIA's interest?"

"That's need to know only. And you don't."

Sam bristled at the dismissal. "Guess I'll need that confirmation first."

The door opened, revealing a hallway full of hotel personnel cleaning the carpet. Sam stepped away without a backward glance at Juan.

As the door closed, Juan hissed, "Don't be a jerk."

Once in his room, Sam flopped on the bed and hit the remote for the TV. Sure enough, the fish channel came on and he stared at it, his mind a blank, while he snagged a beer from the mini-bar built into the nightstand next to the bed. He pulled out the messages. A call from a Ms. Tucker—maybe Harvey's ex-wife, maybe the sister.

Two of the message slips asked him to call the LA office and speak with Supervisor Ricci, between eight and noon. He looked at his watch, but realized he was too brain-fried to figure out the time in LA.

He opened the envelope and found a fax copy of an export license issued to Harvey Tucker. It granted permission for the sale and foreign delivery of fourteen roosters, point of origination in Oklahoma. The routing slip indicated it had come from Customs via Homeland Security, thence to ATF. He couldn't make any sense of that either, and decided to put the messages aside until morning.

More than anything he wanted to sleep, but the man mountain in the elevator had got his adrenaline going. He fervently hoped that something amongst the messages was an actual live lead. All he wanted was to go in-country, make a quick nab, and return home covered in glory.

Yeah, and maybe win the lottery, too.

He channel surfed while he finished his beer. CNN, ESPN, HBO Manila, BBC, some Japanese news channels, stock market reports, and about a dozen channels of local programming. He noted that the local shows went from Tagalog to English and back again in the same sentence.

He switched back to the fish channel, stripped off his clothes, and lay spread-eagled on the bed. The day felt like it had lasted several years.

He didn't want to stay in Manila any longer than he had to. It was too hot, too humid, too polluted, too poor, too crowded— just too. And he didn't like being the lone white face most places he went.

He realized he had caught a glimpse of what Blake had complained about, Blake being one of the two black ATF agents in LA. It was a new experience for Sam to be the guy who stood out because of skin color. He didn't much care for it.

He thought about that for a minute. He didn't think that made him a racist—but it sure made him an easy target.

At last he drifted off, dreaming he was wrapped in a warm, moist blanket. Someone was carrying him on his back through the crowded Manila streets. Around him was the cacophony of multiple languages: English, Tagalog, Taglish, Mandarin, Japanese, Spanish, Portuguese.

Ahead he could see a pale face—Christy's face—receding through the crowd. He tried to call out to her, but he couldn't speak, because he was under water now. He realized he was a fish, and the current was against him.

He decided to just float with it.

After a second restless night, Sam tried calling ATF in Los Angeles at six in the morning. When the switchboard answered he realized that although it was two in the afternoon back home, it was still Sunday there, not Monday. Los Angeles was on the other side of the international date line.

His encounter with Juan Samoa didn't seem like an emergency, so he just left a message for his supervisor Ricci to call, wondering when—no, make that if—he would ever adjust to the time zone shift. He decided to take an extra long shower and see if he could run the hotel out of hot water.

Later over breakfast, Sam showed Bogie the fax of Tucker's license to export roosters. Bogie snapped to its implication at once.

"Tucker was bringing in some fresh stock to sell to the cock fight promoters."

"I don't get it," said Sam. "Cockfighting isn't even legal in the States."

"Except Louisiana and Oklahoma."

"You're kidding, right?"

"It's common knowledge in the Philippines," said Bogie.

"Why would that be common knowledge?"

"Same reason you know the batting averages of baseball players. Cockfighting is our national sport."

Sam chewed on that.

"Why on Earth would someone ship chickens halfway around the world just to kill them?"

From the look he got, he realized Bogie thought he was either joking or being stupid on purpose. Either way, he didn't look amused.

"Not chickens. Cocks. Fighting cocks. Some of the best gamecocks in the world are bred in Oklahoma. Most of them get shipped either here or Thailand."

Bogie downed the last of his fresh mango and took the check. Sam threw back his coffee and followed him to the register.

"We'll check out one of the larger cockfighting arenas, see if we can find who Tucker's customers were." Bogie's alpha-pager sounded and he read the display. "That'll have to wait a bit. They're holding Olivia—our suspect—at headquarters."

nine--

CIA FACTBOOK—RP is the smuggling crossroads of
   the world. The nearly 8,000 islands of the archi-
   pelago make it easy to land cargo for transship-
   ment elsewhere.

Subic Bay is a legitimate free port. Manila Bay often
   acts as a second free port, due to corruption in
   the Customs Office. RP leads the world in smuggling of prescription drugs, weapons, humans
   for illegal immigration, and humans for sexual
   slavery. It ranks among the top five for traffic in
   illegal drugs, industrial espionage, and money
   laundering.

NATIONAL SPORT—Cockfighting, with betting regulated by the state. Such regulation is widely
   ignored. Cockfights are broadcast on television,
   but attendance at the arenas is heavy, due to the
   ability to place live wagers.

MALIGAY TANDANG (HAPPY ROOSTER) ARENA
—10 A.M. MONDAY

The low roof of the cockfight arena served as a lid to keep
the cigar smoke thick as LA smog. About two hundred men
stood or sat on low benches around the pit, where the owners
of the fighting cocks prepped them for battle.

While the front row was well-dressed and smoked fine
cigars, the peanut gallery ran to torn undershirts and misshapen
cigars that smelled like steaming dog turds. The overall stench
could be cut with a machete.

In the fighting pit a bird was extracted from its wicker carrier. Its owner, Chewie, broke a razor blade in half and taped it
to the spur of the roan cock, the crowd's clear favorite. Chewie
was so called because of his full beard, such a rarity among

Filipinos that his cronies thought he resembled Chewbacca in Star Wars.

He stared into the beady eye of his bird, which was beginning to hyperventilate, avian adrenaline pouring through its system. Chewie blew into the face of the cock and ruffled its feathers.

On the other side of the ring, Bong attached a custom-made killing spur to his golden fighting cock. Bong inhaled a hit of rock cocaine and slowly breathed it into his bird's face.

The bird began to thrash. Bong listened to the bets being called out and realized that they were going against his bird. He fluffed his bird's feathers and surreptitiously inserted a pinkie into its anus.

The cock screeched, extended it wings wide, and stretched its neck, all the while shaking like it had palsy. The bettors took note of the bird's display of vigor, and there was a renewed round of betting.

Ollie, the *casador*, took wagers at high speed, using finger signs to transmit figures to his assistant. After a minute the assistant waved for the bookie's attention and signed back. The book had become too lopsided; it was more than they could cover if things went the wrong way.

Ollie turned to the well-heeled cockers in the front row and inquired non-verbally whether they would lay off the bets he couldn't cover. A Filipino politico named Sonny Lagos nodded in the affirmative.

Sonny was a leftover from the Marcos days, and whether he won or lost an extra couple of hundred was less important than getting a chance to see the blood fly. He loved a good match better than sex.

Sonny elbowed his neighbor, Nosaka, who was looking quite dour. Sonny wondered why Nosaka had oiled his hair so heavily this morning. With his narrow shoulders and small ears, it made him look like a seal wearing a hairpiece.

"Come on, Nosaka-san. We cover the wagers, make the match more interesting, OK?"

Nosaka looked as if he had stomach cramps, but nodded his agreement.

The *casador* signaled. With a final fluffing of feathers, Bong and Chewie thrust their birds toward each other, and jerked them back, circling the ring at a measured pace, feinting with the cocks. The roosters grew ever more enraged.

As the squawking increased in volume, so did the cries of the punters, trying to get down last-minute bets, and the noise level jumped thirty decibels. Bong pinched the wing of his bird, causing it to scream and peck madly at his hand. Another round of wagers was shouted out.

Chewie smirked at Bong's crude attempt to make his bird look tough, and his expression set off another bout of activity among the bettors. Ollie scrambled to take in the pesos and dollars, signing hurriedly to his assistant. He checked the crowd and saw they were worked to a fever pitch, but no more bets were being offered.

"Release!" The owners freed their birds, which rushed toward each other. There was a blinding flurry of wings, jabs of beak to head and neck. The birds butted breasts against each other, fighting for domination.

After a few seconds they fell back, to roars of approval from the crowd. Their owners grabbed the birds by the throat and tail, stilling them. With the first round over, the bettors reevaluated the chances for each bird.

Ollie took wagers only from those holding up ten-dollar bills or greater. No time for penny-ante stuff.

As for Chewie, he no longer looked so certain of victory. And Bong wished he hadn't bet his son's tuition money on the fight.

Ollie signaled to let the birds go. They rushed into the center of the pit, squawking and screeching. They butted chests like two frat brothers at a football game, and tried to climb over each other. Pecking and shrieking, the golden cock slashed the roan with its spur, cutting a vital artery.

The roan dropped to the floor, wings flopping feebly, its blood pumping onto the floor.

The golden rooster crowed its victory, but the sound was lost in the roar of the crowd. The venture capitalists surged to their feet, eager either to collect their winnings or to scream curses at the owner of the defeated cockerel.

Chewie collected the carcass of his bird, holding it upside down by its feet so the blood wouldn't drip on his clothes. *Fucking Okie chicken,* he thought to himself. Tonight his family would have to eat "loser stew." Later he would have his boys take the head of this one into the roost as an example to the other cocks that a similar fate awaited them if they didn't learn from the roan's example.

Bong snaffled his bird's head with a burlap sack, and bear-hugged the rooster until it calmed down. He removed the killing spur and made his way to Ollie to get his cut of the book. He could pay for his son's Catholic school for another month.

Ollie's assistant brought a bucket of sand and sprinkled it in the arena to sop up the blood. He raked the fighting area with a bamboo whisk. The next set of gamecock owners brought out their cages and the whole process began to repeat.

In the rear row of bleacher seats, two men feigned interest in the cockfight, using the noise of the crowd to mask their conversation.

Gerard, a Frenchman in his late thirties, was dressed with no more care or taste than a tourist. He smoked cigarettes like someone who wanted to commit suicide by lung cancer within the week, lighting a new Gaulois from the old one. He put his arm around his companion, Riffat, a small Pakistani dressed in workman's clothing.

Because Riff was browner, smaller, and less ostentatiously dressed, he blended with the Filipinos better. He didn't care for the looks—some leering, some wistful—the other cockers gave him. He thought—correctly—that they assumed he was yet another member of Manila's huge gay community (and Euro-fortunate, to boot).

"I'm thinking we should be seeing Mister Tucker here, no?" said Gerard, pitching his gravelly voice low. His exhaled smoke wreathed them both. "Are these not his birds fighting today, the ones from his own ranch?"

"Enough about these birds, my friend," said Riffat. "I can bring the money whenever you wish." He spoke within inches of Gerard's nose, in that unmistakable Middle-Eastern invasion of personal space, his halitosis making a perfect counterpoint to the stink of Gerard's cigarette. "Did you bring the tech sheets?"

Gerard circumvented the question. "You understand if I supply the details of this process, you will be many steps closer to a device that can be delivered in a small package—perhaps even a briefcase." Riffat nodded his understanding, allowing some impatience to show. Gerard continued. "And you also understand that what happens to the chosen people is none of my concern, yes?"

"Why should it be any of your business what happens to the Christ-killers?" replied Riffat. He suspected that Gerard was a devout Catholic—maybe his religion could be turned toward a mutual cause.

Gerard withdrew his arm from Riff's shoulders. He paused, seeming to weigh Riff on the balance of justice and finding him a little light.

Riffat wondered if he had gone too far. Perhaps he had offended the Frenchman.

"You are not understanding me, Mr. Khan," said Gerard. "If certain of your less-than-sane fundamentalist cousins—let us say, just for the sake of argument, from Morocco—no, more likely Algeria—were to deploy these items against France— Well, you see my problem, *non*?"

Riffat shrugged impatiently. "Of course. And I have brought guarantees from the Minister of Defense."

Gerard looked at him quizzically. "Of Morocco—or Algeria?"

"No. Of my country. These devices will be used only for internal defense."

"How do you use a portable nuclear device for internal defense?" asked Gerard.

"Perhaps along the Kashmiri border," said Riff.

"Or in the Indian Parliament?" said Gerard. "Well, this is beside the point."

"We have assurances, in writing, from our—" Riff hesitated. "Our cousins—that your homeland will be removed from the list of active targets, because of your sympathy to our cause."

Gerard gave him the fish eye. "Do you think I am a fool?"

No, I think you are a dog, and the sooner you are out of my life—

"These assurances are verifiable at the highest level," said Riffat. "Not only of my government but of our cousins' governments."

Around them the noise level rose as the crowd readied itself for another cockfight. Riffat spotted a policeman coming through the door, probably looking to make some arrests, take some payoffs, and pay for his mistress' rent. Riff touched Gerard's sleeve and pointed discreetly. The two men rose from their seats and worked their way to the exit.

"Show me the funds, show me these guarantees," said Gerard. "If I can confirm them, we can consummate this deal."

As they made their way outside, Gerard thought to himself that being a broker of industrial secrets was an excellent job. Others brought him merchandise, which he was able to resell at a profit. He seldom had to put up any cash himself.

It was a perfect spot for an entrepreneur with balls of brass. Low capital investment, high turnover. Almost no overhead, other than the occasional bribe to the local police. And the baksheesh was always reasonable. The Filipinos were a people remarkable for their lack of greed.

Gerard looked sideways at the little Pakistani and smiled. *True believers are such simpletons.*

Riffat smiled back. *Infidels always think money is the key to happiness.*

The policeman passed by the two foreigners without a glance. As it happened, he was a relatively honest cop. He wasn't there to shake anyone down. He just liked placing a bet on a good cockfight.

The poorer patrons, though, moved away from him, leaving him a seat. To them it was not yet clear whether this police officer was off duty or not, and it was always safer to give a cop some space, stay out of his line of sight.

NBI HEADQUARTERS—MONDAY 9 A.M.

Sam and Bogie watched the interrogation through the one-way observation glass. They sipped from bottles of water, trying not to melt down in the small space. On the other side of the glass Garcia was in the barrel, grilling Olivia.

Olivia had been detained at NBI when she tried to post bond for Chito. Garcia had been on call when she was brought in, and Sam and Bogie had hurried to NBI headquarters once they received his page.

Her mascara had run from the heat and sweat, but not from tears. She was as hard and self-possessed as any woman Sam had ever seen being questioned. Her answers were flat and clipped, communicating little or nothing.

Now and again she goaded Garcia, trying out little insults and epithets to see if she could make him lose his temper. It was clear to Bogie and Sam that Olivia would never give up any information of value.

Bogie switched off the intercom, and they watched her performance in companionable silence. It didn't take a lip reader to see she was calling Garcia a limp-dicked faggot. Bogie resumed an ongoing amiable argument they'd been having.

"Barbara Stanwyck in *Double Indemnity*," said Bogie. "Black and white. Of course."

Sam thought again. "Kathleen Turner in *Body Heat*. Way sexier in living color."

"Lana Turner in *The Postman Always Rings Twice*," said Bogie. "Black and white and four stars, according to Video Hound."

Sam snorted. "No contest. Same title, Jessica Lange, in color. On the kitchen table, with Jack Nicholson. And no one cares how many stars." Olivia caught his attention as she spat at Garcia. "You know, I've never worked vice, but I can't figure out what makes a whore bring all her money down to the station to spring a low-life pimp like Chito."

"Family values," replied Bogie. He looked appraisingly at Olivia as she jerked open the top of her blouse in an attempt to cool off. "You want to know why a woman with her looks ends up on her back for a living? I first ran into Olivia when I was working vice, about ten years ago. You think she's good-looking now, you should have seen her back then."

He lit a new cigarette. "I worked vice for five years, and I can give you twenty-five reasons why they say they're in the business; but the older I get, the less sense I can make of any of them." He drained the last of his water and turned to Sam. "So, you want to be the good, understanding cop or the nasty, foreign cop?"

Sam laughed and got up. The room was so small they both had to stand and do-si-do to get out of the room. Sam's bottle *tinked* against the mirror, unnoticed by him, as he pulled the door shut behind him.

In the interrogation room Olivia heard the small sounds of the men leaving the observation booth. When she judged they were in the hallway outside the door, she slammed her face against the desktop and pushed her knuckle into her eye. Garcia's jaw dropped in amazement as she burst into uncontrollable sobs, tears streaming from her eyes.

By the time Sam followed Bogie into the interrogation room, she had covered her face with her hands and was cowering away from Garcia. Bogie grabbed Garcia's arm, jerking him away from Olivia.

"What the hell are you doing, Detective?" Bogie switched to Tagalog. *"Never strike someone being questioned!"* Bogie turned from Garcia and raised Olivia's face from her hands.

Her transformation was breathtaking. She looked like a frightened schoolgirl. Bogie gave Garcia a hard stare. "Give the clipboard to Agent Haine. Wait for us back in my office."

Garcia looked pissed off, as if he couldn't believe he was being shooed from the interrogation. "I never touched her. She's a lying bitch."

Sam glanced back and forth from Olivia to Garcia. He decided to believe Garcia. He gave Olivia a malicious look. "I'll take over for you, Garcia."

Garcia left in disgust, slamming the door. Bogie drew a chair up next to Olivia. Lowering his voice, trying for an air of calm, he asked "Can I get you some water, a tissue, or—?"

"No, thank you, sir." She sounded like a wounded child.

Sam decided it was time to assume his role. He flipped through the Polaroids and held up the picture of the woman in a pig mask, breasts bared.

"Without the mask I'm not sure. Maybe if you'll pose more like the picture—" Sam grabbed the collar of her blouse as if to tug it open.

Bogie knocked Sam's hand aside. "Enough!" He turned to Olivia. "No one—no one—in this station will touch you again."

Sam was taken by surprise. It looked like Bogie was not just playing good cop. Sam backed off, as far as the six by six room would permit.

Bogie stared Sam down. "We don't want a Rodney King, eh, *kano*?"

This got under Sam's skin. "I'm not sure you noticed, but the whore is the suspect here, not American justice."

"Which one is the bigger whore?" said Bogie, still staring at Sam.

For an instant, while she was still dry-sobbing, Olivia let her delight show, just before Bogie turned back to her. But Sam saw it. He glared at the clipboard and asked flatly, "So where were you on the night of August 18, Miss de la Cruz?"

Olivia looked confused. She glanced to Bogie for support. Sam couldn't suppress his sarcasm. "Yes, August 18. You know, the night good ol' Harv Tucker stuck his johnson in the light socket and went to reside among the morning stars."

Olivia looked up meekly from her damp little hanky.

"Is this amusing, Agent Haine? The death of one of your fellow countrymen?" said Bogie.

"Murder is never amusing, Detective Lorenzano," said Sam. "But whoever offed this bozo is just one of Darwin's elves, far as I'm concerned."

Olivia sniffled into her hanky—or perhaps she was just stifling a laugh. She composed herself, and asked Bogie, distress in her voice. "Darwin's elves, sir? Please, I do not understand."

Sam responded before Bogie could pat her hand. "Survival of the fittest. Someone removed a little pollution from the gene pool." He looked back at his clipboard. "I hope to shake that elf's hand personally and thank him."

The door to the interrogation room burst open, and an irate Captain Velasquez entered, startling Sam and Bogie. Olivia offered a malevolent smile behind their backs.

With his girth and blood pressure, Velasquez was built neither for bursts of speed nor high emotion. He wheezed for breath as he took in the bruise blossoming on Olivia's face, the tear-streaked mascara, the blouse tugged awry. He addressed her, ignoring the two detectives.

"Miss de la Cruz, you're free to go."

Bogie couldn't believe his ears. "What are you—?"

With a vicious gesture, the Captain motioned him to silence. Olivia maintained her best schoolgirl demeanor as she demurely struggled to hold her blouse together. With a barely audible "Thank you, Captain," she made her way from the room.

Velasquez pulled the door shut before he spoke to the two men. "Chito Rivera's being released, also. On his own recognizance."

Bogie shrugged and his expression went flat.

It was too much for Sam. "What's going on, Captain?"

"I won't waste my breath explaining to you. The office of the fiscal has requested—no, make that demanded—that both of you report at once." He paused for a beat. When they didn't start moving he said, "That means leave now! Don't make the fiscal wait. It's not good for anyone's career."

With that he followed his belly out of the office, wheezing heavily.

Bogie and Sam gathered up their paperwork. "What's a fiscal?" asked Sam.

"Like one of your prosecuting district attorneys," said Bogie.

"Must carry even more weight here than it does back in the US," said Sam.

Bogie looked at him as they left the interrogation room, as if deciding what to tell him.

"It's not just the office. It's the officer. Fiscal Santos comes from a powerful family. One brother's a senator. The other is governor of a province. And her father was on the Supreme Court."

Sam did a mental double take and asked *"Her* father?"

"Under Marcos," added Bogie.

OFFICE OF THE FISCAL—10 A.M. MONDAY

Daddy had gotten his little girl into Oxford, one of her brothers into Harvard, the other placed at the Sorbonne. He wanted his children to have classmates from around the world, classmates who would graduate to become movers and shakers.

Once in school, the kids pulled their own grades, and they all graduated *cum laude* or better. Jennifer Santos was the fastest-rising assistant fiscal in the country. Smart, well connected, and well educated.

She was part of the competent oligarchy that ran the country pretty much as it saw fit. She and her brothers were the new generation of Filipino pols who wanted to pull the RP into the twenty-first century—and leave behind the baggage of corruption from earlier administrations.

Bogie had filled in the background information as they rode across town, but he had failed to mention that Miss Santos was in her early thirties and stunning.

Now Sam and Bogie sat in too-small chairs in front of her imposing desk, two truants called before the principal. Sam's eyes were drawn to her toe, tapping beneath her desk as she reviewed the files in hand.

Sam wasn't a fashionista, but Christy had been in the garment industry. He could recognize shoes that cost a week's wages, silk hose, a designer label businesswoman's outfit. With a start he realized he was staring and raised his eyes to a neutral position.

Jennifer grew more irritated as she read through the files. She looked up to lock eyes with Bogie.

"Where is the search warrant for Club de Sex?"

Bogie evaded a direct answer. "Finding a body in a dumpster is probable cause to search the premises—"

Jennifer cut him off. "Since the dumpster was in a public alleyway, then 'the premises' would be defined as the area surrounding the dumpster—not the interior of a private business."

She looked at the file and flipped over another page. "On what basis did you hold Mr. Rivera without either charging or arresting him?"

"He was detained as a material witness, held for questioning—" began Bogie.

She cut him off again. "Material witness? Who gave information that puts him at the scene of the crime? You can't even place him in the club on that evening."

Sam thought he would try to help. "Rivera and de la Cruz have a—" He hesitated as he tried to find the right choice of words. "What you might call a business relationship. He'd have known where she was that night."

Jennifer shot him a withering glance. "Business relationship?"

"Yes, pimp and whore, to be specific," added Bogie, enjoying Sam's discomfort. Jennifer seemed unfazed.

Sam looked at Bogie, wondering if the policeman had offended the fiscal. "Don't worry. She's heard the word before," said Bogie.

Jennifer's eyes blazed. "You are perilously close to having a formal complaint filed against you, Detective."

Sam hoped to smooth things over. "Chito seemed like the best lead—"

"You're an expert on our legal system, Agent Haine?"

"No, I'm not," said Sam.

"That's apparent," snapped Jennifer. "But even an ATF agent must have heard of habeas corpus."

She slapped the file shut and rose to dismiss the two men. They hurriedly came to their feet as well.

"Detective Lorenzano, I'm going to keep an eye on your conduct on this case. This isn't the first report I've had of your slipshod methods. I am sure you realize that if you were to taint the evidence because of sloppy police work, I'd have to drop this case rather than prosecute it. That is *not* going to happen."

She shifted her eyes and pinned Sam with a laser-like glare.

"As for you, Agent Haine, you are part of this investigation as a courtesy extended between friendly governments. Don't abuse that courtesy."

She dropped her eyes back to the work on her desk and sat down. The men were released, forgotten in the load of the day's work. Sam and Bogie exited as unobtrusively as possible.

Jennifer was already scanning the next file when the door opened and Sam returned. He indicated the notebook he had left on the floor beside his chair and bent to retrieve it. He hesitated.

"I haven't been spanked like that in quite a while."

Jennifer listened with disinterest, returned to her reading. "You were staring," she said, and raised her eyes as if to evaluate his looks. "Quite rude of you."

Sam halted, taken aback. "I didn't realize I was so—"

"Obvious?" She waited a beat. "Nine tonight."

Sam started, confused by the shift. Then he got it.

"Pick me up here," said Jennifer. "We'll take my car and driver." She didn't even glance up, just kept working. Sam waited a beat, then made for the door.

Outside on the hot sidewalk, Bogie finished a cigarette in three long drags. When Sam caught up to him, he said, "There's a bar near here where a lot of ex-pats hang out. We can inquire about Tucker. Besides, I need a beer after that little business."

He turned on his heel and walked off, leaving Sam to follow in his wake as they pushed their way through the crowd of Filipinos sweltering in the sun.

ten--

METRO MANILA JAIL— 10:30 A.M. MONDAY

Olivia sat on a bench near the holding cells, waiting, trying not to show her anxiety. The detainees kept up a constant yammering that frayed her nerves. Distant cell doors slammed shut, and she could hear the occasional stream of cursing as prisoners disputed whose turn it was at the communal commode.

She worked hard to block it all out, so much so that when Chito put his hand on her shoulder she jumped at his touch. Up close she could see his torn shirt, the black eye, bruises on his neck as if he had been choked. Chito sat down beside her.

She had been keeping up her façade for a long time and now it crumbled. She cried—real tears this time. She brushed the bruises on his face and neck with her fingertips.

Chito held himself stiffly, trying to hide the pain. At her touch he, too, wept silently. Olivia pulled him into her arms, and he rested his head against her breast as she comforted him.

Behind the desk, Garcia watched sardonically. *Looks like some freaky Madonna and Child. Maybe I can crucify them both.*

When Olivia and Chito walked out of the station, Garcia signaled for Saddul's attention. The detectives waited a few moments and followed the two.

> PHILIPPINE BEER—San Miguel Corporation is the largest publicly-traded food, beverage, and packaging company in the Philippines. Founded in 1890 as a brewery, the company has over 100 facilities in the Philippines, Southeast Asia, China,

and Australia. San Miguel Beer has long been a favorite beer of the United States' sailors and soldiers stationed in the Philippine Islands.

OTTO'S BAR—11:30 A.M. MONDAY

The bar was home away from home to a lot of mid-level business executives. The owner, a retired US Air Force quartermaster by the name of Otto, had thought it clever to call his place "Working Late at the Office." That way his semi-alcoholic regulars could answer appropriately when their wives called them on their cell phones to find out why they weren't home yet.

Otto had found that his US pension stretched a long way in RP. He didn't need to work, but standing behind the bar drinking up the profits, shooting the shit with passing businessmen, and porking the B-girls who rented space at his bar had proved to be a dream retirement. If a Budweiser gal showed up, he'd have figured he must have died and made it to Heaven.

Otto had three ex-wives along with some indeterminate number of Air Force brats. He was damned sure they weren't all his own, so he left them all behind when he moved to the RP. He felt that twelve thousand miles was just about the right amount of breathing space he needed between himself and those harridans.

In fact, the only fly in his ointment was paying off the local beat cops. But as long as they didn't squeeze too hard, he was about as happy as a bitter, thrice-divorced alcoholic with a football-sized liver can be.

Right now he was entirely unhappy to see the uniform at the door. This was a departure from the usual schedule.

Otto's cup of unhappiness overflowed as he watched two plainclothes cops push past the beat cop. He couldn't figure what a *kano* was doing with a flip. Without being asked, he opened two San Miguels for them.

Bogie pulled Harvey Tucker's photo from his inside jacket pocket and flashed it toward Otto like it was a free pass to Disneyworld. "You ever see this guy? He's a countryman of yours."

Otto glanced at Tucker's picture without interest or attention. "Don't know."

"Maybe you lost track of him, since you get so many Americanos in here," continued Bogie.

"Told you I don't know." Otto pushed back the two dollar bills Sam had put on the counter. "It's on the house."

Sam pushed the money back across the bar. "We'll drink 'em, so we'll pay for them."

Bogie and Sam carried their beers to a booth. Bogie took a long pull, but managed to lose none of his hangdog expression.

Sam, however, was buzzing right along. He looked at Bogie and conjectured that he was replaying the tongue-lashing the fiscal had given him.

"Same crap we put up with stateside," said Sam.

Bogie made a sour face. "Makes you feel right at home, does it?"

"Yeah." Sam grinned, but turned thoughtful. "I know I'm not the world's most sensitive guy regarding cultural differences and all. Still, I'm beginning to think we have more things in common than not."

Bogie gave him a long stare, and did an excellent Bogart imitation.

"Including a taste for bossy dames?"

Sam was embarrassed that he was so transparent. He took another swallow of his drink. Damned if he wasn't developing a taste for the local beer.

Bogie's pager went off, he pulled it from its holster, and beeped his way through four pages of text.

"Good luck for a change," said Bogie. "Garcia followed Olivia to a bank and later to a cockfighting arena. She dropped something off with the owner."

Bogie rose and motioned for Sam to follow him. They

headed for the exit. Bogie pulled aside the uniformed cop who was hanging out near the entry.

"This isn't payday."

"What the fuck is it to you?" answered the beat cop. Sam watched from a few feet away.

"If I were Internal Affairs this would be the first day of your suspension," said Bogie. "Don't pretend. And don't be stupid. You squeeze the *kano* owner too hard and sooner or later there will be someone else in your shoes, walking your beat. And if you're as dumb as you look, there will be someone else in your woman's bed, too. A guy who still has a job."

The cop bristled at the insult but was unsure who Bogie might be.

"You got it wrong. I was just stopping by for a cold one."

"You're still on duty, mister," said Bogie. "Just wave hello to the bartender and get back to your beat."

The cop left, disgruntled.

Sam offered no comment, but asked instead, "I thought Olivia was meeting Chito for his release. So what happened to him?"

"He's being shadowed, too," said Bogie. "Olivia's more important. We'll walk to the arena from here. We can ask after Tucker at the same time."

Bogie and Sam made their way through the usual throng of working-class Filipinos that seemed to be on the streets at any hour of the day or night. Beneath a flyover (which Sam now knew was Filipino for freeway overpass) several families had set up housekeeping in large cardboard boxes.

Between the pasteboard shanties, street vendors sold kitsch bric-a-brac from TV trays. Chartreuse Santa Claus dolls vied for space with shoddy artificial flowers in a variety of unnatural hues.

Here and there some entrepreneur had a hibachi going, but Sam couldn't make out what was on the barbie. From the odor he didn't think it was shrimp, unless it had died about two weeks ago.

He tried to remember if they ate rat here, or if that was in

Thailand. He didn't suppose it mattered. Ever since the Donner party, people always said whatever it was, it tasted just like chicken.

Sam drew an occasional inquisitive glance, but not that many more than Bogie. Their suits and self-confident carriage marked both of them as outsiders.

Bogie resumed their debate. "Bogart in *Maltese Falcon*."

Sam waved it aside. "No black and white films. It's the twenty-first century."

Bogie reflected for a few seconds. "All right, Steve McQueen in *Bullit*."

"Great car chase, but Hackman in *French Connection* is a better detective," said Sam.

"How about Dirty Harry, *Magnum Force*?"

That almost satisfied Sam. "Yeah, he's a great detective—but not believable. The truth is, we're much more regulated than that in the US, especially in the big cities." He thought as they pushed through the crowd for a few yards. "How about Chow Yun Fat?"

That pleased Bogie. "You like John Woo films?"

"Only those before he went Hollywood," said Sam.

"What do you think is his best? *The Killer*?" asked Bogie.

"Nah. It's gotta be *A Better Tomorrow*."

Bogie nodded. "I don't agree. Still, I take your point."

Half a block from the arena they had to forge their way against the flow of disgruntled bettors making their way home. By the time they made it to the door, the rush had slowed to a trickle and the place was almost empty, just two laborers cleaning up trash left behind by the crowd.

The smaller of the two held a garbage bag, while the larger one swept debris into it. The sweeper was huge, worked nights as a bouncer, and looked like he might have been the clone-brother of the doorman at Club de Sex.

Sam and Bogie peered about as their eyes adjusted to the gloomy interior. Sam called over to the cleaners. "Excuse me, sir."

There was no response. The cleaners ignored the two detectives.

"They hire deaf mutes for this job?" said Sam.

"They think it's a shakedown," said Bogie.

Sam was put out by this explanation. "Why is it every time I go someplace with you, people think—" He broke off, realizing where that was headed. "Doesn't anyone trust a cop in this country?"

"I thought you lived in Los Angeles." said Bogie.

Sam snorted at the jab. "Yeah." He decided he wasn't going to let the two nimrods sweeping up ignore him. Raising his voice he called to the cleaners, "Hey! You! I want to talk to you!"

The cleaners looked up sullenly, muttered angrily to each other. Sam pointed to the sweeper and crooked his finger to call him over.

In no more than a heartbeat, the sweeper became enraged. From across the arena he charged Sam at a dead run, his broom held before him like a medieval lance.

With an oath, Bogie knocked Sam's beckoning hand aside and tried to step between Sam and the sweeper. He was about half a step too late, and the sweeper rammed Bogie in the solar plexus with the broom head, knocking him to the floor.

Stepping around Bogie the sweeper screamed out in Tagalog, *"I'll show you who's a fucking dog!"* He came after Sam, his lips pulled back in a snarl.

Sam had never seen a person actually foam at the mouth before. He backpedaled, dodging a wild swing from the sweeper's broom. "Back off, big guy." He brushed back his coat and unsnapped the restraint of his service pistol holster.

Bogie lurched to his feet and grabbed Sam's gun arm. "Don't shoot!" he croaked to Sam. "Misunderstanding!"

With Bogie holding Sam's arm, Sweeper had a chance to bring the broom head down across Sam's back with enough force to break the handle. Though the blow stunned Sam, his adrenaline was surging. He pushed Bogie aside and waded into the sweeper, pumping with both fists.

Bogie was still gulping for breath as he tried to break up the fight. For his part, the sweeper was in a steroid rage and saw both of the cops as enemies. He rained blows on them without regard to race, creed, or country of origin.

Meanwhile, it looked to the trash bag boy that Sam was going to use the beating as an excuse to shoot the sweeper. He grabbed his partner from behind, in hopes of stopping the fight. But Sweeper was no longer thinking, just fighting. He shook off Bag Boy, bellowing *"Kano bakla!"*

Sam didn't need to understand Tagalog to know that his manhood was being impugned. He landed a solid right to Sweeper's head, but it didn't even faze the man. Sweeper grabbed Sam in a bear hug and squeezed.

With his air gone, Sam struggled. He knew he had no more than seconds before he lost consciousness. He wriggled one hand toward his waistband to draw his gun.

Bag Boy could see where things were going. He tugged effetely on the sweeper's elbow, but even with Bag Boy's impediment to Sweeper's freedom of motion, Sam was losing the fight.

Bag Boy dropped to the floor with a thud, where he rested quietly, no longer interested in the activities of the day. Bogie had rejoined the fray, removing Bag Boy from the action by belting him with the broken broom handle. He followed up by whacking Sweeper's bald dome twice, with no effect.

Sam was turning an interesting shade of purple. This must have pleased Sweeper's sense of aesthetics, because he smiled maniacally as he tightened his grip. Bogie came up behind Sweeper, pulled the broken broom handle across his Adam's apple, and applied pressure.

Sweeper bellowed his anger, shook his head, but wouldn't release Sam. Sweeper's eyes watered, then bulged, as the wood cut off his oxygen. Ultimately he loosened his grip, allowing a limp Sam slid to the floor. Moments later Sweeper himself went down like a felled tree.

Bogie leaned over from the waist, hands on his knees, breath rasping. Sam rolled over and tried to make it to his knees, but couldn't muster the energy.

"And what the hell happened with this janitor—slash — Hulk?"

Bogie looked sour, but amused. "You gave him a mortal insult. Dogs are summoned with your finger crooked." He demonstrated, finger bent. "If you want a person to come, you do this." He made an open handed sweeping gesture.

Sam couldn't believe what he had just heard. "And for that I almost died?"

A door opened and the stump-like arena manager came in. When he saw his cleaning crew unconscious on the floor, he pulled his skullcap tighter on his head, gave a shout, and trotted over to the detectives. He screamed in some provincial dialect, spraying Sam and Bogie liberally with saliva as he shrieked at them.

Sam didn't know or care what the guy was yelling. He lay on the floor and inspected the man's appalling dentition. Light glinted from two front teeth, sheathed in gold as they were. The rest of his teeth were missing, broken, rotted, or some combination of the above.

Goldie (which turned out to be his unsurprising nickname) switched into broken Tagalog and shouted into Bogie's face. *"What fuck going on here? Pay 'insurance' three days ago. What kind protection this, you assholes? What you do my nephew? Why Godzilla on floor? I call beat cop, he bust your head."*

He might have gone on like this forever, but Bogie menaced him with the sharp wooden handle.

"You own this toilet?" said Bogie in English.

Goldie switched to English, which was as rough as his Tagalog. "Who you, asshole? And who asshole friend?"

Sam had regained his voice, though he was still on all fours, panting like a dog. "Police."

"Where uniform? No look like polices to me," said Goldie. "Look like some kinda *kano* fuckhead and faggot friend."

Bogie took another ragged breath. "No uniform. I'm a detective—NBI. He's with the United States police."

Sam had recovered enough to see some humor in Goldie's tirade. "Why is it that everyone assumes we're a couple, Bogie?" He paused for dramatic effect. "Hey, which one of us is the cute one?"

"You both ugly faggots," said Goldie. "Know what I thinkin'? I thinkin' you two no polices at all. I thinkin' I get my real cop arrest your ugly faggot asses. You s'posed to be some plain clothesed poe-lices you better show ID quick. Yeah, I thinkin' you better show me badges."

Sam fumbled for his shield, but stopped at a peremptory signal from Bogie. "Stay out of this, Sam," said Bogie, a certain edgy glee in his voice. "I've been waiting my whole career for this."

Bogie straightened to his full height, whipped out his pistol, and pointed it dead center between Goldie's eyes. His whole demeanor changed as he assumed the role of the bandito in *Treasure of the Sierra Madre*. With a heavy Mexican accent he said, "Badges? Badges! We don't need no stinking badges!"

Sam laughed, and couldn't stop. Goldie wasn't nearly as amused and looked like he had just dropped a load in his pants.

"All right, all right," Sam told Bogie. "Sometimes the old black and white films are the best."

In his closet-sized office, Goldie was hunkered down in a chair across from Sam. His desk must have been liberated from a grade school classroom. Through the open door Sam watched as two beat cops took the sweeper into custody.

Sam listened as Bogie finished a call. "Thank you, Judge Vasquez. I appreciate your aid in this matter." Bogie paused while the judge responded. "Yes, I look forward to it, sir."

Bogie hung up and turned to Sam. "OK. We have authorization to search the premises. No problems later with Miss

Santos." He directed his attention to Goldie. "But I don't think we need to search too hard. I'm certain our friend is going to cooperate and just point out what Olivia de la Cruz left with him."

Goldie paled at this suggestion. He crossed himself, muttering, "*Manananggal!*"

Sam looked to Bogie. "What's he saying?"

"He says she's a vampire."

Sam looked at Bogie, shaking his head. "Are we talking fangs-in-the-neck bloodsucker here, or is this a cross-cultural vocabulary problem?"

Bogie was about to answer, but Goldie rushed ahead. "She suck away my life. I do this, I dead." He made a brushing motion with his hands indicating he would have nothing further to do with this.

Bogie pulled out the few drawers the office held. He handed a stack of files to Sam. Goldie gabbled in protest and Sam eyeballed him. He'd restrain Goldie if necessary, but he wanted to watch his face to ascertain when Bogie was getting close to the goods.

"I don't get it," said Sam while he methodically thumbed through the papers. "Just when I think I understand Manila, something crazy happens."

"What are you talking about?" said Bogie.

"This yahoo talking about vampires, for one thing."

"I took a world literature course in college," said Bogie. "Every culture that anthropologists have studied has some variation of the vampire legend."

Sam continued working through the files. His eye was caught by Goldie squirming in his seat, so he focused on his files. He pulled out a thin package wrapped in brown paper. "Bingo."

Bogie came over to look at the package as Sam opened it. Inside was a portfolio full of technical drawings and a research report. On top was a hand-scrawled note, not in English. Below that, in another hand, something was written in a curling script.

eleven--

Jennifer worked alone at her desk, annotating a stack of documents. Though she worked at a steady pace, the stack never seemed to get smaller.

The door opened and her assistant, Carla, put her head inside the office. "I am going home now, Miss Santos. Is there anything else you need?"

"No, thank you. I'm going to work a while longer."

Carla pursed her lips in mock disapproval. "Those files won't go anywhere. Take a break."

Jennifer smiled, but focused back on the task. Carla left and Jennifer heard the lights click off in the outer office. A few moments later, the door to her office opened again, though no one entered. Busy, Jennifer didn't bother to look up.

"Did you forget something, Carla?"

When there was no immediate response, she raised her eyes. She could see the darkened hallway through the door, which was ajar. Taking care to be quiet, Jennifer opened a desk drawer and withdrew a stun gun.

A shadow crossed the door frame.

"Don't be alarmed, Fiscal Santos. I was waiting for your assistant to be out of hearing."

A man took a step into the room, pausing to light a cigar. His arrogance and sense of self-importance were at odds with his clandestine behavior.

Jennifer recognized him as a former business associate of her father. The two men had fallen out over the validity of some four-century-old Spanish land grants, and now Sonny Lagos was a congressman heading a land reform movement. He had been yet another minor source of corruption during the Marcos regime, and she was not happy to see him in her office.

She thought it ridiculous that he was still called Sonny, even though he was in his late fifties, and had the beginnings of a paunch. Since she had last seen him he had styled his hair and had his teeth capped. *Thinks he's a politician on the way up, does he?*

She returned the stun gun to its drawer, making sure that he got a good look at it as she did so.

"What do you want of me, Congressman?"

"Respect for your elders, for a start," said Sonny. After a long pause during which Jennifer remained impassive, he continued. "After all, we got you this job."

Jennifer was not taking that bait. "I *keep* this job because I am good at it. Not because of your so-called influence."

"Wrong. You keep this job at our behest," he snapped. "And now we have a request to make of you. Drop this investigation of the murdered *kano.*"

At the reference to the Tucker case, Jennifer made several connections. As a prosecutor she reviewed many cases that never moved forward because they lacked enough evidence for a likely conviction, and Sonny's request brought together several strands from open cases.

Bogie had told her that Tucker sold gamecocks to the arenas, and she knew that Sonny was an avid fan. In conjunction with the information from the American ATF agent, she saw that cockfighting might be the cover for a deeper connection: Tucker running guns to Sonny for his new political party. *Perhaps he's arming a private militia.*

She put on a confused look and asked, "Why would a congressman be interested in the death of an unknown American?"

Sonny didn't buy her act and breathed stertorously through his nose.

"If you persist in this stupid behavior, there will be consequences."

"Don't threaten me." Jennifer leaned back in her chair. "Even congressmen are no longer beyond the law."

Sonny held his anger in check with visible difficulty. He

was unused to opposition. He pulled a folded poster from his coat and handed it to her.

"The Homeless Coalition has become a force to be reckoned with," he said. "There will be a rally at the opening of the Intramuros apartment complex."

Jennifer unfolded the poster. Her body tensed as she read through the copy. "A CALL TO ARMS! Why are you homeless?—Who has stolen your land?—These are the criminals who control your lives!"

Her eyes flicked up to Lagos, and back to photos on the poster in disbelief.

"Quite good likenesses of your parents, don't you think?" said Sonny. "Five hundred copies of this can be posted in less than two hours. Volunteers are easy to—"

"You bastard," said Jennifer.

"Such language." Lagos clicked his tongue. "I told your father a foreign education would ruin your Filipina modesty." He stepped to the door. "I'm sure you've noticed that sometimes these rallies get out of control."

MANILA STREETS—7:00 P.M. MONDAY

Sam made his way through the dense foot traffic, the folder from Goldie's office in a portfolio beneath his arm. In the smog-diffused light he thought this was the flyover where he and Bogie had seen the hibachi and the Santa Claus figures ,but now they were nowhere in sight. Since there were cardboard shanties everywhere he looked, he wasn't sure if he was back at the same spot or not.

He looked at the street sign, but the name didn't stir any memories, either. Confused about which way he should head, he flagged down one of the omnipresent bicycle rickshaws called pedicabs. He had no idea what the ride should cost, so he just showed the driver a five-dollar bill.

"Can you take me to the NBI offices near here?" He glanced

at the ID photo the driver was required to display. "You know where it is, Manny?"

The pedicab driver gave a broad smile, probably because tourists never knew the right price for anything. "Sure, boss. No problem."

Sam had no way of knowing that this one fare would feed the cabbie's whole family today and tomorrow. He put the five spot back in his pocket, climbed in, and leaned back against the sprung seat.

He felt like he had been dropped into the film set of Blade Runner. Sidewalk vendors hawked their wares in a language that sounded like a mix of Spanish and Hawaiian. A group of children in black and gray plaid parochial school uniforms bought fried squid-on-a-stick from a pushcart. The signs on the buildings were half English and half Tagalog. The graffiti was pure East L.A., with plenty of spider script.

Forward progress slowed as the pedicab moved into traffic. A blind beggar, an old man with three long gray beard hairs, was led through the traffic by his sighted helper, a small girl in a bedraggled red party dress three sizes too large. She led him up to Sam's pedicab.

Both she and the old man stood next to the vehicle, silent. They asked for nothing, didn't try to sell him anything, had no dance to offer. They just stood there.

The cabbie made a brushing motion with his hand, trying to get them to leave, to no avail. The little girl seemed fascinated by Sam's suit and his light skin, and the old man appeared content to wait with his helper.

It wasn't often Sam sat this close to poverty, and he felt uncomfortable. He remembered the airport cabbie who had warned him about giving anything to the beggars. Somehow this felt different to Sam.

Is that her father? Or did he buy this child to be his helper? Maybe he's training an apprentice and he's not even blind. Sam revised that last thought as he took a closer look at the man's opaque corneas. Cataracts or trachoma or something worse.

At last the girl moved on, the old man's hand on her shoulder. The driver maneuvered his cab onto the median, circumnavigated a few autos, and got back into the press. The cab inched along as shadows lengthened.

Sam saw a squat bus off to his side, making its way with its right wheels riding the sidewalk. It was painted in psychedelic patterns of watermelon pink and Day-Glo green. Mirrors and plastic baubles glued to its surface reminded him of Mardi Gras. Back in the States, Sam could have sold it instantly to some Dead Heads.

Like a fighter jet, this vehicle had the name "Rambo" painted on its side. Sam wasn't sure if that was the nickname of the bus or the driver. The driver's compartment sported fuzzy dice, a fringe of brilliant orange cloth balls, and a once-white angora dash cover. Even from twenty feet away, Sam could see that the tires were completely bald, with patches of white fiberglass belting showing through.

"What is that thing?"

"A jeepney, sir. Berry cheap transportation. Crowded and dirty, sir. Only low class people use them."

The jeepney stopped and several passengers emerged from its interior. Two others let themselves down from the roof where they had perched. New passengers pushed up the step at the rear of the vehicle, putting coins into the hand of someone inside. Three young men clambered onto the roof, hoping for a free ride.

The collector inside shouted for the driver to stop. Both driver and collector jumped out to confront the roof-riding freeloaders. Within a minute the situation had escalated to a screaming match. Sam watched as four male riders clambered out, eager either to find out what the trouble was, or to see if they could make some.

The driver had left the motor idling. It was a hot evening, and with an abrupt eructation the jeepney's overburdened engine boiled over, spraying steam into the pedestrians on the sidewalk. Screams of pain were added to the din. The driver and fare collector found themselves the center of an ever-shrinking circle of outraged pedestrians.

The passengers still inside the jeepney peered through the windows. Sam thought they must have decided it was time to find alternate transportation. They jumped out and moved away through the angry crowd. From fifty yards away a traffic cop blew his whistle to see if he could persuade the jeepney to move along. He made his way toward the mob.

Sam found this more entertaining than the cable TV channels in his hotel room, so he settled back to watch things develop. It was then he saw Chito emerge from El Zorro, a strip club some twenty yards ahead. Chito hadn't seen him, and Sam decided this was his chance. He jumped from the cab to follow on foot.

The driver squawked in Tagalog. To Sam's ears the driver's non-English protests were lost in the general hubbub. He pushed toward Chito.

Chito was far more adept at making his way through the crowd. He did that inoffensive Filipino wriggle that allowed him to pass between the tightly-meshed bodies.

Sam was more salmon-like in his progress. He would surge forward, making some headway, but struggling with every step. Sam saw that he was losing ground and began just bulling his way through. He drew ever more hostile looks from the pedestrians.

Sam couldn't believe that he was falling behind. He decided to take more direct action and yelled at the top of his lungs. "Chito!"

Chito looked around when he heard his name, clearly unhappy that someone had called attention to him on the street. Because of Sam's relative height, Chito spotted him in the crowd at once.

At that moment the driver rammed his pedicab onto the sidewalk, blocking Sam's progress. He screamed curses about the "son-a-bitch robber," creating a blockage in the pedestrian flow. In an instant, dozens of interested onlookers surrounded them. Sam saw they were ready to be entertained by a crazy *kano* and a possibly/probably drunken pedicab driver.

Sam regressed to his college football days. He lowered his head, stuck out an arm, and plowed through the crowd, drawing cries of anger from those he pushed aside.

Indignant young men around him muttered at the outlander's rudeness. On the fringe of the crowd an old woman fell as she stepped off the curb. Her yelp of pain convinced Sam—and many of those in the mob—that some new outrage was being perpetrated. Meanwhile, the cabbie never let up in his howling for payment and again tried to ram his vehicle into Sam.

Sam could no longer move forward. "Chito! Stop where you are! I want to talk to you!" His voice was aggressive and demanding, the kind of voice that most antagonizes Asians.

Chito stopped and sized up the situation around Sam. He shouted to the crowd in Tagalog. *"He's some asshole who tried to pick me up at the bar. He won't take no for an answer."*

The crowd pressed in around Sam. An entrepreneurial pickpocket who had seen an opportunity to increase the day's profits had already lifted Sam's wallet, but when he spied the gun in Sam's waistband, he backed away quickly. The seething crowd carried him away from Sam.

"Where's my five dollar?" the cabbie screamed in Sam's face. He switched to Tagalog in an aside to the crowd. *"Who do these cock-sucking foreigners think they are?"*

Sam could feel things were getting out of hand. He stood still and smiled in what he hoped was an amicable manner. Chito looked back, flipped Sam off, and melted into the crowd.

Sam tried to control his anger at losing Chito as someone brushed up hard against him. Sam felt for his billfold, realized it was missing.

"Hey! Someone took my wallet!"

Somehow neither the pedicab driver nor the crowd was convinced.

"Maybe money in your notebook, sir!" said the driver in English. "Give it to me, I find it!"

Helpful hands tried to assist the driver, attempting to pluck the portfolio from Sam's grasp. Sam began a tug-of-war and decided to show his badge to let the citizens know who he was.

The pickpocket was still nearby, waiting for someone to clock Sam so that he could snag either his passport or badge. When he saw Sam reach beneath his coat the pickpocket shouted, "Watch out! He's got a gun!"

The crowd got uglier by the instant. A few of the braver (and larger) Filipinos pushed against Sam, shoving him back and forth. Sam fought to maintain his balance. Someone pushed a lit cigarette into the back of his neck, and he barked in pain.

He whirled about, looking for the culprit. Since about seventy-five per cent of the people on the street were smoking, it wasn't hard to find someone who could be guilty. He collared the most likely miscreant and shook him.

"I'm not an ashtray!"

As angry shouts went up from the crowd, two cops began swinging their nightsticks with abandon, moving toward the heart of this problem on their beat.

Sam saw them coming and felt a wave of relief. He didn't mind admitting to himself that he was scared, and it was good to see the guys in blue. His relief was short lived as one of the cops whacked him in the head and he went to his knees, stunned.

The second cop pulled back Sam's coat and jerked the pistol from his waistband in elation.

"What we got here?" he asked his partner. "A real bad guy, maybe."

He fingered his billy club. Beat cops might not be well paid, but on occasion they got the chance to crack heads, and that gave a sense of satisfaction worth many pesos.

The first cop checked Sam's holster. He paled when he saw the US ATF badge. He showed it to his partner.

"Oh, *tae!*"

They pulled Sam to his feet, brushed off his clothes, and moved him through the crowd to a quieter spot. One cop looked into Sam's pupils to see if he had a concussion. The other pushed the gun back into Sam's waistband, also replacing the badge and its case.

The pedicab driver had followed along, hoping to claim his five-dollar fare. Once Manny saw the flash of Sam's badge, he retrieved Sam's portfolio notebook and parcel from the ground with a dexterous swoop. Figuring the notebook alone might fetch a couple of dollars, he pedaled away from the scene as fast as the crowd allowed.

A block away he stopped to go through the packages. He didn't find currency or any papers of obvious value. He saved a nice ballpoint pen for himself and tossed the papers from the notebook into a dumpster.

Just then an old woman called out for a cab. He pedaled back to the main road, thinking about where he might sell the notebook.

twelve--

As he walked toward Dirty Harry's Bar, sweat poured down Chito's face—from fear, not the heat.

Saddul palmed a small snub-nosed pistol. It looked as if he were just a friend of Chito's walking beside him.

The closer they got to the bar, the more desperate Chito became.

"If I'm seen going in there—" he whimpered.

Saddul pressed the gun into Chito's back.

"Don't get stupid. Cuz I can see the headlines now: Cheap Pimp Killed in Escape Attempt." Saddul shoved Chito on ahead, making him stumble.

Bogie shifted in the booth, moving stiffly, still recovering from the blow to the stomach.

"We never caught the sweeper or his helper."

The gathering in the cops' bar was morose. Bogie and Garcia picked at their *meryenda* with little appetite.

With one hand Sam held a bar towel with some ice in it to the back of his head, hoping to halt the throbbing before his date with Jennifer. With his other hand he pressed a cold bottle of beer to his forehead. His time in Manila felt more and more like a nightmare.

"I lost Olivia when she went into the ladies room at El Zorro," said Garcia. "Musta gone out through the window."

"I managed to get mugged and lose the evidence Olivia left at the arena," said Sam. "Productive day."

There was a brief fuss at the entry. With mock

politeness, Saddul ushered Chito through the door into Dirty Harry's. He steered him toward the bar, scanning for Bogie and the others. Once he spotted the detectives he pushed Chito towards them.

"You shitheads!" said Chito.

A few off-duty policemen looked up at the commotion. They all knew Chito by sight, and once they realized who it was, they went back to their meals.

Sam couldn't believe his eyes. He nodded to Saddul. He got up and stood to face Chito.

"Nice work."

Chito ignored Sam and directed his remarks to Bogie.

"She told you to get off my case."

Sam and Bogie both realized Chito had to be referring to their meeting with the fiscal. They exchanged a glance before Bogie responded.

"I don't know what you're talking about. I thought Detective Saddul brought you by for a friendly drink, see if we couldn't have a little chat—off the record."

Chito grew ever more agitated, looking toward the open door of the bar.

"If anybody I know sees me in here—" He switched to Tagalog. *"They'll kill me."*

"We have guests," Garcia answered in English, with a nod toward Sam.

"I thought a tough guy like you knew how to handle himself on the streets," said Saddul. He pulled a tissue from his pocket, snorked into it, and tucked the soiled tissue back into its hiding place.

Chito appealed mutely to Bogie, behaving as if they had some special bond.

"You're signing my death warrant. If Olivia ever meant anything to you—"

Bogie stared back at him, nothing on his face.

"Tell us who killed Mr. Tucker, and we'll arrange protective custody," said Garcia. "Otherwise you're free to go."

Sam looked a question at Bogie, and Bogie nodded.

Chito looked around the bar, searching for a non-threatening face. The off-duties eyeballed him dispassionately.

It didn't look as if anyone gave a rat's ass whether Chito lived or died, inside the bar or out. They all just hoped his death wouldn't interrupt their *meryenda*.

Sam caught Chito's eye.

"You know, I've been wanting to ask you something." He reached out, caught Chito's balls, and squeezed hard. "That crowd was gonna lynch me. What did you tell them?"

Chito's eyes bulged from their sockets. He spoke with difficulty. "I—told them—you were trying—to—grab my balls."

Sam acted as if he were holding a hot potato. The nearby cops and detectives hooted at his embarrassment. Sam got up and shoved Chito toward the door.

"I hope your friends are right outside." He pushed Chito into the street, calling out "And heeeeeeere's Chito!"

Chito whipped his head around, checking the street for onlookers who could identify him. He spoke to Sam over his shoulder as he hustled away.

"You'll be hearing from her again. Believe it."

Sam wondered how and why Chito was connected to any fiscal, much less Jennifer Santos. It heightened his sense that his whole trip to Manila might be a fever dream. He walked over to Saddul.

"So why bring him in here if we're just gonna let him go again?"

Saddul held up one finger. "If anyone saw, there'll be a contract out to kill him by nightfall. So either 'A,' he gets scared and asks for protection, which we will provide if he tells us what we need to know." He held up a second finger. "Or 'B,' he thinks he can talk his way out of his situation, and he gets himself killed. We cross one more problem off our list."

Sam had difficulty believing he had heard right. "Look, I'm not a big proponent of civil rights for criminals, but—" He stopped, unsure where he should take the conversation.

"I just gave him an incentive to cooperate," said Saddul. "We'll see if it works out."

Pasay Warehouse—8:30 p.m. Monday

Olivia had freshened her makeup and pulled her hair into a bun. Her look of schoolgirl innocence was belied by a slight twist in her smile.

"What did you do with them?" She was almost pleading. "You must tell us. We have to know." She seemed desperate for an answer. "When you tell us, the pain will stop."

The pedicab driver was unrecognizable. One eye was swollen shut. His nose had been mashed to a pulp, and it still bled across his mouth and chin, staining the few teeth he had left.

His lips moved slowly and painfully as he tried to speak, his breath coming in ragged gasps, his whisper barely audible. His voice was long gone, the result of an hour of unbroken screaming. The empty tobacco warehouse had echoed with his agony, but the concrete block walls muffled all sound.

Olivia leaned closer to listen, her perfect features juxtaposed with the ruins of his.

The cabbie's lips moved again. "I—don't—know."

Olivia turned away, saddened by what she knew would follow.

The driver lay spread-eagled face down on a workbench, one arm now twisted obscenely behind him, long since dislocated. The other arm was pulled taut above his head. A screwdriver had been driven through his hand, pinning it to the table.

From the shadows a Japanese businessman watched. Mr. Nosaka was clad in Armani, his oiled hair freshly cut. His Rolex flashed, reflecting light from the single overhead bulb, as he motioned Olivia away from the driver.

Nosaka grabbed the screwdriver and twisted it, grinding the tendons and bones of the cabbie's hand. His body arched in pain, and his throat constricted as he tried to scream, but only a gurgle came from his tortured larynx.

Nosaka picked up Sam's ballpoint pen and held it in front of the driver's nose, the ATF insignia visible. He clicked it, trying to get the cabbie's attention, twisting the screwdriver all the while.

"Is this bringing it back? Have you remembered yet?" Nosaka asked.

The driver seemed to swim up from some dark place. He opened his remaining eye and looked at the pen, but he was so far gone that he couldn't register what it was. Nosaka dropped the pen and let go of the screwdriver. He grabbed the driver's hair with both hands and slammed his head against the table top once—twice—

"This is getting us nowhere," said Olivia. "He doesn't know who has it."

Just as well that Nosaka had stopped—the cabbie was dead. He let the man's head drop to the table with a hint of satisfaction at a job well done. He took a tissue from his pocket and applied it to his forehead, blotting oily perspiration.

"Perhaps he really did just throw them in a dumpster," Olivia said, careful not to put a challenge in it. She wondered why Nosaka-san was so obsessed by these papers. "Perhaps it was just coincidence that put the documents in his hands to begin with."

"I don't believe in coincidence."

Nosaka indicated that they were finished, and Olivia accompanied him to the doorway. She gave instructions to a waiting thug to leave the body at the entry to the *baranggáy*.

"With a calling card," said Nosaka.

"My people will keep searching," said Olivia. "We'll find the papers or whoever has them at this time."

Nosaka handed Olivia an envelope filled with cash. "As usual, your helpers' services are much appreciated. This matter must be resolved at once."

FISCAL'S OFFICE—9:15 P.M. MONDAY

Illumined by her desk lamp, Jennifer worked in a golden pool of light in an office that was otherwise dark. The pile of folders had diminished but was still formidable. The phone rang and she answered distractedly.

"Yes? Oh, Agent Haine. Aren't you early?"

She glanced at her watch, realized how late it was, and mouthed *dammit*. She cradled the phone between her shoulder and chin as she slipped on her shoes.

"I should have warned you. After 8 p.m. you can't get past the security post in the lobby." She pulled on the jacket to her business suit. "I was already on my way out when the phone rang. I'll be right down."

She gathered the Harvey Tucker files into a pile and put them into the shallow top drawer of her desk. She locked the drawer and flicked off the light.

On a landing halfway up the curved marble staircase a small combo played show tunes. The musicians were not just good, they were record studio quality. The Filipina vocalist sounded like a younger version of Aretha Franklin.

Sam was enjoying himself, though he knew he was blowing a week's per diem on this one meal. He had the feeling that Jennifer might be as interested in him as he was in her.

"Try it, you'll like it," she said.

"I've already tried the local beer," said Sam. "It's a good brew. It's just that I prefer a Coors with my steak. I don't think that's too much to ask."

"I'm not talking about the beer," said Jennifer in a sultry voice.

Images strobed through Sam's mind of what else he might try and like with her.

Jennifer pointed to the small mound of *bagoong* on his plate. "I meant the *bagoong*."

Sam looked at the glutinous paste. "What is it exactly?"

"Shrimp eggs. Sort of like caviar."

"Bah-gong, eh," said Sam. "I'm not a big caviar fan."

"Buh-goh-ahng," she corrected. "It's the real flavor of the Philippines."

Hesitantly Sam dipped his spoon into the fishy mass and resumed his argument.

"It's not cultural imperialism to serve American beer in the Philippines. It's just good business. You have an international clientele in this country, especially in the five-star hotels."

He put the whole spoonful of the paste into his mouth. Jennifer opened her mouth to warn him, but it was too late. First his nose wrinkled as if he had just sniffed an expulsion of sewer gas. His face contorted as he rolled the stuff on his tongue, trying to escape the overwhelming flavor.

He grabbed his Coors and chugged it, practically gargling with the beer before his face returned to normal. He gestured toward her beer and she nodded assent. He downed hers as well.

Outwardly Jennifer acted as if she were somewhat embarrassed by his behavior, as the waiters standing nearby frowned in disapproval. Sam looked at her over the bottle and wondered if, secretly, she was pleased at throwing him off balance this way.

Having finished Jennifer's beer, Sam looked at the bottle with approval.

"Thank God for San Miguel."

From the kitchen doorway a busboy watched the flirtation between Sam and Jennifer. His scowl was interpreted by the other busboys as disapproval at the sight of an upper-class Filipina dating a *kano*. They were right, but there was more to it than that.

He pulled out two small ID photos from the pocket of his white uniform shirt and checked them against Sam and Jennifer's faces. He made his way to a pay phone near the lobby and placed a call to Congressman Lagos' office.

thirteen--

BARYO PASAY—11 P.M. MONDAY

Yellow crime scene tape cordoned the area around a body that lay beneath a tarp next to the shantytown entryway. Several uniformed police kept curiosity seekers back. Pickpockets worked the crowd, always glad of an opportunity to improve their earnings.

Two homeless families clamored for attention at the edge of the crime scene. Every night they slept on the sidewalk in a spot now enclosed by the police tape. They demanded their right to spread their cardboard and blankets.

"We have to get some sleep," the father asserted. "We have a busy day tomorrow."

The second homeless man, cousin to the first man, joined in.

"You cannot keep us from our sleeping spot. We know our rights."

The police had lost patience with their demands.

"Less interfering with police business," said the senior beat cop. He waved his baton. "If you don't quiet down, I'll drive you away, and you'll sleep in a gutter tonight."

The two homeless wives shrieked their outrage. "You heartless pigs," said one, a wizened thirty-five year old. "May you never escape purgatory."

"Show some Christian charity," said the second woman, who had been a close runner-up in the withered dug competition. "May the saints protect us from your evil eye and evil heart."

Talk about the evil eye upset the nine children the two families had between them. They wailed in fear.

To make the misery complete, it began to rain again. Harder this time.

Garcia and Saddul had received the call about 10 p.m. Traffic had eased, and it only took them half an hour to make the three-mile trip from the police station to the entrance of the *baranggáy*.

A photographer, Jojo, was already there, waiting for them. He worked freelance, both for the police and the newspapers, carrying a variety of press passes and badges that generally allowed him access to any site. He had been a few streets away doing "red pavement" shots of a jeepney accident for a tabloid when he heard the police call on his scanner. When Garcia and Saddul walked up, he motioned them to one side.

"I already took the ID photos, details of the wounds on the body, and the body position," said Jojo. For a man who had seen an untoward amount of human misery through his camera lens, he was a little uneasy. "This isn't the usual 'peasant kills peasant' kind of thing."

He paused, took a breath, looked around the crowd to see if someone was watching. He thought better of telling them any more and stepped aside so they could get to the body.

Garcia and Saddul squatted next to the corpse and pulled back the tarp to reveal the face. Saddul was shocked at the condition of the man's face.

Garcia flinched as well, but acted more concerned that he might get blood on his cuffs. Garcia motioned a uniformed policeman over.

"Anyone here know who this is?" asked Garcia, pointing at the crowd of onlookers.

"No, sir," said the policeman. "We asked the headman of the *baranggáy* to identify the deceased, but he said he didn't recognize the face."

"That's no surprise," said Saddul. "No one could recognize that face. Did you go through his pockets for ID?"

"Yes, sir. There was nothing in his pockets." The policeman hesitated . "Perhaps you should look at the right hand of the deceased, sir."

He stepped away from them, not wanting to step on the toes of those above him. Garcia and Saddul got on opposite sides of the body and pulled back the cheap sheet of plastic.

"Not much blood on the sidewalk," said Garcia. "He didn't die here."

Saddul gingerly raised the right arm of the corpse. He pointed first to the wrist.

"Looks like he was tied up."

He rolled the wrist so Garcia could see into the hand. A ballpoint pen penetrated the palm.

Garcia looked at Saddul. "What's this?"

"It sure ain't the murder weapon." Saddul pointed at the logo on the cylinder of the pen. "Look closer."

Garcia leaned in and saw the ATF insignia. He looked at Saddul. "How many of those do you suppose there are in Manila on any given day?"

"Zero or one?" said Saddul.

"That's my guess, too," answered Garcia.

"Bogie's gonna love this."

A thin woman with wild hair and an infant on her hip pushed her way to the front of the crowd. When she saw the body she let out a shriek that nearly broke Garcia's eardrum.

"Manny! Manny! What's happened to you?"

She threw herself on the body, sobbing hysterically. Saddul and Garcia looked at her with some distaste. Two uniformed policemen came over and took her by the arms, trying to pull her away. She clutched the blood-soaked shirt of her dead husband.

As the cops tugged, the woman, the infant, and the body were jerked along the pavement in a daisy chain. There were angry grumbles from the crowd at the disrespect the police were showing to a wife and mother in her time of grief.

Eyes open wide in fear, the infant remained absolutely quiet throughout the tug-of-war, clutching at his mother's blouse. Garcia thought to himself that even the babies learn how to stifle their own cries in the *baranggáy*. It was one of the prices of survival.

Saddul and Garcia turned control of the scene over to the forensics team.

The homeless families saw that fortune was beginning to favor them again, and they hurried to reclaim their allotted space on the pavement, pushing their flattened cardboard boxes back into place, covering the chalk outline on the broken sidewalk.

In the ensuing emotional storm, no one noticed the Chinese ideograms scratched on the pavement next to the dead man. By the next day the rain and the crowd had erased them. It didn't really matter, though. If the beat cops had seen them, they would have scuffed them away before the homicide detectives had arrived. Too much of their income was derived from payoffs made by the men who left such gang markings.

MANILA HILTON—11 P.M. MONDAY

Jennifer was halfway through an enormous ice cream sundae. Four different flavors of ice cream, as many kinds of syrup, whipped cream, nuts, M&Ms, and a cherry. Sam picked at his cheesecake as he watched her in awe.

"God, I wish I could do that," said Sam.

"I'm sure the waiter will take your order."

"I meant I wish I could eat four thousand calories of dessert."

"I knew what you meant. I was just teasing." Jennifer smiled at him.

And when she did Sam thought a cherry bomb had exploded in his crotch, the reaction was so immediate and strong. In a strained voice he said, "You've got to be careful with that."

"With what?"

"That thousand-watt smile. You just lit up this side of the room and people are putting on sunglasses."

"That's corny. But original. I'll take it as a compliment," she said.

"Good. That's how it was intended."

She put aside her spoon, having done as much damage as she was going to do to the mountain of ice cream.

"Shall we go? I have an early morning briefing."

Sam wriggled in his chair, not quite composed enough to get up.

"Let me finish my cheesecake. I was so impressed watching you, I forgot to keep working on my own dessert."

Jennifer thought she'd twist the knife, just a little. "A gentleman never keeps a lady waiting." Sam thought she was enjoying watching him squirm. "I really do have to go. I can send my driver back for you—"

Sam couldn't believe the way he was being dismissed, and it served to cool him off. "That's OK. I'll catch a cab."

"I enjoyed the dinner, Agent Haine," she said as she rose from the table. "Thank you."

Now we're back to Agent Haine? "Perhaps we can do it again, Fiscal Santos." *On some cold day in—*

"I'd love to," she replied. "You have my office number. Call." She turned and walked away.

If he hadn't received such mixed signals, he might have followed her from the restaurant. As things were, he just watched the excellent view as she exited.

Man, I love a woman in a tailored business suit. He sat up as he realized that her outfit could have come straight from some nineteen forties film noir.

Maybe Bogie is onto something.

fourteen--

THE HORNDOG'S GUIDE TO MANILA—VIP rooms at the strip clubs and karaoke bars cater to those gentlemen who can afford to pay for private performances.

You can have a private, up-close and personal chat with a *good girl*; get a lap dance or hand job from a *nice girl*; or you can cut a deal to take a *game girl* back to your hotel room. Prices range from five to fifty dollars.

No sex is allowed on the premises of a strip club, since these are not brothels. Brothels are illegal—and besides, the police payoffs are prohibitively expensive.

Each Guest Relations Officer, or **GRO**, as the girls are called, reports her deal to the mama-san as she leaves. When the GRO returns to the club, she has to cough up a third of her take to the management.

Leaving the club premises for sex means that the GRO must collect her own fees, risk being picked up by police at the patron's hotel, and she must avoid abusive clients on her own. On the plus side, she meets much wealthier clients, ones who don't want their faces in the papers. It is an arrangement that satisfies everyone.

MAKATI ARMS—9 A.M. TUESDAY

Bogie looked over the shoulder of the beautiful clerk at the Makati Arms reservation desk as she tapped search parameters into the computer. He marveled that Manila produced such a plentiful supply of beautiful women from such poverty. Filipinas had won the Miss Universe title twice, a feat unequaled by any other third world country. He decided it had to be the mixture of Filipino, European, Polynesian, Malay, and Chinese genes that produced women of such international appeal.

Bogie read the clerk's name tag reflected on the screen of the computer monitor, as the screen filled with guest information.

"Raven, can you bring up Mr. Tucker's previous visits during the past year?"

"I would have to search a different data base, sir. It is not accessible from this workstation."

"How far back can you search at this station?" he asked.

"Just thirty days, sir."

"Let's sort the last month's registrations, looking for guests with foreign passports."

She typed, and pointed to a tool bar at the bottom of the screen. "More than eighty per cent of our guests are foreigners. More than six hundred a month."

"That's too many," said Bogie. He thought. "Did Mr. Tucker charge his meals to his room?"

Raven entered a few keystrokes. Several pages of billing detail scrolled by on the screen. She moused through the data, highlighting several entries. She moved those to a new window, and printed out the information Bogie wanted.

Bogie took the list. "So he ate most meals here, and always with a guest at his table?"

The clerk looked down, embarrassed. He scrutinized the list again.

"Lots of alcohol. Champagne most often. What am I not understanding?" said Bogie.

The clerk continued to study her shoes as she spoke. "Mr. Tucker was well known here, sir. He often brought GRO's to the hotel for dinner and entertained them in his room." She looked at Bogie again. "Many of our guests prefer not to sleep alone."

"I see," said Bogie. "Is Olivia de la Cruz a frequent guest also?" Raven's expression showed that she knew who Olivia was, but she shook her head no.

He stared at the itemized list. "A week ago he charged a

lunch for three people. Do you know who might have been at the table with him?"

"How could I know that, sir? I work at the registration desk. Perhaps the maitre d'—"

"Where can I find him at this time of day?"

"I'll give you his home phone number, sir." Raven pulled out a personnel directory and wrote rapidly on the back of a hotel business card. "And here is my home number as well." She looked him directly in the eye. "In case I can be of any assistance."

Bogie smiled. "I'm sure I'll be in touch, Raven."

CLUB BOOM BOOM—10 A.M. TUESDAY

At the far end of the narrow gallery a Filipina mama-san in her sixties sat foursquare on a bar stool. The Frenchman Gerard peered into the "aquarium" of Club Boom Boom, looking down the cramped corridor which sat about three feet above street level, just next to the dressing room for the pole dancers who worked the club.

A one-way mirror covered one wall, and there was a bench running the length of the room so the male customers could sit and watch through the mirror as the girls dressed. On the other side of the glass several half-clad Filipinas in their mid-teens were applying their makeup, the elevation of the gallery allowing the men on the benches to peer into the cleavage of the girls as they primped. Mama-san perused the patrons, checking to see if any funny business was going on.

Gerard moved along the glass wall, groping each girl mentally. He paused when he saw that the last two girls looked to be pure Chinese—and only eleven or twelve years old. He slipped his hand into his slacks and began to play a little pocket pool.

The mama-san was impatient for Gerard to make a choice. It didn't matter who he chose, as long as he didn't make a mess on the floor for the next customer. Her Japanese guests were fussy about stepping in someone else's residue.

Not like those Frenchy bastards. Jap pervs pay top dollar. The mama-san looked at Gerard, peeping at his crotch.

"Hey! I know you!" said the mama-san, recognizing Gerard. "You keep pecker in pocket now. No want trouble with you."

"Where did you get the Chinese girls, Mama?"

"They my daughters," lied Mama-san directly. She had hit menopause ten years before either of the girls was conceived, nor were these girls even minimally Filipino. "You like Chinese? Make you special deal. Ten dollars US for one. Eighteen for both."

Gerard looked uncertain.

"I don't take no fuckin' Euros. Only US dollars. You want pay in Euros, cost you twice as much."

"No, no. The price is good. But I am thinking I cannot take girls so young to my hotel room."

"No problem-o. Four dollars more, I rent you bedroom at nephew's house," said Mama-san. "Just down street. Convenient." She scratched absently at her hair bun. "Clean."

Gerard moved near the glass as the youngest Chinese girl leaned in from her side to check her lip gloss, her breath leaving a thin haze on the mirror. Without looking away from the girl, he spoke to Mama-san from the side of his mouth, his voice lowered because his face was no more than six inches from the girl on the far side of the glass.

"This one has pimples. Perhaps worse. I do not desire any diseases, Mama-san."

Mama-san smiled sourly to herself. They had reached the negotiation stage. "Why you insult me? No disease here. Daughters get regular check up with doctor. Ex-US Army surgeon, top-notch guy."

Something behind Gerard caught Mama's eye and she clammed up. Gerard felt someone take a seat close to him, and he turned to the newcomer, whose body eclipsed Gerard's view of two-thirds of the gallery.

Juan Samoa leaned his bulk forward until his forehead

bumped against the one-way mirror. The Chinese girl child was startled by the tiny thump from the other side of the mirror and pulled away from the glass. She sat back in her chair, motionless, waiting for instructions to come over the intercom.

Juan smiled at Gerard. "When you tap the glass, it scares the fish in the aquarium."

Gerard looked confused. "Why are you here? We have no business together this night."

Juan cut his eyes toward Mama-san. She turned to face away from them, temporarily deaf. "Olivia wants to do you a favor."

"I am getting my girls here tonight," said Gerard. "Perhaps I will return to your establishment tomorrow, but it is not certain. I like to spread my business around."

"Different kind of favor," said Juan. "This is about a missing package. One meant for your Pakistani friend."

"I don't know what you are talking about." What does he know of the technical plans? "I have no package that is missing. I know no one from Pakistan."

Juan looked into Gerard's eyes and leaned in close. "If you *should* discover that a package of yours has gone missing—if you happen to meet someone of Pakistani descent—Olivia can be of help to you."

Gerard tried to back away from the behemoth without offending him. "My friend, my company in France exports goods to eager customers around the world. I import items for which I may find buyers elsewhere. I am a trader, and Manila is the best crossroads at which to do business."

Gerard searched his pocket for a match to light his cigarette as Juan continued to scrutinize him. There was a thin film of sweat on his upper lip.

"Yes, I take some small pleasures while upon the road, and I often use the services of Miss de la Cruz and yourself." He exhaled a plume of smoke that filled the small space. "I fail to see how our businesses can intersect. I deal in goods. You deal in services."

"If you persist in being stupid, then perhaps the package

will find its way into other hands," said Juan, his voice flat. "Do you understand?"

Gerard gave a French shrug. "What package?"

But to himself he thought, *How has Riffat screwed things up? You never can trust these merde-for-brains Pakis.*

DAVAU, MINDANAO—NOON TUESDAY

Riffat needed a cigarette. He needed real coffee. And to converse in Arabic, not some forsaken jungle tongue.

Oh well, he would spend but one night with the Abu Sayef. He would drop the funds and instructions from Al Qaeda, retrace his route to Davau, and leave this pesthole behind. In two days he could retrieve the plans for the triggering device from Manila and go home to Islamabad.

Riffat had flown from Manila to Davau, largest city on the island of Mindanao. From there he had boarded a bus to ride five hours into the countryside.

The highway began well but lost its integrity about two hours outside the city. From there on it was paved sporadically, between potholes and stream crossings. The bus stopped at each tiny village, taking on a few passengers, letting off a few.

Goats and piglets were assigned to the roof, along with their owners. A six-inch-high railing was meant to keep them from falling off, and usually did, since the bus broke fifteen miles per hour only on rare occasions. The animals were hobbled so that in their terror they wouldn't try to escape. Now and then a chicken was smuggled inside the bus, beneath a rider's shirt.

In Davau, Riffat had blended well on the bus, being the same shade of brown as the locals, but after an hour of exchanging passengers, he was recognizable as a foreigner. The faces surrounding him were less cosmopolitan, darker, with more Malaysian features. And the locals got smaller the farther they were from the city, a result of poverty and poorer nutrition.

An hour before sunset he got off the bus at a collection of *nipa* huts, their dry thatch catching the red rays. There were no electric lights this far into the bush, and the sole phone was located in the village police station. He knew from past experience that it worked infrequently, as did the local police.

An occasional Coleman lantern broke the gloom around the clearing that served as the village center. Riffat walked over to a small hibachi where chicken was being grilled. The cook looked up and handed him a sliver of bamboo with bits of skewered chicken.

Riffat gave him a hundred-peso note without exchanging a word.

The chicken vendor made the huge overpayment disappear into the recesses of a ragged camouflage shirt, which had doubtless been issued to a US GI during the Viet Nam era. He stood, dumped out the remainder of his charcoal, wrapped the remaining chicken in a banana leaf, and walked into the jungle beyond the village.

Riffat followed amidst the stridulations of the insects and peeping of the frogs. A seemingly endless column of fruit bats flew overhead, their two-foot wingspans crowding the dusky sky. Riffat looked up, wondering how the flapping of all those leathery wings made no sound at all. Their flight was eerie in its silence.

The two men walked by moonlight for almost an hour before they heard the wailing cry. It was the final call to Isha, the last Muslim prayer of the day. Riffat and his guide found their way inside a small hut, where a dozen men in skullcaps had spread their prayer rugs.

Riffat joined the others in prayer, observing the rites, while letting his muscles relax. Twenty years ago, when he first started making these trips, it had been an adventure, full of excitement. Even today he still believed that jihad in the Philippines was crucial to the establishment of a Muslim Pacific sphere of influence.

But now, by and large, jihad made him tired. Force the infidels out of the Visayas, drive the damned Catholics back to Luzon. Once the Christians could be isolated there, the Mindanao National Liberation Front could use Cebu and Davau as staging areas for the rest of the Pacific Rim. The mental recitation also had the feeling of ritual, like the prayers.

In the meantime, his legs were cramping from the unaccustomed hike. And these provincials ate food that tasted like dung. And the women were homely. And there was no air-con—

Riffat stopped himself from going any further down that train of thought. He was becoming as soft as Gerard, who even though (or maybe because) he was an infidel, had a nose for finding good food and willing women.

Manila Streets—Noon Tuesday

Chito beckoned the group of ragged street children into an abandoned storefront. The corners of the room were filled with feces, and the stench forced him to breathe through his mouth. However, the number of flies per cubic foot of air made this hazardous, and he pulled the neck of his shirt up to cover his mouth.

The kids ranged from eight to ten years old. They were so undernourished, even the oldest could have passed for six—until you looked in their eyes. These children had seen too much misery, been beaten too often, fed too frequently from garbage cans, been used by too many pervs.

They all knew the truth. And the truth was that any one of them would kill—or be killed—for a good meal. They would betray their best friend for a better spot on the street to run their begging scams. They would pimp their sister or their brother for a dry place to sleep.

They were survivors. If they got sick or lost just a step of their speed, another kid would take their place. And then they would disappear.

Not one of them suffered from depression. Kids who were depressed got eaten by the street. None of them worried about the future—at least not past the end of this night. There was no point worrying about something you might never see.

These were the lost boys.

Because they were who they were, they hovered in the entry to the building. They had learned it wasn't smart to get too close to an adult in an out-of-the-way place. Adults had funny ideas about the games kids wanted to play. They knew Chito by sight, or they wouldn't have come even that close.

He pulled ten money-rolls from his pockets. Each roll consisted of low denomination notes and totaled a hundred pesos. The kids moved closer, still just out of arm's reach.

"I need ten of you to search the dumpsters around the *baranggáy*. I know that if you don't beg today you won't be able to eat, so—"

Chito pulled papers from inside his shirt, poor quality photocopies of the cover sheet of the Frenchman's report. He showed the boys the seal that was stamped there. "Whoever finds papers like these—" He paused to make sure he had their full attention. "I will give one thousand pesos."

There were more boys than there were money-rolls, and the tougher ones shoved the weaker to the rear as they pushed forward to take them. A little fellow at the back called out, "Mister Chito, if I find the papers will you give me the thousand pesos?"

The older boys hooted at the idea of this runt finding papers which they were being paid to look for. They found it even funnier that he thought he would be able to hang onto them if he did find them.

Chito grinned. "The reward is to whoever brings me the papers. By tonight."

The older boys moved away, while the younger ones crowded in to look at the imprint of the seal.

"I'll be back here at sundown. If you find it earlier, leave a message at Club de Sex," said Chito. "And if you think one of you can just take my hundred pesos but not look for my papers, I'm sure these boys," he gestured to the smaller children, "will tell me where to find you."

fifteen--

Bogie and Sam met at the NBI office to go over their material. This case had acquired its own momentum, accreting new crimes as the investigation rolled along. Garcia had earlier dropped off the forensic report of the pedicab driver's death, including the photos Jojo had developed overnight. They worked for twenty minutes without a dozen words passing between them, reviewing the data.

"What's wrong with this case, Bogie?" said Sam. He knew plenty of things about the case had to be bothering Bogie as well.

"Every case is complicated," said Bogie.

Sam realized Bogie wanted to hear his analysis before offering his own ideas.

"But this is like peeling an onion. I knew Tucker was setting up a weapons buy, a whole cargo container-full. That's why he was here. ATF knows that he had an arrangement with some intermediary who was brokering the deal."

Bogie gave him an inquisitive look.

"We were going to pass all the info along to the Philippine government after we cracked the case," said Sam. "Tucker's death muddies the water. Sellers don't kill customers. Did Harv welsh on a deal? Did he try to put the squeeze on someone?"

Sam picked up the crime scene report concerning the dead pedicab driver.

"Is this connected? Maybe, but the main reason we think so is because I thought this man had possession of papers from someone unknown who wrote a note in French, and we believe that Olivia had left these same papers for safekeeping at a cockfighting arena." Sam held up one finger.

"And, of course, he had your ATF pen," said Bogie, straight-faced.

"Stay on track." Sam held up a second finger. "Tucker sold gamecocks to that particular arena, but also to several others. Does that make this particular arena a real link?"

He waggled his second finger, as if undecided whether it should stay up. "And a Frenchman known to be involved in industrial espionage liked to hang out at the same sex club where Harv bought it."

He held up a third finger. "Is this another link in the chain of evidence? They could just be coincidences."

"They could be. But even though Manila is a big city, the number of people with real power—either on the surface or in the underworld—is quite small," said Bogie. "We're always finding that the crime rings overlap and interlock. Drug money buys foreign sex slaves. Sex slaves produce money and services to bribe police. Corrupt cops turn a blind eye to smuggling. Smuggling of guns and weapons pays for influence with politicians."

"And the big wheel keeps on turning," said Sam. He had run out of ideas.

Bogie pulled the photos from the folder and looked at one that showed the driver's mangled hand. He showed the picture to Sam. "See those scratches on the ground by his hand? Was he trying to draw something? Guy like him probably couldn't read or write."

Sam inspected the image. "What am I missing? He wasn't just robbed, he was tortured." He shook his head. "Does this make sense to you?"

"Not yet." Bogie put the photos back in their folder and pulled the file jacket for Tucker's death, checking the photo of Tucker's body in the dumpster. "No drawings or messages scratched on the inside wall of the dumpster."

He stacked the two folders together and sat back in his chair. "You've never explained why ATF was so worried about this particular shipment."

"Did the shootings in Waco a few years back make the news here?"

"Sure. Seemed like just another 'crazy *kano*' story."

"It touched a nerve in the US, big time. Kids were killed. ATF looked like a bunch of uncaring incompetents. And the public wondered how the Branch Davidians accumulated such an arsenal."

"All Americans own guns." Bogie smiled, acknowledging the exaggeration. "Well-known fact."

"They don't own the kind of stuff those whackos had. So when we heard that a group calling themselves the Texas Freemen Militia was looking to acquire automatic weapons, it tweaked our tail. No one wants terrorists, either foreign or domestic, on American soil. The last thing we need is another Texas shootout."

"Better to have the next shootout in Idaho or Montana, eh?" said Bogie

Sam did a slow burn. "That's not funny. You have no idea how many separatist groups there are in the US, all of them wanting to set up their own little utopias, get the Federal government off their backs."

Bogie raised an eyebrow

"The great state of Nevada refuses to share tax information with the IRS," Sam continued. "A Chicano group wants to break off the Southwestern states and call it Aztlan, after their Aztec ancestors. A black organization wants a chunk of the South to set up an African-American homeland. Assorted white supremacists want autonomous Christian enclaves, not to mention the polygamous Mormons."

Bogie raised his other eyebrow.

"They all do anything they can to hamstring the ATF, because the one thing they have in common is a need for firepower—" Sam stopped himself, took a drink of bottled water. "I'll get off my soapbox. It's not something you'd understand without being there."

"Americans are so insular. You haven't heard about the various liberation fronts here in the Philippines?" said Bogie. "Or our Muslim minority that tried to assassinate the Pope—the Pope!—when he visited here? Or the Communist insurgency? Or the land reform movement? Same problems. Same games. Same guns. Different names."

"All right," said Sam, "so I'm an uneducated American who doesn't read the Manila Times."

They sat in uncomfortable silence for a bit, mulling over the case, their lives, their countries, their careers, the screwed-up state of the world. And it wasn't even lunch yet.

"You remember *Chinatown*?" asked Bogie.

"With Nicholson and Dunaway? Of course. Great film noir."

"We'll skip whether a color film can be noir for a second," said Bogie. "Remember the plot? At first it seemed like a case of a philandering husband, then a murder, then maybe land fraud. Turned out it was really about water."

"Yeah," said Sam reflectively. "Why the hell was it called '*Chinatown*'?"

"Don't get off the subject. My point is maybe there's some bigger picture," said Bogie, "something we aren't seeing yet."

"Wait a second." Sam sat up with a start. "That first night we were working together. I was still jet-lagged, hadn't slept properly yet. I dragged myself to my room. A guy came up to me on the elevator, said he was CIA. Told me to back off investigating Tucker's death."

Bogie's eyes snapped. "When were you going to mention this?"

"I told him to go to hell," Sam continued, as if Bogie hadn't spoken. "Said if I was getting new orders, they had to come through my boss. I went to my room and crashed. Made a call in the morning, but it was Sunday at the ATF office, and the duty officer didn't think it rated as an emergency, said someone would get back to me."

"Yeah? So what does that all mean?"

"I'm not sure. But I never got any change of orders," said Sam. "Although that could just be the usual snafu of a new bureaucracy, what with Homeland Security trying to coordinate fifty-seven agencies that all used to be autonomous."

"So why bring this up now?" asked Bogie.

"I just remembered that I saw the same guy again," said Sam. "Kind of hard to miss him, in fact. Looked like some huge Polynesian football player."

"Where was this?"

"He was in the crowd that roughed me up by the flyover."

"Huge Polynesian guy?" Bogie picked at a cuticle distractedly. "Goes by the name of Juan?"

"That's what he told me. Juan Samoa. You know him?"

Without answering, Bogie picked up a phone and dialed.

"I'll see if RP Intel knows of any CIA activity on this case and if a Juan Samoa is involved."

"So what's the connection?"

"If it's the same Juan—and it will be—he's part owner of Club de Sex."

MR. AND MRS. SANTOS' HOME—5 P.M. TUESDAY

Jennifer's driver pulled into the semicircular drive of her mother's home. The house security guard recognized Jennifer through the tinted window and waved her through the gate.

Her Mercedes mini-van bottomed out as it crossed the rainwater swale, since it weighed five hundred pounds more than its suspension was designed for. The Kevlar panels and bulletproof glass made the vehicle safe from ordinary armed kidnap attempts, but the mini-van tended to wallow in turns.

Petie, her driver, had taken a three-day course in evasive driving while serving in the presidential guard under Marcos. Now that Marcos was long gone, most of the elite military units had either been dissolved or their cadres had resigned from the military. Petie had been lucky enough to become personal bodyguard and driver to the daughter of a member of Marcos' inner circle.

Even beyond that he had a tremendous loyalty to Jennifer. She paid him well, and she never failed to treat him with kindness and respect. Being around her he had come to understand the meaning of *noblesse oblige*, though he had never heard the term.

J ennifer opened the van door herself and strode to the front entry, which was opened by a young woman from the provinces. Jennifer paused, giving the maid time to recognize her. The young girl froze, afraid to speak to someone so far above her station.

Jennifer saw the girl's discomfort and put on a kind smile. "You must be the new maid. My mother told me about you," she lied. "Is Mrs. Santos at home?"

The maid took a breath. "Yes, Miss." She opened the door all the way, gesturing for Jennifer to come in out of the heat. "I will tell her you are here, Miss."

Before the maid could move, Jennifer's mother's voice came over the intercom. "Jennifer, can you join me upstairs? I have something to show you."

The maid disappeared into the "dirty" kitchen, the one where food was actually prepared, to tell the cook to make snacks and drinks. Jennifer went up a flight of stairs and found her mother standing before a closed doorway in the hall. Like a game show hostess she pointed dramatically.

"And what is behind door number one?" said her mother.

Jennifer laughed. "You are such a drama queen, Mother." She walked over to the door, did a double take.

"Where did this come from? You added a door to the hallway?" She opened the door, revealing a walk-in closet filled with shoes. "You moved your shoe closet?"

"Of course not. This is a new closet I just had built. I used a part of your father's study. He isn't practicing law any longer. All he does is golf."

"Are you trying to compete with Imelda? How many shoes do you have now?"

"I don't even speak to Imelda any more. But you are missing the best part. Press that button, there."

Resigned to playing a bit part in her mother's show, Jennifer pressed the button. The shoes began to move.

"Motorized racks, to bring what I want to the front," said her mother. "I got the idea at a dry cleaners."

"This seems excessive, even for you. In fact it's related to why I came over."

Her mother bristled at the criticism. Jennifer paused, knowing she wasn't going to react well to what she was going to say next.

Still, mother is easier to talk to than father, and she might be able to cajole Daddy into changing their course of action.

"I don't think you should attend the opening of your new apartment complex," said Jennifer. "Sonny Lagos threatened a demonstration by the Landless Coalition and there could be violence."

"What has that to do with my shoes?"

"The plan is to pelt you with old shoes," said Jennifer. "It's common knowledge that Imelda has five thousand pair. And they call you 'Imelda's little sister'."

"That's crazy, comparing me to that social climber. And anyone with enough sense to come in out of the monsoon knows that when you find a style of shoe that flatters your legs and feet, you should buy a pair in every color available." Mrs. Santos spoke faster, waving a shoe for emphasis. "It's my money. Why shouldn't I have as many shoes as I wish? I like shoes—"

"I know, Mother. In fact, everyone knows. The poorest peasant from the province knows," said Jennifer. "That's the problem. Even the people who lost their homes when you cleared the land for the apartments—"

"Those weren't homes! It was a shantytown, just cardboard and flattened oil barrels. That part of Manila was a slum. Your father and I have created something of beauty and—"

"Yes, they were shanties, but those shanties were home to the people who lived there—"

"And now they live in a different shanty, so they haven't

lost anything. And the city has gained decent housing!"

Jennifer sighed. They had run through this argument too many times before.

"You're right." That caught her mother off guard. "The apartments *are* beautiful. But I am afraid for your safety. Please don't attend the grand opening."

Her mother calmed herself with visible effort.

"I'll tell your father what you have said. It will be his decision." She paused, ready to take up a new topic. "Although I am not sure he wants to hear anything from you after the way you have been carrying on."

"What on earth are you talking about?"

"I'm talking about the way you were flirting with some foreign policeman at the Hilton restaurant. Half of Manila saw you there. Your father is embarrassed."

"Embarrassed?"

"At your age I had been married for three years and given birth to my first son—"

"And all I have done," said Jennifer with some heat, "is become the youngest female fiscal in the history of the RP—"

"Besides which, I had married into one of the leading Filipino families—"

"You were already from a 'leading Filipino family' yourself!"

"My point exactly! Date your own kind. Don't embarrass your grandmother, your aunts and uncles, your brothers—" She paused to wring all the drama she could from the moment. "Your parents."

Jennifer bit her tongue. She took a final look into the closet as if there might be answers hidden amongst the footwear, something that would explain why mothers thought they had the right to run their daughters' lives. She pulled the door shut.

"I better be getting back to the office, Mother."

Her mother wasn't ready to let go yet.

"It was bad enough when you were dating Bogie. His father's a nobody, but at least he's Filipino."

"Did he call you to tell you who I've been dining with? Has Bogie been spying on me?"

"Spying on you?" Her mother looked at her with surprise. "You don't know him at all. No wonder you couldn't hold onto him."

"I was the one who broke it off, Mother! Not Bogie!"

Her mother just smiled that know-it-all, superior, "when-you're-older-dear" smile, the one that daughters hate so much.

sixteen--

Though it was not yet eight in the morning, both temperature and humidity were over eighty. Bogie leaned against the wall just outside Club de Sex. His shirt stuck to him like a poultice. He stubbed his third cigarette against the wall and dropped the butt.

A five-year-old girl snatched the smoldering stub from the sidewalk and hurried away. She straightened out the crumpled paper, tamped the tobacco back in, and put the remnant into a small tin, a treat to be savored later.

"*Batà!*" called Bogie. "Youngster!"

The girl looked over her shoulder in apprehension. She sized up the man in the rumpled suit as a cop, but that didn't make her feel safe. She walked back hesitantly.

Bogie held out a five-peso coin as he squatted down to talk. "For breakfast." She grabbed the coin, but Bogie didn't release it. "Don't you know smoking's bad for you?"

"What do you want, sir?"

Up close he could count her ribs through the paper-thin Hello Kitty blouse she wore. He pulled a twenty-peso coin from his pocket. "I want to buy back my cigarette. I wasn't finished."

The girl made the two coins disappear and pulled out the tin. Her body tensed as she held out the crumpled cigarette. She was ready to run from this crazy man at the first sign of trouble.

Bogie took the cigarette and stood up. The girl sprinted away, not stopping until a dozen people were between her and Bogie. She paused to look at him over her shoulder, shook her head, and melted into the crowd.

Bogie crumbled the cigarette butt between his fingers

until it was powder, let the wind take it. He absent-mindedly pulled out his pack to light up, then grimaced, and put it away.

Olivia came from the rear entrance of the club, in a lime-green metallic sheath dress. Though she was dead tired, she still looked good enough to make her gay bartender reconsider his orientation. She walked down the alley, rolling her ass like she needed one more customer to make the night's quota.

Bogie waited until she had passed him, caught up and took her by the elbow.

"Let me buy you breakfast, Miss de la Cruz."

Olivia tried to slip her arm loose, saw it wasn't going to happen. "This isn't your style, Detective. You're the one who *doesn't* shake us down."

"I'm not shaking you down, I'm taking you to breakfast."

Bogie pulled her to a halt in front of a sidewalk vendor, a skinny little dude who would have looked at home in Ethiopia or Calcutta, all teeth and eyes. A small grill was covered with smoking fish heads, eyes bubbling. Bogie got each of them a fish head on a bamboo skewer. Olivia planted herself at the grill, back to Bogie, and made a production of pouring soy sauce into every orifice and crevice of the piscine snack.

Bogie decided to get right to the point. "Two days before Harvey Tucker died, you had lunch with him at his hotel. There was also a third party there. I'd like to know who it was."

"I don't know what you're talking about," replied Olivia, sucking the eyes from the fish. One, two, they came out with satisfying little pops.

Her insolence irritated Bogie. "Right. Well, you know that little mole on your lower back? Okay, so we both know who the dominatrix is in those photos. That puts you with the deceased twice in three days."

Olivia licked her lips. "I don't recall anyone else at lunch with us."

"I don't think you're the murderer," said Bogie. "I'm trying to do you a favor."

Olivia gave him a sidelong glance. "Is this sweet talk?" She delicately pulled flesh from the cheek of the fish with her teeth. "My other dates take me to nicer places."

"Come on, Olivia. You know who did it. Save yourself some grief and help me find him."

"Find him?" Olivia was amused. "So you're positive the murderer is a man?"

Bogie looked at her. "You just moved up the list of suspects, Olivia. You're surprising me. I don't often misjudge character."

"You've no right to judge my character." Her voice hardened. "You don't know jack about me. Except what I charge." She was furious now and spat the last word: "Bogie."

Dropping the remains of her fish head at Bogie's feet, she spun on her heel and melded with the morning crowd.

Otto's Bar—Noon Wednesday

Goldie walked into "Working Late at the Office" to find Riffat already waiting for him. He stopped first at the bar to have Otto pour him a tall gin, straight up.

Riffat watched in irritation from the corner booth in the rear. He munched some deep-fried *meryenda*, wondering what the stuff was. He looked up when he heard Otto's coarse laugh. Both Goldie and Otto were staring at him, chuckling. He hated wasting time while Goldie shared some infidel joke with the bartender. He wanted to smack the grin from that whoreson's face.

"Hey, Goldie," called Riffat, "what do you find so funny?"

Goldie sauntered over, still smirking, the gin having replenished his confidence. "I just wond'ring 'bout *halal* butchers."

Riffat grew still. Goldie had crossed a line. "What are you saying?"

"I ask Otto what means *halal*. He said he think it some rules for how you kill the pig, if you a moose-leem."

— 117 —

"You do not dare to speak of the true faith in this way, you piece of filth. Islam is not for joking."

Goldie looked at him with false obsequiousness. "I sorry, boss. My mistake. I thinking you find special butcher who fix those pork rinds for you."

Riffat looked in horror at his plate. He sputtered and coughed out the remnants of his snack. He tried to hawk up the forbidden flesh so assiduously that he choked. He reached for Goldie's glass, thinking it was water, and took a large gulp. Eyes bulging, he sprayed the harsh liquid over the tabletop.

Goldie and Otto both burst out laughing at Riffat's reaction. "Must be some of that halal gin you got there," howled Otto.

When Riffat recovered his voice he said, "I'm going to kill you, Goldie."

"This no way talk with friends. Whuss your problem?"

"The problem is that certain papers are not where Gerard left them."

"Sound like mebbe you should talk with Gerard," said Goldie.

"Gerard told me he put the papers in your office."

Goldie assumed a false look of contrition. "I gotta tell you," said Goldie, "Some cops came and hook them papers right outta my office."

"Cops?" said Riffat. "What cops?"

"Cops. With badges."

"But it was you who was paid," said Riffat. "You were given money to keep those papers safe."

"Maybe you fill out complaint form," said Goldie. "Maybe Gerard get refund." Goldie stopped to tap his finger to his temple. "But I don't thinking so."

"Yeah," chimed in Otto, from behind the bar. "Cops with badges are an 'Act of God'—sorry, 'Act of Allah'—and void all guarantees."

"You be finding complaint form in little room out back," said Goldie. "They comin' in rolls."

"Two ply," added Otto.

NIGHTLIFE IN MANILA: Hang on to your tushies! Manila
has the second largest gay population in the
world. The lush life is celebrated in Mani-La-La-
Land, with over a hundred clubs catering to all
your most decadent desires.

Try Lash LaRoue's if you like leather and bondage.
If you're butch and lezzy, then Johnny Bulldog
will be your cup of tea. Bi-curious capitalist? Try
Buy/Sell. Into fun with food? The Produce Market
may be up your alley, so to speak.—

Travel Tips from the Gay Caballero

MAKATI ARMS—9 P.M. WEDNESDAY

At last Sam understood the fish channel. Three days
in-country and the fourteen-hour time zone shift still had
him wired every night from two a.m. till seven a.m. the next
morning. He wondered if he would ever acclimate. If he tried
to watch any normal cable programming, it set his mind spinning, and sleep wouldn't come at all.

But the fish. They swished sedately through the water,
unhurried, without pattern to their movement. The aquarium
scene was neither daylight nor nighttime. It was some indeterminate limbo light. Predators never intruded. The fish never
ate or defecated or procreated. Just swam. Lazily.

Sam had looked at the screen up close the first night, trying to decide if it was a video loop of a real aquarium or some
sophisticated computer animation. He couldn't tell.

The sound track was a low burble, almost musical, yet still
mechanical. It didn't call for your attention. But it blocked out
the night noises of the hotel.

Sam felt his forehead, wondering if he had a temperature.
He got up from the king-sized bed and padded naked into
the bathroom of the suite, splashed tepid water on his face.
He looked at the clock: nine-thirty p.m. and he felt like he hadn't
slept in weeks. He was counting on his jet-lagged circadian
rhythm to bring him alive by the time he met Jennifer

at Club Peanut. He pulled out his razor and shaved.

He looked at his clothes, immaculately laid out on the bed. Sam had discovered the hotel's laundry and dry cleaner. They were cheap, fast, and of a higher standard than he was used to, a perk of a society where labor was plentiful. His clothes had knife-edge creases. His shirt had been boiled, bleached, pressed, and starched, until it practically glowed in the dark.

If he left his shoes outside the door of his hotel room, they were shined overnight for free. His haircut had cost him five dollars at a shop in the mall that was attached to the hotel.

I could get used to life in a five star.

CLUB PEANUT—10 P.M. WEDNESDAY

The taxi dropped him right at the door to the club. Sam had sprung for a new tie to go with his best navy suit, the one with almost unnoticeable pinstripes. The maroon of the silk tie perfectly echoed the pinstripes. Sam paid the driver, over-tipping, as usual.

A tall hooker gave a low whistle as Sam got out of the car.

"Ooh, ladies!" she called out to two more over-sized working girls. Her voice was husky. "Look what we got here. Some fresh white bread."

The three women crowded around Sam, blocking him from the club entry. "Don't you just love those blue eyes of his!" said one, more heavily made up than the other two.

A second reached out and patted Sam's hair. "And his hair is so fine—curly, too."

"Come with me," said the third. "I show you my curly hairs."

"Girl, you're too low class for a man this good lookin'," said the husky-voiced hooker. "But I'm thinkin' maybe this white bread wanna make sandwiches with some wheat bread." She looked Sam in the face. "What you say? You want to take me and my sister back to your hotel? We can teach you something new."

Sam tried to be polite as he pushed between them and made for the door. "I'm meeting someone inside, ladies."

"If he won't do you, then come on back out here," said the second girl, her Adam's apple bobbing in excitement.

Sam caught a glimpse of himself in the glossy door leading into the club. *I guess I don't look so bad for thirty-five. Hell, I don't look bad for thirty-four.*

The interior of Club Peanut surprised him, after his experience at Club de Sex. No eardrum-popping bass line, no strobes. Instead, low lights, a live jazz band playing something cool and downbeat.

Huge photos on the walls. Color blow-ups of Marilyn Monroe, Madonna, Cher, Liza Minnelli. Older black and white pictures of Ginger Rogers, Judy Garland, Ruby Keeler, Bette Davis.

The club was full of well-dressed couples, and Sam was glad he'd made the effort to look sharp. He spotted Jennifer at a table at the edge of the small stage and made his way over.

Two waiters had attached themselves to Jennifer as her personal servants for the evening. Sam stood and watched as they fawned over her, knowing they were hoping for record-breaking tips.

Still, he didn't blame them. She was one of the few women who could wear a designer cocktail dress and make the designer look good. The dress was a purple so dark he thought at first that it was black. It was made of some velvety material he had never seen before. It clung. In all the right places.

Around her neck was a minuscule gold chain. It supported a black opal the size of a half dollar. It was the largest one Sam had ever seen outside a jewelry store.

Sam stared long enough that one of the waiters looked up and came to his side.

"May I help you, sir?"

"I'm here for the lady," said Sam. "Bring me whatever she's having. No, wait. I don't want it if it involves *bagoong*."

The waiter smirked and went to the bar.

Sam walked over and took a seat. "Wow."

Jennifer colored prettily. "I was beginning to think you weren't coming."

"I thought I'd get here sooner. I didn't realize the traffic was still jammed at ten p.m."

"Yes, rush hour is five a.m. to midnight."

Sam laughed, but stopped as she looked at him quizzically. "You're not joking?"

"I'm a very serious person." She showed him a fetching dimple. "I take it you like my pendant?"

Sam raised his eyes a few inches. "What pendant?" he deadpanned.

She showed him the dimple again. "Move your chair over next to me."

Sam did and was going to ask for a closer examination of the pendant when the lights dimmed. The jazz band died away, and a spotlight illumined the stage.

A tuxedo-clad host came out carrying a hand mike and did the standard comic shticks required on all continents by the International MC's Union.

Jennifer leaned close to Sam and whispered, "Since you're from LA, I thought you might like a little taste of Hollywood."

Sam wasn't sure what to make of that, but he loved the perfume she was wearing. He decided it was smarter to say nothing and just enjoy the fragrance.

The host was winding down. "And so, without further ado, heeeeeeere's Cher!"

Silver lamé drapes were whisked aside, and a beautiful Filipina in a sleek gown did a Norma Desmond slink as she made her way into the spotlight. Her straight black shoulder-length hair shimmered as she walked.

A recording of "Gypsies, Tramps, and Thieves" came on at 108 decibels, and she lip-synced to the playback. She was good. She had Cher's movements and mannerisms down to a nicety.

The audience shouted its admiration for the performance. A couple at the next table both called out to "Cher."

"You go, girl!" said the first baritone.

"You're perfect, honey!" came the second baritone.

Sam sneaked a glance at the couple next to him. He was handsome. So was "she." *Though that is a gorgeous gown he's wearing,* thought Sam.

Sam looked back at the stage as Cher made her sultry way to the edge and performed for her admirers. Sam leaned over to Jennifer. "I think she has a five o'clock shadow."

"He tells me the pancake can only cover for a couple of hours," said Jennifer. "And this is the second club he's performed at tonight."

"You know Cher?"

Jennifer turned to look at Sam, trying to judge if he was kidding. "So do you. That's Garcia." Sam still looked blank. "From your office. He's working the case with you."

Sam's head snapped around as he stared at Cher, catching the lascivious wink she offered him. Sam gulped his drink.

"I could have gone all night without seeing that," Sam said to Jennifer.

Jennifer leaned close so she could whisper. "He asked me to bring you to the club. He said he thinks you're cute, in a *kano* kind of way."

"And I could have gone all night without hearing that."

Jennifer laughed musically and took his arm. "Don't worry. I told him I was pretty sure you had other interests."

"Pretty sure?"

"Let's get some supper somewhere else when he's done with his act," said Jennifer. "The Bette Midler that's on next isn't that good."

"Will it be a regular restaurant? I don't know if I can take any more surprises tonight."

Jennifer looked at him. "You don't want any more surprises tonight? How disappointing."

Sam nearly unhinged his jaw. "Hey, don't I get take-backs?"

Jennifer smiled as the lights came up. Garcia stopped by their table first, kissing each of them on either cheek, before starting his grand tour of the club. Sam turned a bright red but managed to say, "Great act, man. Uh, Cher."

"See you at the office tomorrow," said Garcia. "But not too early. I'm feeling lucky tonight." He turned to Jennifer. "*Looooove* your dress. You must tell me where you bought it."

Sam thought, not for the first time, that Manila seemed like an absurdist play staged in some gargantuan theater-in-the-round. As he and Jennifer made their way across the club, he noted the eyes tracking their progress. First, Jennifer's stunning dress and fashion-model looks. Next the eyes always switched to him—to his butt, to be more precise.

Gee, I feel special.

seventeen--

Juan Samoa sat on a piling, smoking one Marlboro after another. He flicked the butts into the water, his eyes scanning the harbor. The docks had settled into relative quiet for the night.

Shortly after two a.m. he heard a faint plashing of paddles. Leaning forward to peer into the light mist that lay like a dirty gray skin across the bay, he almost fell into the water when someone touched him on the shoulder.

"Not much time. I need to get out of the bay while the mist can still hide us."

The speaker was a small-boned Malay, with a blue tattoo on his neck. He was dressed in black denim that faded into the night shadows. He held out a note for inspection.

Juan snapped on a mini flashlight and recognized the handwriting. He flicked off the beam. He peered at the messenger and realized that the tattoo on his neck was an Arabic phrase but couldn't make out its meaning, since most of it was below the collar of the Malay's jacket.

"I brought operating funds for MILF," said Juan. "And a list of businessmen whose companies will ransom them without hesitation. The key targets are a Japanese infidel named Nosaka and a French businessman, Gerard Laveau."

"Good." The Malay waited, sensing there was something more.

"You need to know something else. Riffat—"

The Malay stood silent, the tension building, as he waited for Juan to continue. "Yes?"

"Riffat has been giving money to your rivals, the Abu Sayef. He says they are looked on with greater favor because they are ruthless with their hostages. He says there is room for only one Islamic revolution. He says—"

Juan stopped to light another cigarette. Now the Malay could no longer his hide his unease. He shifted his weight from one foot to the other.

"He says what?"

"Abu Sayef has been directed to absorb the members of the Mindoro Islamist Liberation Front, effective at once."

"Have we no say in this?" asked the Malay. "Why should not MILF absorb the Abu Sayef?"

"That is why I have given you this list. Make your devotion and ability known. Outshine the Abu Sayef—"

The Malay held his breath. He knew that the real message, the reason he had been called here tonight, the reason he had risked his life to come to the Christian capital, was about to be revealed.

"Eliminate the Abu Sayef. You have supporters other than the Saudis, and they—" Juan looked down, and took a drag on his cigarette. He pulled a pouch from inside his jacket. "I can't say more—not at this time."

The Malay took the pouch, glanced inside, saw cash and a note. He salaamed and moved away into the mist.

> **"When will we achieve equity?** When we take back the land that is ours! The Spanish stole it from us four hundred years ago. The Americans promised it to us one hundred years ago but then took our country for themselves. Only after Filipinos shed their blood to help America repel the Japanese did they finally *give* us the right to run our own lives.
>
> "And *still* we have no land reform. The time has come for all Filipinos to stand shoulder to shoulder, to dispossess the landlords, to fight for what is ours. VOTE POPULIST PARTY!"
> *Unidentified speaker at political rally*

MANILA STREETS—8 A.M. THURSDAY

Frankie crouched behind the dumpster, staying in the shadows, and tried to plan his next move. It was a full day since Mister Chito had offered a thousand pesos for the papers with the funny marks, and Frankie didn't know what to do next.

A feral cat came sniffing at his bare toes, but he picked it up by the scruff and hoisted it into the dumpster. He didn't have time for cat games.

Frankie was six, though he often pretended to be four, especially with *kano* women tourists. They found it hard to resist his enormous, tear-filled eyes. He could make the tears come in less than five seconds. It was his best begging ploy.

He had been on the streets for as long as he could remember. Some of the older kids told him June was his sister. She was maybe twelve, thirteen years old. He hadn't seen her since she started working the streets. He knew the men who paid for her services didn't want a kid brother hanging around, watching. Anyway, it had been months since she had last come looking for him. He didn't think he could find her soon enough to get her help.

He scrunched the papers against his chest, checking to make sure none of them showed outside his ragged shirt. He hated carrying them, but there was no place safe to leave them. The older boys knew all his secret places. *They'd steal these away super fast. Everyone needs a thousand pesos.*

Worse, he knew the older guys would hurt him bad if they found he was hiding them.

Frankie breathed harder, worrying that he might meet one of the boys. But he couldn't just squat in the shadows forever. He had to get to Chito's club and claim his reward.

He thought about that. Some of the boys would be waiting to ambush whoever showed up with the papers. *Yeah, that's something Bobby would do. Bobby will beat me up and take the papers.*

There was a sudden rustling in the dumpster followed by a prolonged squeal. That lucky cat found his own breakfast. His own stomach growled, and he thought how easy cats had it. Rats were plentiful, and not all that smart. He sometimes caught them himself, but could never bring himself to cook one and eat it. He sold the ones he snagged to the drunks down by the rails. They'd eat anything.

He wondered if he could make a deal with Bobby. Somehow he didn't think so. Bobby wouldn't see any reason to split the reward money. Split his head, maybe, but not the money.

"Hey, kid. Beat it."

A grungy worker from the restaurant that backed onto the alley came up to Frankie. He didn't look menacing, but Frankie kept a wary eye on him as he approached.

"The boss says we don't want no lost boys living back here. You gotta get movin', hey." The worker looked at Frankie, squatted down to his level. "I'll give you five pesos, OK? You go buy some breakfast, yeah?"

He held out the money, but Frankie knew that trick. He just stared at the worker until the man put the coin on the ground and backed away. When he was sure the busboy couldn't catch him, Frankie snatched at the bit of copper. "Thanks."

"But you gotta go now, right? Boss'll fire me if you don't, yes?" The man watched him worriedly until Frankie got to his feet and darted into the sunlit street.

Frankie barreled into a white man, dodged quickly to one side. Unfortunately, he didn't see the *kano* lady at all. He ran into her knee and was knocked to the ground.

He knew how to play this one and immediately burst into tears. It was always good for some coin, but right now he needed more than just a peso or two from rich foreigners.

Five minutes later he was in a taxi while the nice *kanos* took the little lost boy back to his apartment. The cabbie had looked at Frankie with skepticism when he told him he lived at Club de Sex, but a quick exchange in Tagalog had let the cabbie know the score.

Once they got to the club, Frankie poured on the tears again, claiming he was too afraid to go to the door alone. The white man had the cab wait while he walked Frankie up the stairs to the back of the club and pushed the buzzer. A grumpy Olivia opened the door a crack and eyeballed the mismatched pair on the landing.

"I bet you didn't know the little guy was out this time of the morning, did you?" said the *kano*. "Maybe you should keep a closer eye on him." He rested one hand protectively on Frankie's shoulder and looked at Olivia's tight-fitting sheath with clear disapproval.

Frankie pulled down his collar just enough so Olivia could see the papers. She flashed a big smile at the man.

"You are so right, sir. This little rascal is always getting away from home." She swung the door wide, and motioned Frankie inside. "Go on and have some breakfast." He darted inside, peered around the door frame.

She smiled again at the man, saw the cab at the alley entry. "Thank you so much for bringing him home. May I pay for your cab?"

"No. We were on our way to the airport anyway. Glad we could help the boy. He was crying his eyes out because he was lost."

"I'm sure he was."

eighteen--

The celebration began at dawn and promised to last all night. The Phil-Cap Corporation wanted to launch the new apartment complex with as much publicity as possible.

It had hired a dozen local bands to provide live music at four locations, one on each side of the square that fronted the complex. Each band played a one-hour set, then had a two-hour break before performing again. The bands had pooled their gear to get the most amplification possible, so the noise level was formidable.

The Santos family, sole shareholders of Phil-Cap, were hosting an enormous barbecue in the center of the square, serving roasted chicken to anyone willing to wear a sash proclaiming "Better Homes for Happier Families—Santos Apartments." There was no shortage of street people ready to wear a ribbon in exchange for a free lunch.

The press had also been invited. They got to set up their cameras near the speakers' stage and had access to an even better buffet reserved for the guests of honor—the deputy mayor and the provincial lieutenant governor. Both luminaries were related by marriage to the Santos family.

The more enterprising freeloaders got a sash, ate their chicken, danced away into the crowd, and discreetly dumped the sash. They then got back in line to repeat the process.

Some of the lost children donned the discarded sashes. Local merchants gave them trays of already opened (and watered down) San Miguel to sell to the merrymakers, counting on the sashes to make it look like part of the planned celebration.

The average Filipino eats fish every day (if he is lucky) and only gets chicken on birthdays and Christmas. Free barbecued chicken improved their meager daily food allowance so that it now included a beer or three. Soon the celebration was in full swing, with much raucous song and dancing in the streets.

The TV cameras loved the spectacle.

At noon the politicians ascended the stage and began a series of self-congratulatory speeches. The Santos family was praised in terms usually reserved for beatification services. On cue from professional rally cheerers, the crowd roared its approval.

Jennifer's mother and father, looking much like visiting royalty, sat on the platform appearing pleased and benevolent. They graciously accepted the paeans offered.

The TV cameras loved them.

Mr. Santos leaned across to his wife and said, "I thought Jennifer was going to join us. I don't ask much of our daughter, but she won't even do this small thing for us."

Mrs. Santos gave a small wave of acknowledgment to an acquaintance on the other side of the dais. She stage whispered to her husband, "This isn't the time to discuss this, Alejandro. But we are going to have to take a firmer hand with her."

From a boulevard facing opposite the speakers' platform, a flatbed truck pushed into the edge of the crowd. Sonny Lagos sat next to the driver of the truck, hiding his identity behind denim work clothes and sunglasses.

Thirty young men carrying armloads of placards mounted on wooden staves jumped down from the truck bed and fanned out into the crowd. The young men began passing out simply-worded agitprop broadsides, featuring photos of Mr. and Mrs. Santos.

As the flyers circulated, the cheering grew less enthusiastic. From the podium the deputy mayor, who had been gassing for fifteen minutes, sensed that the mood of the crowd was changing, but couldn't make out why.

Lagos' truck revved its engine to power the on-board generator that drove a huge amplifier. In the cab Sonny keyed his microphone and addressed the crowd. His amp was bigger and cut through both the crowd noise and the deputy mayor's blather.

"Citizens of Intramuros! Why do you celebrate this abomination, this misuse of resources? Where this obscene apartment building sits there was once a *baranggáy* of more than one thousand homes. Homes of honest people just like you. Can such honest people afford to rent these new apartments? Can YOU afford to rent them?"

As his voice echoed around the square, people craned their necks, trying to discover where this new orator was located. The echoes made it difficult, and two-thirds of the crowd faced the wrong way, toward the nearest sound-reflecting surface.

The deputy mayor gave up trying to out shout the super-amp. He pulled out his cell phone and called for riot police.

"The answer is NO!" continued Sonny. "The PEOPLE'S housing has been stolen by these capitalist pigs—pigs who already are wealthy beyond my understanding. But are these pigs content? NO! They are greedy pigs, always wanting more. What they want, they take! And they take it from you—the people—the true heart and soul of Manila!"

A ragged cheer went up from the agitators who had dispersed throughout the crowd.

"Citizens!" roared Sonny, "You have pictures of these greedy pigs in your hands. And there they sit on the speakers' platform. Let us go show them how we—we, the landless—we, the homeless—we, the poor—how WE feel about their greed!"

At this point the first personnel carrier of the riot squad arrived. It entered from the far side of the square, opposite to Sonny's truck. The crowd standing just in front of them was just then seeing copies of the flyer.

Most people in this quarter had no idea what was going on, why there had been two simultaneous speakers from opposite sides of the square. Worst of all, in their view, they couldn't understand why the music and dancing had stopped.

The riot squad deployed quickly. RP riot police are schooled well in crowd control and know that the best defense is a strong offense. During fifty years of independence and democracy, the riot police have had plenty of practice quelling civil disturbances. The order of business is to break heads first, ask questions later. They leapt from their carrier, truncheons swinging.

The TV cameras loved this, too.

A great cry of pain rippled through the crowd as the riot police worked to cut a strategic swath across the middle of the square. Men fell beneath their blows, bleeding from head wounds. Riot police the world over have discovered that faces dripping blood generate the quickest flight by onlookers.

Women dropped to their knees to assist their fallen menfolk. In turn, the panicked crowd trampled them, the screams of the injured women adding to the chaos.

The thirty young men who had been distributing placards gathered other men about them, calling, "Follow us! We must save the women. Our comrades have fallen!"

They brandished their wood-handled signs like the makeshift weapons they were designed to be and plowed through the crowd, heading for the riot squad. Dozens of men from the throng picked up placard staves and followed their lead. An enterprising TV news cameraman followed along.

The TV cameras were going to love this, too.

The oligarchs of the Philippines have outlasted colonial rule under the Spanish and the Americans. They even survived the Japanese occupation. They have lived through numerous regime changes, many of them more or less violent.

The private bodyguards of the Santos family drew their hand weapons, formed a protective ring around Jennifer's parents, and backed them toward an armored van. Once the couple was safely inside, they walked ahead of the van, clubbing people out of the way, making sure the van never halted as it made its way from the square.

After half a block the crowd thinned, and the van's driver accelerated, scattering the bodyguards and other pedestrians. In moments the van had passed from sight.

In the square, the riot police had bulled their way to the speakers' stand, allowing the remaining dignitaries to escape. The stick-wielding protesters had also reached the stand, and a pitched battle began. The riot squad fired tear gas canisters into the crowd, causing another wave of panic, and thirty-seven more tramplings.

The TV cameraman videotaped one quick thinker as he wrapped his hands in sashes, picked up a canister, and lobbed it through a window of the apartment complex. The canister set the drapes ablaze, and smoke poured from the broken window. A ragged cheer rose from the crowd, captured by the news videographers.

A second contingent of riot police arrived to find their way blocked by the flatbed truck, now abandoned. Protesters rocked the truck onto its side, plugging entry to the square.

Sonny motioned to the driver to flip a cigarette into the gas tank, and the ensuing explosion and vehicle fire claimed fourteen lives. This equaled the number that were beaten to death by the police or crushed to death by the panicky crowd, bringing the day's total to twenty-eight dead, one hundred fifty-three injured.

Sonny and the driver disappeared into the Brownian motion of the mob. When they emerged a couple of blocks away, Sonny stepped into a waiting limo, where he stripped off his denim work clothes. He threw the clothes and the sunglasses from the car window, certain that street people would recycle them within minutes.

Sonny pulled on a long-sleeve white shirt, expensive slacks, and a sport coat, becoming Congressman Lagos once again. The driver saw that his employer was ready to move.

"Where now, Congressman Lagos?"

"Let's go down to the TV network and sit in with the video editors. I believe this will be the main story on tonight's newscast."

It took less than half an hour for the fire department to douse the flames in the apartment complex. There was little real damage.

Sonny Lagos turned out to be right. "Riots at Santos" was the lead story on the six o'clock news.

And the TV cameras had loved it all.

In a city of thirteen million, where there is a chronic housing shortage, it was not surprising that all units of the Santos Apartment were rented and occupied as scheduled by members of the new middle class. None of the new tenants had bothered attending the grand opening fiesta and riot.

They were too busy earning an upwardly-mobile living.

nineteen--

B ogie punched in the now-familiar number and waited for someone to answer. A receptionist came on the line and transferred Bogie to yet another agent at RP National Security Agency. He spent the next two minutes confirming his own credentials as an agent of the National Bureau of Investigation.

"Look," said Bogie, "you are the fourth NSA man I have spoken with. Someone in our government must have the authority to speak with CIA's Manila office. I want to find out if they are investigating the same murder case I am working on. An American, Harvey Tucker, from Texas. Turned up dead in a dumpster behind a sex club."

There was a lengthy pause while the NSA agent considered his options. Bogie spent his time doodling on his notepad. NSA—CIA. NBI—ATF. ATF—CIA?

"I already heard from the other three agents," said the NSA agent. "And each told you that we at NSA have no direct liaison with the CIA. Why have you persisted in calling me?"

"Because I don't believe that our governments have no direct communication with each other!"

"I didn't say that. Of course our governments speak to each other. That is why there is an American Embassy in Manila."

"Why can't you get an answer for me?" said Bogie. "It's a simple question."

The NSA agent sighed, and addressed Bogie as if he were a backward child. "Governments speak to each other. Covert operations of governments do not. There can be no answer to your question. Just as there would be no answer—at least not to you—if you asked if NSA were interested in Mr. Tucker's death. If it were an actual National Security Administration issue, it would—by definition—not be something you need to know. You would receive no answer."

"Just so I'm clear," said Bogie, "either you don't know or I don't need to know."

"I think you have your answer." And the NSA agent hung up.

"Have a nice day," snarled Bogie into the dead phone.

Bogie walked to the water cooler, smoked a cigarette, went to water the porcelain, and made a general nuisance of himself in the hallways of NBI. At length he cooled down and returned to his desk.

He went on the Internet, and Googled for US Department of Alcohol, Tobacco, and Firearms, finding out it was now ATF and Explosives. He discovered it was part of the Department of Justice, having been transferred from Treasury. It had the highest return on dollars spent: each dollar used for enforcement resulted in thirty-five dollars of fines and revenue collected.

He moused through the department organizational chart until he found the phone number for the International Programs section of Firearms Enforcement Branch of the Firearms Technology Branch of the Firearm Programs Division. They had three operational sections: Miami, New York, and Los Angeles. He dialed the Los Angeles office and asked for agent Sam Haine.

"I'm sorry, he's out of the office," said a pleasant voice.

"Can you have him call me back?" said Bogie.

"I'm afraid he's on assignment."

"Perhaps I can speak with his supervisor. This is National Bureau of Investigation Agent Lorenzano in the Philippines."

The receptionist put him through, and Bogie was able to have an even less rewarding discussion of the interaction between CIA and ATF than before. All he could confirm was that Sam Haine was an agent of ATF. And that Agent Haine was on assignment in Manila to investigate the movements of Harvey Tucker.

Bogie thought he had seldom spent two hours to less purpose. He considered the possibility of taking up his father's offer to help run his factory—or taking his retirement savings to a small island and seeing how long he could make it last—or quitting smoking—or getting retrained in traffic enforcement.

He headed for lunch.

Club de Sex—11 a.m. Thursday

Juan walked up the steps to the rear entry of Club de Sex. His key let him in, but he still needed to enter a code to disarm the alarm system. He heard an answering beep from within the club's business office.

Olivia poked her head into the corridor, one arm concealed by the doorjamb. When she recognized Juan, she returned the Taser to her purse. "Why are you here so early, Juan?"

"I heard Chito's boys got the papers back."

Olivia nodded, but said nothing.

"I'm going to deliver them to Riffat myself," continued Juan. "He's been making a hassle, talking shit about us."

"I have another buyer," said Olivia. "Someone with stronger financial resources."

"Stronger than Saudi oil money?" Juan thought. "Well. Isn't this why they invented Xerox? Give me the papers, I'll copy them and deliver both sets this afternoon."

Olivia gave him an appraising look. "We've been together a long time, Johnny."

Juan returned her look. "We're a great team, Livvie."

"Exactly," she said. "So don't fuck this up for us."

Juan took the papers and pecked her on the cheek. "Lighten up, Livvie. I'm just going to the copy shop." He turned and walked down the hall. He called over his shoulder, "I'll be back by the time the club opens."

Juan walked a few blocks to the public cyber cafe and took a seat at a PC that had a scanner attached. He flipped through the documents and found a page that was all text. He scanned it to determine the original font used to generate the document.

He opened a word processor, formatted for that font, inserted a burnable CD-ROM, and loaded text into the word processor. His CIA handler had told him to take any numbers and alter them. Double the first, triple the second, cut the third in half, cut the next to one quarter. Scramble each one so that the plans became useless, like blueprints with incorrect dimensions. He also had a list of key pieces of hardware for which he was to substitute names of similar-sounding devices.

It took him twenty minutes to match the page layout, paragraph formats, headers, and footers. He printed out two trial runs that were still a bit off. He shredded the printouts and made a few more adjustments.

At last he was satisfied that his new pages would substitute exactly for the three pages he had extracted from the original document. He went to a copier and duped his pages.

They were still too clean, so he crumpled the copied pages, flattened them once again, and copied the copies. Two more generations away from the originals, and his faked docs were a near-perfect match. He collated them with the originals and ran two complete sets. He scanned the pages he had extracted and saved them to the CD.

Juan went to the checkout and had the clerk Fed Ex the disk to the home of a certain Arthur Trent at a US address, one of the CIA postal drops that were changed every month. For the point of origin, he used the address of the cyber cafe and had the clerk sign as the sender.

Juan paid with cash, put the two copies of his document into separate envelopes, and left the store. Once outside he breathed a little more easily. There would have been no reasonable explanation if someone had found him altering these papers.

Just two deliveries and he would be safe again.

twenty--

Sam sniffed the curried rice and pork. There were at least forty other food stalls in the basement food court of the mall, and cooking aromas of cuisines from around the world mingled together in a heady mixture.

McDonald's, of course. And a competing burger joint called Jolli Bee, with a huge cartoon-ish bee for a mascot. Arby's Roast Beef. Innumerable little seafood stands, serving everything from urchins to squid to *balut*, those hideous unhatched duck embryos.

Rice balls, fried rice, white rice—but no brown rice. Fifty varieties of potato chip: onion flavored, sour cream, lime, honeyed, with bananas, barbecued, with cayenne—even plain, if your imagination were so stunted. Bottles of banana catsup, mango catsup, soy catsup, papaya catsup. Jars of peppers, pickled bits of mango, pickled eggs. It was the most diverse food bazaar he had ever seen.

He ate a forkful of his curried pork and smiled.

Bogie pulled up a chair across the small table from Sam and set down his tray of KFC chicken and ribs. Bogie dug in, and they ate in companionable silence for a bit.

"Afterward I'll treat you to something very Manila, 'dirty' ice cream at a stand just outside," said Bogie

Sam looked dubious. "Dirty ice cream?"

"Just means 'peasant' or 'street.' It's like the 'dirty' kitchen at Jennifer's parents' home," said Bogie. "It's where the peasant cook prepares the actual meals. But Mrs. Santos has her 'clean' kitchen where she makes a show of preparing things for her guests."

"What makes you think I've been to Jennifer's parents' home?"

Bogie had the grace to be embarrassed. "From the gossip around the office— I thought she might have taken you there to show off her—" He looked away.

"And how do you know what kind of kitchen Jennifer's mother has?"

Bogie drummed his fingers on the table. "I got the tour, too."

Sam put it together. "Small world, isn't it?" He felt an irrational twinge of jealousy. "Have I stepped somewhere I shouldn't?"

Bogie waved it off. "That was five years ago. When Jennifer first joined the Fiscal's Office—and I was still a detective on the way up."

"That implies you think you're on the way down. That doesn't square with what I'm seeing. If you're on the way down, why do you get the high profile cases?"

"Yeah? Why?" Bogie stared at him without expression. "So, you ever notice that all the best noir detectives were war veterans?"

"We changing subjects now?" Sam waited for Bogie to answer, saw it wasn't going to happen.

"Remember Alan Ladd in *The Blue Dahlia*?" said Bogie. "William Bendix was his Army buddy. They didn't mind bending the law as long as justice was served."

"All right, all right, I'll play along," said Sam. "I suppose you have a cinematic theory that explains all this."

"Some guy who's been through a war, seen his buddies killed, doesn't know why the bullets passed him by. He's been thrown into battle by idiots who've never seen combat and who were sitting a thousand miles behind the front line. He's killed guys on the other side, guys his own age, could have been his friends given a different situation."

"Okay," said Sam. "So in his own mind, at some level, maybe the level when he was a kid in Sunday school, he's a murderer. He does bad things just because he's told to, by people he never sees and doesn't know. He's breaking the law, but also being told it's the right thing to do."

"And maybe he's a little attracted by the violence," said Bogie. "You know the cliché, 'never so alive as when facing death.' Perhaps he thinks he ought to pay for some of the things he's done."

Sam studied his food for a while. "So what are you telling me? You're not above breaking the law if you're doing the right thing? You love being a cop because you get a chance for some of the old ultraviolence?"

"I'm not talking about me. I'm talking about film noir. How the protagonist's ultimate guide is loyalty to his buddies, the guys who fought beside him, not some abstract sense of good and evil."

Sam took another bite of the pork. He wondered if Bogie was offering him something. But what? He chewed in silence for a bit. "Too deep for me."

Bogie pushed some rice to the side of his plate. "How is it you happened to get this assignment? Why you in particular?"

"I'd been tracking this Aryan militia group in Texas. When ATF realized the guns were coming in via the Philippines, my name came up because I'd been here once before."

"R&R when you were in the military?"

"Not exactly. My father wanted to commemorate his father's death. He brought me, my sister, and brother along."

"Your grandfather died in the Philippines?"

"He was stationed at Subic, before World War II. He was lucky enough not to be in Subic when it was bombed on December 7th." He took a breath. "He was unlucky enough to be on leave in Manila when the Japanese invasion began. He didn't survive the Bataan March."

Bogie started. He licked his lips as if to speak, but Sam went on.

"My dad was three years old at the time. He grew up not knowing his own father, and he brought us to the fiftieth reunion of the survivors of the Bataan death march. That was in '92. We were here for three days."

Bogie pushed away his plate. "I was more fortunate

than you. My father survived Bataan." He paused, seeming to struggle with something. "He was fifteen. He was able to slip away into the forest and live off the land."

"Your father? How old are you?

"No, no. The right question to ask is how old my father was when I was born."

"All right. How old?"

"Forty-two. And in the RP that is quite late in life for a poor man to have a child. It was a last attempt to prolong his youth. I don't know if it worked out exactly the way he hoped, but he is still among the living."

Sam looked at Bogie, waiting for him to go on. "Is there something I'm not understanding here?"

"Like you said before, Filipinos and Americans have a lot in common." Bogie waited for a long moment before he went on. "Perhaps we'll visit my father while you're here."

Sam leaned back from the table, finished with his plate. He sensed there was more to this than what Bogie was saying, but for the life of him he couldn't figure out what. By now he knew there would probably be no answer if he asked directly. "Let's try some of that ice cream."

Outside it was in the nineties. As they stepped into the humid, sun-bleached street, their shirts adhered to their backs. They hugged the building edge trying to stay in its shadow as they made their way to a sidewalk vendor.

Bogie ordered up two dishes of mango ice cream and handed one to Sam. Bogie took his spoon and began slurping his down, trying to beat the sun's effort to turn the ice cream into a drink.

Sam took a big mouthful of his—and stopped with his mouth half open, unsure whether to spit it out. Did they have the same anti-spitting laws here as they did in Singapore? He swallowed hastily, trying not to gag.

"What the heck do the cows eat around here?" said Sam.

"Grass, I suppose," said Bogie. "Why?"

"Milk tastes a little different from region to region in the US, based on the type of grass that grows best there, whatever breed of cattle's most suited to that climate. So I wondered—"

Bogie spooned a huge bite of dirty mango ice cream into his mouth, smiling.

"Why are we talking about cows? This is made from carabao milk. Much higher milk fat content than you are used to."

"You're telling me you raise reindeer in the Philippines?"

"Reindeer? No, that's a caribou," said Bogie. "This is carabao. You know—water buffalo."

Sam looked into the carton of stuff made by milking a buffalo that ate god-knows-what out in some swamp.

"Yeah, well, it's a little rich for my taste. You want the rest of mine?"

Bogie grinned and took Sam's carton. He ate a huge, melting spoonful. "The taste of Manila, man."

"I'm gonna guess they make cheese from carabao milk, too. Will you be sure to warn me?"

Bogie looked thoughtful as he finished the ice cream. "I don't think we make any cheese at all in the Philippines. Every time I see some for sale it's from the US or New Zealand." He concentrated, scanning his memory. "In fact, I don't think they make cheese anywhere in Asia."

"After tasting carabao milk, I can see how so many Asians came to be lactose intolerant." Sam stopped at another sidewalk vendor and bought two soft drinks. He gave one to Bogie and chugged his own, trying to clear the cloying taste of carabao from his palate.

Bogie's beeper went off, and a second later so did Sam's. They each pulled out their pagers and read their respective messages.

"Olivia says she has something for me," said Bogie. "Wants me to meet her in thirty minutes at the club."

Sam smiled as he put away his pager. "Jennifer wants me to call her ASAP. I'll go back inside and use the pay phone. I'll page you later and catch up."

Sam dialed Jennifer's office and was put through to her. "Hi, it's Sam. I didn't expect a call from you so soon—"

"Give me the number where you are right now. I'll call you back."

Sam gave her the pay phone number and stood watching the shoppers in the mall. The good feeling generated by a call from a beautiful woman had been replaced by something leaden in his gut.

He picked up part way through the first ring. Jennifer's voice was a little breathless, and she was on a cell phone.

"I had to dash outside," she explained. "I couldn't risk being overheard in my office."

"Is there a problem?"

"Did you watch the news last night? The Manila news?"

"No, but I caught an item on BBC, something about riots in Manila, at some apartment—" Sam paused. "The Santos Apartments. You weren't there, were you?"

Jennifer took a long breath before she spoke. "No. I had been warned away by an old—" There was a gap long enough that Sam thought he had lost the call. "—family friend."

"Were your parents injured?"

"No, their personal security people kept them from harm. But I got a call from a worker at one of the local networks. He saw some of the raw footage of the riot. He has a copy of the tape and thinks I should see it. But I can't review it in the Fiscal's office. My family has too many political enemies, some of whom work here."

"What about the TV station? No. Scratch that. Can I get it analyzed at NBI?"

"My family owns part of a video post-production house, a place that finishes commercials. I'll give you the address and have a courier bring you the tape. I don't want Bogie involved."

"You don't want Bogie knowing about it?" Sam thought that last bit over. "Are you saying Bogie is implicated?"

"No. But I need to see this information first, without leaks to the police. Will you do this?"

"All right. Bogie is away for a bit."

"When you are viewing it, call me on my cell phone. I was told to look for footage of the men in the flatbed truck."

Jennifer's personal driver delivered the tape to Sam. The driver said he would wait for Sam to bring it back.

Sam took the tape into the high tech offices of the video finishers. He didn't know if it was professional courtesy or his sparkling personality, but the Filipinos were unfailingly helpful to him.

A video tech put in the tape, a professional format digital cassette from the news crew. Sam scrolled at high speed until he found the flatbed truck footage. When he saw two men get out of the cab, he had the tech pick a frame, blow it up, and enhance it as best he could. They printed it out both in color and black and white. It wasn't a great photo, but the faces were recognizable.

Sam picked up the phone and dialed Jennifer's cell. She answered half way through the first ring. "I'm in my office."

"I understand. The faces are recognizable, though I don't know who they are. Should I ask around the office to see if anyone can—?"

Jennifer cut him off. "No! Just give the tape and pictures back to my driver. Don't act as if this is a big deal. If anyone asks, let them think it has something to do with your current investigation."

"Okay," said Sam.

"In truth, I'm afraid that it probably does intersect with the Tucker case. I'll know after I see the photo. Call you soon."

Sam thanked the tech, put the items into a large envelope, and took them downstairs. He thanked the driver for waiting, which amused him greatly.

"It's my job, sir. I drive, I wait, I drive. It's a good job." The driver sensed he hadn't made himself clear to Sam. "The car has air con. And I get to wear this uniform."

If there was any irony in the driver's speech, Sam couldn't detect it. He shook the driver's hand, adding to the man's amusement.

"I want to thank you anyway," said Sam.

Then he went back upstairs and got the video tech to print out a second set of photos.

twenty-one--

YANKEES GOING HOME!—In a surprise announce-
ment, President George H. Bush has set the date
for a speedy withdrawal of all US troops from
the Philippines. Clark Air Force Base, after being
devastated by the eruption of Mt. Pinatubo last
year, has been permanently closed, and awaits
final decommissioning of weaponry.
The withdrawal follows the controversial rejection
by the RP Senate of a new treaty to retain the US
bases in the RP. Subic Naval Base, the largest US
port in Asia, will be closed in six months. The US
leaves behind some $3 billion in assets. Arrange-
ments are being made to hand over control of
the base and its assets to a Filipino consortium
as soon as possible.

Manila Times
November 24, 1992

ROAD TO OLONGAPO—1:00 P.M. THURSDAY

Chito's Ford Escort was a beater, even by the standards of
rural Luzon. Olivia had warned him never to drive as nice
a car as he could really afford. That would just attract kidnappers and/or extortionate policemen. Better something junky
and safe.

He didn't care whatever she had to say about his clothes,
though. He wasn't going to look like a peasant.

Though it was less than a hundred klicks from Manila to
Subic, the trip took four hours: two to get out of the city, with
its multi-lane gridlocked freeway; and two more to negotiate
the two-lane highway that wound through the hills, meander-
ing into Olongapo, the border town that sprawled next to the
old base.

Chito stopped in at the American Bar to throw back a couple of drinks with the owner, American Mike. Three of Mike's four grandparents had been American citizens, and he lived in the vain hope that the American base would reopen.

Back when Subic had been the principal US Naval Port in Asia, the bar used to have a string of fifty B-girls to service the huge contingent of Navy personnel. The town was littered with their bastards. Business had fallen off sharply, but there were still a dozen girls working the bar.

Chito checked the local talent to see if any of them might be good enough for Club de Sex. He was surprised to find half the girls were Chinese.

"What's going on, Mike? How'd you get so many Chinese working here?"

Mike had long since lowered his IQ some twenty points via cannabis aroma therapy; otherwise, he wouldn't have been so open.

"Subic being a free port and all, it's easy to get new girls delivered. And the Chinese are cheap. I buy their contracts and passports for a grand; they have to pay me back twenty K."

Chito was incredulous. "Twenty K? What's the other nineteen K for?"

Mike laughed wetly. "Shipping and handling."

"I remember when it was all Filipina talent in here," said Chito. "What are those local girls doing now?"

"Most of them went back to their families, nannies to their nieces and nephews. Some moved to Manila, but the competition is tough. Quite a few mail order brides leaving here, too. Sailors from all over the world got fond memories of the girls from Olongapo."

"Maybe you can hook me up with your supplier," said Chito. "We're paying too much for our Chinese."

"Sure, I'll introduce you to the man." Mike thought it over, seeing new possibilities for income. "But if I do that, I gotta charge you an agent fee, buddy." He saw Chito give him the stink eye. "It's just business, you know that. I'm only gonna charge you one, two per cent. Net. FOB. No delivery."

Chito took American Mike's proffered hand and shook on it. "Great doing business with friends," he said without enthusiasm. "Where can I meet him?"

"He's got a place in the jungle over near Clark. I'll take you."

The monsoons were dumping water on Olongapo like someone had opened a hydrant, and streets were running two feet deep. A long file of young girls in their Catholic school uniforms waded across the street, the rich brown water swirling around their thighs. They hiked up their plaid skirts to keep them out of the mud, to the great satisfaction of the teenage boys following them.

The shopkeepers would have appreciated it, too, if they hadn't been so busy sandbagging their entries, trying to keep the water out.

American Mike drove a military surplus personnel carrier painted in jungle camouflage. Although Chito thought it looked cool, it rode worse than his Escort.

"You gotta love this high clearance, man," said Mike. "The aitch-two-oh slides right underneath, while we're sitting high and dry." He smirked at Chito, who was bouncing in his seat. "Not like that turd you drive. Fucker'd be underwater, and you'd be dancin' on top, waiting for the rescue team."

They passed beyond the city limits of Olongapo, and the water became shallower. The carrier thumped over something invisible in the turbulent flow. The jolt tossed Chito six inches into the air and brought him down hard on his coccyx.

"This thing's beating my ass black and blue," said Chito.

"Hey, I heard you like it that way." Mike snuffled a laugh, and dug out a cigar-sized doobie from the map box. "Fire this mother up, OK?"

Chito got the joint going and took a long hit. It helped take the edge off the pain in his backside, and he passed it over to Mike.

"You sure you're all right to drive? I mean, what with the rain, and the dope, and the fact that you can't see the road?"

"Hey, I know this road like the back of my hand," said Mike expansively, waving the joint. "I can get you where you want to go, daylight, pitch dark, rain or shine, what have you."

It was at that precise moment that the vehicle took a drop, one wheel bottoming out in a two-foot-deep pothole. As the car rebounded, Mike's forehead hit the steering wheel, and the joint was snapped off against the dashboard.

Mike sat up straighter and shook his head, trying to clear away the stars. "Forgot about that pothole." He stared at the broken joint. "You best search on the floor for what's left of this. Don't want it to go to waste."

Chito scrabbled around amongst the Twinkie wrappers, soda cans, and used tissues till he found the weed and pinched out the cherry.

"So where we headed?"

"Ever hear 'bout the missile silos over by Clark? Most of 'em were covered a meter deep in ash when Pinatubo blew. After the US left, the air force base was all divvied up. Some of it for resort hotels, some for golf courses. Lot of the old service housing is just sitting empty, still got a foot of ash on top of the roofs."

"What are you, a realtor? I just asked where we're going."

"Take a look in that map box. You'll find a picture of a guy inside some kinda cave. But it's not a real cave, see. It's one of the missile silos."

Chito dug through cigarette butts, a pack of condoms, Zig-Zag papers, Styrofoam clamshells from McDonald's, and a mound of other debris. After a minute of ever more impatient search, he turned up a dog-eared photo. As advertised, it was indeed the inside of a kind of cavern. Inside the cavern was a missile. Chito didn't know what kind of missile it was, but figured it had to be worth something to the right buyer.

But what got his attention was the man standing next to the missile: Harvey Tucker, the jerkoff who'd laid that beating on Olivia. He turned away so Mike couldn't see, folded the picture in quarters, and put it in his watch pocket

CLUB DE SEX—1:30 P.M. THURSDAY

Bogie tried the entry to Club de Sex, but it was locked. He went to the alley behind the club, kicking trash aside as he went, and climbed the stairway to the rear entry. It was locked, too. He knocked. Waited. Knocked again, harder.

He pulled out his cell phone and dialed Olivia. An answering machine picked up. Bogie took a deep, calming breath, realized it wasn't helping, and barked into the phone.

"What are you playing at, Livvie? I don't like wild goose chases."

Olivia picked up. "Bogie. What's the matter?"

"You know damn well."

"Where are you calling from?"

"I'm standing on the landing at the rear entry!"

"Come in out of the sun. You'll get heat stroke," said Olivia, and buzzed the entry lock.

Bogie jerked the door open and strode down the short hallway to her office. Olivia stuck her head out of the doorway, hand in her purse. Once she saw Bogie was alone, she buried the Taser back at the bottom and motioned him inside. She could see he was still steaming.

"Take off your coat, Bogie. I'll get you something cold," she said, turning to the small fridge in her office

Bogie took her wrist, and spun her back to face him. "Cut the crap. Why did you call me over here?"

Olivia winced at the force of Bogie's grip. He saw it in her eyes and eased up a fraction, but didn't let go. Olivia's blood was up in a millisecond.

"The fuck you talking about? I didn't call for a cop."

Bogie pushed her into a chair, pulled out his alpha pager,

and thumbed buttons until her message came up. He showed it to her. "Yeah?"

"Call my service, see if I asked them to forward you a message in the last twenty-four hours."

"Good idea," said Bogie. "Dial them now."

Two minutes and a pint of ice-cold beer later, Bogie apologized. "So who's playing practical jokes?"

"Come on, Detective. You know the drill better than I do. Do you have any enemies? Disgruntled partners? Angry coworkers?" She paused for a beat, and added lightly, "Jealous lovers?"

Bogie scowled, but couldn't keep it up.

"Oh my, you almost smiled, officer." Olivia plucked a compact from her desk drawer and touched up her makeup. "Let's see. You brought me in for questioning four days ago. You dropped by at dawn for a snack two days ago. And now this. I haven't seen you three times in a week—oh, for about five years, wouldn't you say?"

Bogie stubbed out one cigarette and lipped another, not responding.

"And then Miss Fiscal figured out you weren't such a great stepping stone after all. Poor upstart boys from Olongapo don't get to be chief, no matter how smart they are."

"That's enough, Olivia." But he could see that Olivia was on a roll now, and she wasn't going to stop until she dumped her load.

"Did you weep, poor boy, did you gnash your teeth?" Olivia snapped her compact shut. "Unrequited love sucks, doesn't it?" She dropped the compact back into the drawer of the desk. "But even after she was finished with you, you never came back here. Why was that? Couldn't stand slumming after screwing a society bitch? Didn't want that 'dirty' poon anymore?"

Bogie looked away. "It wasn't that, and you know it."

She fought back angry tears. "Then what was it?"

"I was—shown—my confidential file. Certain items were holding up promotion."

Olivia studied his face while he glanced about the room

restlessly, not returning her gaze. "Well, well." She sounded disappointed.

"I thought I was going places," he said, without conviction.

She looked at the floor. "And now you've made senior detective."

"Yeah, I'm an overnight success."

"Seems to me you just lost five years. When do you suppose you'll get them back?"

Bogie turned his face to her and gave a thin-lipped smile. "We both know I'm not going anyplace else."

Olivia eyed him gravely for some time.

Finally, he made a crooked smile and put on his best Bogart imitation. "I think this could be the start of a beautiful friendship."

Olivia gave him back a wan look. "You quote any more movie lines, and you're out on your ass."

She stood up from her desk and stretched. It was a well-practiced move. Both she and Bogie knew it, but it didn't stop him from appreciating her performance. She closed an accounting ledger and moved it to the desk drawer.

"I'm finished with the books." She put away a calculator, a pen, a stapler, and a box of paper clips. "Two hours before I open the club."

Bogie took the unlit cigarette from his mouth and put it back in the pack. "Livvie, we can't just pick up where we left off." He caught Olivia's glance as she looked at him over her shoulder. "Can we?"

Olivia reached to the far corner of the desk and flicked off a balled-up piece of paper. Her eyes never left Bogie's.

"You always liked a clean desk at the end of the day. Isn't that right? Something about that big slick surface, so cool to the touch."

She leaned against the edge of the desk and scooted her buttocks up onto the desktop, knees slightly apart. As small as she was, her feet dangled above the floor a couple of inches. She swung her feet back and forth into the knee well, like a schoolgirl. And every time they swung, her sheath skirt hiked up just a bit more.

"Take off your shoes and socks, Bogie. Stay a while."

Bogie smiled sardonically, removed his shirt and tie, but not his shoes.

Olivia mock-scolded him. "You've got to do what Livvie says. You get much better traction when you can dig your toes into the rug."

Bogie laughed. "I'd forgotten." He kicked off his shoes and shucked his socks, with a smooth grace.

Olivia pouted. "Dear, dear, I hope you haven't forgotten anything else." She blinked, and lowered the pitch of her voice a bit. "Or do you need help remembering? Is that it? Or maybe lessons? From Mama-san?"

Bogie took her by the shoulders. "Not like that, Livvie. No games. I always wanted you—just you. No acting." He kissed her, pulling her in close, needy. While she undid his belt, he unbuttoned her silk blouse. As he slid the blouse off her shoulders, she stiffened.

"Please, let's turn off the lights, Bogie."

"But we used to like the lights on—"

She closed her eyes as he continued to slide her top off. He saw the scars, felt the fine crosshatching of raised tissue that covered her back. Bogie pulled away from her so that he could look into her face.

"Livvie—"

He closed his eyes. Bogie reached for the wall switch and turned off the overhead lights, leaving just the faint illumination through the transom to the hallway.

"I don't need you to see me, Livvie. I'm not getting any younger."

When he reached out for her, she grabbed his face roughly and pulled it between her breasts. "I want this, Bogie," she said into his ear, her voice harsh with emotion. "More than you know. But I will not be patronized." She leaned back, using her leverage to pull him atop her on the desk.

"Livvie—"

She wrapped her legs around him, pushing her toes into the waistband of his boxers, and tugged them down around his thighs.

Whatever Bogie had been going to say was lost. The scent of her warm flesh rose up and enveloped him in a cloud of pheromones that obliterated all thought. His lips worked their way along her sweat-sheened breasts, to her collarbone, up her neck, behind her ear.

Now he could smell fragrant oil in her hair, could feel her nipples hard against his chest. He kissed her open mouth, tasting the peppery chips she'd had at lunch. Her sharp nails dug into his lower back, giving him a jolt of pain, as she pulled him inside her.

Everything focused as he rocked her against the desktop, his toes scything through the nap of the carpet. He pushed her closer and closer to the edge, listening to her moan, gasp.

"Bogie. Bogie. Don't—you—"

But they were both falling together into a place with no words.

It was about time to open the club when Bogie left. He looked like a guilty schoolboy, and Olivia almost felt sorry for him. She walked over to the club's surveillance room and watched him leave on the video camera that monitored the alley at the rear entry.

When he was gone, she punched up the video feed from her office, rewound, and played back the low-light high-gain video of the two of them making love. She dubbed a digital video copy and erased the images from the video hard drive recorder.

In the counting room, she opened a safe and put the mini-DV cassette in an envelope. She wrote "FOR JUAN OR CHITO— Open in case of my trouble" on the outside of the envelope, sealed it, and closed the safe. She hesitated before spinning the tumblers.

She looked up as she heard someone signal for entry. The

face of Tiki the bartender showed on the monitor, and Olivia buzzed him in. A new business day was starting. She turned back to the safe.

God, that was the best sex I've had since he left me. She spun the dial. *Still, safety first.*

A tape of the lead homicide detective having sex with a prime suspect would discredit any evidence that turned up. She frowned at the thought of turning Bogie against her again.

And that was better sex for him than anything that skinny cow Jennifer could offer.

She hoped it was true.

> **LAND REFORM AFTER MARCOS**—After the ouster of Marcos, there was a brief period of liberal urban land reform. Any unused city property was able to be homesteaded. Occupancy for as little as twenty-four hours, improvements as minor as the construction of a cardboard and tin shanty, could establish ownership.
>
> Property tax bills for the huge holdings of the wealthy families were astronomical, so they often went unpaid. Under the new regime, a single year of tax delinquency clouded the title.
>
> The homeless squatted in parks, alleys, abandoned railway lines, sidewalks, vacant lots, riverbanks, and the old Spanish colonial cemeteries (owner- ship of which was unclear since the US-Spanish War).
>
> The unintended consequence of this reform was the formation of goon squads. Wealthy landowners paid thugs to clear their properties each night to forestall homesteading claims.
>
> *A History of Philippine Land Reform*

After the riots at the Santos Apartment Complex, private security services cracked down on squatters anywhere near holdings of the wealthy. Three nights of carnage left dozens dead and hundreds injured. Since the dead couldn't vote and the injured were homeless and broke, there was little political incentive to curb the violence.

Within a week an uneasy truce had been reached. The landless stayed away from valuable real estate, and the goon squads stopped killing them.

Sonny Lagos led teams of aid workers and nurses into the bloodiest areas, making sure the media recorded his efforts to ameliorate the situation of Manila's poorest citizens. Because Lagos was not a fool, he knew he was a prime target whenever he was out in public.

A para-military-style parade accompanied the relief team, brandishing posters with his likeness. Other than the poster staves, they were always unarmed, but seemed to revel in their matching shirts, sashes, and the pageantry. Sonny kept his personal thugs and/or bodyguards undercover, mingling among the homeless.

Sonny Lagos' new party made the evening news often. Lagos had his political organizers work among the landless enclaves wherever they sprang up. He began a voter registration drive that he believed would take him far up in the government.

He knew he would incur the hatred of the old families of Manila, but he was willing to risk that. He already hated them—especially the Santos clan that had taken so much of his family's land.

Once he was mayor of the city—or better yet, governor of the province—he would begin to dismantle those vast estates. He had made it his business to know which congressmen and senators were willing to sell their votes. He could provide the monetary catalyst for the first true land reform in RP history.

Sonny saw himself as in the "happiness business." When he paid off the legislators, they were happy to take the money. When his party assumed power, all the organizers and pols would be happy.

And when the landless had a few square meters to build a shanty upon, they would be happy. It was true that the families whose land was expropriated would be poorer—but on the plus side they would be better off spiritually.

And if ten million Filipinos became landowners, who would complain if he kept a few crumbs for himself?

But a few crumbs from each estate would make a very nice cake indeed.

twenty-two--

SLAIN AMERICAN MAY HAVE BEEN KIDNAP VICTIM—The fate of Mr. Harvey Tucker, late of Texas, USA, is being investigated as a kidnapping gone awry. If so, he would be the forty-seventh person abducted this year. The Minister of the Interior has begun a probe into the link between terrorist groups and the recent spate of kidnappings of foreign nationals.

"These so-called separatist groups—the Abu Sayef and the MILF—are no more than criminals, intent on ransom, not justice for their people," said an assistant to the Minister. "We must put an end to this lawlessness if foreign investment and foreign tourism are to grow in RP."

Manila Ex-Pat News

DAVAU, MINDANAO—1 P.M. THURSDAY

Once he returned from delivering funds to Abu Sayef on Mindanao, Riffat knew he would have to complete his transaction with Gerard. He sincerely wished that he would never have to spend another minute with any other Frenchman. However, the French had developed the biggest industrial espionage network, since they passed with ease among the countries of the west, using their white skin as a passport of trustworthiness.

Riffat thought the French surpassed even the Americans in their pursuit of money. His government found it much easier to buy the technology they needed from the French, rather than spend a decade training a group of nuclear scientists and engineers to reinvent their own.

Though he wasn't a scientist, he knew from his own Internet research that it required no more than five kilos of fissionable material—something about the size of a coffee can—to create a one kiloton nuclear device. The practical difficulty was engineering a shell of explosives around the fissile matter that would detonate simultaneously at all points, thereby creating a pressure wave to implode the dense metal and start the nuclear chain reaction. And the whole package still needed to fit in a small suitcase.

Riffat had spent the night in a seedy hotel, awaiting his shuttle flight to Cebu City, and on to Manila. Once he had the plans, he planned to fly on to Singapore and thence to Karachi. At six a.m. he went to the desk and had the clerk retrieve his airline tickets and the packet of cash from the hotel safe.

Outside he had to squint against the morning sun, holding tight to his battered suitcase. There were no taxis waiting at the curb—which was unusual—so he flagged one down. A wreck with a taxi sign pulled over, its Malaysian driver grinning from ear to ear. The squat cabbie jumped out with the motor still running and sprinted around the car to grab Riffat's luggage.

"Where to, boss? Airport, yes? I'll put your suitcase in the trunk. Safer that way," said the cabbie.

Riffat growled and climbed into the rear of the cab, settling deep into the concave seat. "I have a 7 a.m. flight. I didn't think I was going to make it on time."

"This your lucky day, boss. I get you there super-quick." The cabbie slammed the rear door, climbed into the driver's seat, tromped the accelerator, and pulled away from the hotel in a miasma of blue smoke.

Riffat stared out the side window, trying to discourage conversation. He was sick of Filipinos and ready to get out of the Philippines, righteous business or not.

He caught sight of the cabbie grinning at him in the mirror. Two blocks away from the hotel the car made a quick turn into a narrow alley and slammed to a halt. The cabbie sat there, still grinning, racing the motor.

Riffat gaped at him. "What are you doing? I told you I have to catch a plane—" Icy fear shot from his sternum to his crotch. Riffat spun on his buttocks on the slick plastic upholstery, looking for a way out. A door opened on either side of the alley, and three short, vicious-looking Malays surrounded the cab. They pulled open the doors and got in, two pinning Riffat between them in the rear seat, while the third took the front passenger seat, showing Riffat an Uzi machine pistol.

"You did a good job, brother," said the gunman to the cabbie, without breaking eye contact with Riffat. "Let's go." He made sure Riffat understood that the Uzi was still aimed at him though it was out of view below the seat.

Riffat said nothing. He knew there was nothing to say until he met with the leader of the kidnappers. The men on either side of him had clamped onto his arms, and neither of them seemed inclined to conversation.

The taxi fought its way out of the urban traffic, heading for the suburbs. They rode in silence for about forty minutes around the edge of Davau, and pulled into a disused rice warehouse. A hundred feet inside they jerked to a stop, and even more men circled the car.

The driver cut the engine, and Riffat's captors got out, leaving him alone in the rear seat. One particularly ugly Malay—with a scar marking a diagonal from the left eyebrow down across his face and disappearing into his collar—leaned in the window of the cab.

"Riffat? Riffat Khan?"

Riffat gave a curt nod, trying to quell his panic. "I have money in my suitcase. I'll pay you to let me go. You can have it all. Just leave me my tickets so I can fly home."

But Ugly wasn't paying attention. He pulled a cell phone from his pants pocket and hit a number in memory. He gave Riffat a bleak stare while he waited for someone to pick up.

"Mr. Samoa, the package was just delivered," said Ugly. "It's sitting right in front of me."

"I can pay you!" shouted Riffat, hoping the person on the other end could hear him. "My friends will help." He looked to Ugly. "Just let me talk with him, we can work something out!"

Ugly pushed a button putting the cell phone in speaker mode, so everyone could hear. "This package is no longer necessary," came Juan Samoa's voice. "Dispose of it. Payment as usual."

The line disconnected, and Ugly looked at Riffat with a feral grin. "I guess he don' wanna talk with you."

Riffat's voice rose half an octave. "I will give the money straight to you! And the tickets. You can cash them in too—"

"You know what I been hearing? You been playin' house with the Abu Sayef?" said Ugly. "That's what I heard."

The cabbie spoke up. "What's next, boss?"

Ugly just shrugged. "We got ten hours before it's dark enough to move out. Let's see if we can make him last that long.

Riffat shrank in on himself, curling into the seat cushion. The kidnappers looked at each other, eyes glinting in anticipation of the entertainment to come. Two of them reached in and jerked Riffat from the car.

Riffat looked to them imploringly. "But I'm a Muslim," he pleaded. "We fight the same jihad."

One of the men carried a short, curved knife. He reached down and stabbed through the back of Riffat's left leg. "You're a traitor to Islam." He twisted the blade and jerked, cutting the Achilles tendon.

Riffat squealed and fell to the ground, blood gushing from the leg wound. He grabbed his leg, trying to stanch the bleeding, but recoiled in pain when he grabbed the naked tendon protruding from the back of his calf.

Another man pulled a bandana from around his neck and tied it around Riffat's leg, pulling it tight to slow the flow of blood. Riffat was still screaming, but he looked at his helper with a glimmer of hope.

Bandana Man was through helping Riffat. He looked around at his comrades. "Ten pesos says he can still make it to the door in less than thirty seconds. Any takers?"

"I'll take that bet." Knife Man bent down and placed the point of his curved blade against Riffat's right calf. "I think that was the signal for you start running for the door. Unless you want me to cut your other leg."

Riffat tried to scramble to his feet, but his left leg gave way. As the Malays placed their wagers on the concrete floor of the warehouse, Ugly took out a pocket watch and began calling the time.

"Five seconds. Eight. Ten."

Riffat dragged his left leg while pushing ahead with his right, blood trailing behind him. The men paced along beside him, some calling out encouragement, others reviling him, depending on which way they were betting.

"Seventeen. Twenty."

Ugly paused to shake his watch.

"I'm not sure I wound this thing. Seems to be running kinda slow."

One of the men stood on Riffat's cuff, pinning him in place. "Give me the watch and I'll wind it!" He mimed winding the timepiece until the others pushed him off, laughing. Riffat resumed his agonizing half-crawl toward freedom.

He was still fifteen feet from the door.

"Twenty-eight. Twenty-nine. Thirty." Ugly made a sound like the buzzer on a low budget TV game show. "Back to square one!"

The men collected their bets and dragged Riffat back to his starting place. Bandana Man went over to Riffat and squatted beside him.

"I was betting on you, man, and you let me down. I tied up your leg, tried to make things better, and this is the way you treat me."

Riffat just stared at him. Shock had taken over, and he couldn't feel his leg any more. He started to shiver.

"You listenin'? You cost me ten pesos," said Bandana Man. "I think I should be compensated, don't you?" He looked around for Knife Man and motioned for the blade. He reached over and began sawing at Riffat's ear. "I don't know if this is worth ten pesos—I mean, maybe it is to you—but at least I keepin something to show for my trouble."

Riffat blubbered as Knife Man pulled his ear free. His shivering increased until his whole body convulsed.

Bandana Man passed the knife back. "Our racehorse looks cold. Maybe we should warm him up."

The others laughed and got to work. It didn't take long to pour a small pool of gasoline on the concrete floor about thirty feet from Riffat. The pool was connected to a trail of petrol that stretched to his legs, split into two branches and continued on toward the door.

Knife Man took a stance near the pool of fuel and struck a match. Bandana Man jerked Riffat's head around to make sure Riffat saw what was up.

"Fifteen pesos says he makes it to the door before he gets too warm," called out Ugly. With a whoop they placed their wagers.

Riffat wondered how long it would be until he saw Allah.

NBI—3 P.M. THURSDAY

Bogie stared at his pager, as if it would yield up answers by force of will. He was grumpy enough to ignore Sam steaming on the other side of his desk.

"Seems more than coincidental that we both got paged at the same time, doesn't it?" asked Sam. "Are those pagers issued by the NBI? Who had use of this one before me?" He drummed his fingers on the edge of Bogie's desk.

The noise irritated Bogie, and he gave Sam a sharp glance. He was surprised to see that Sam had mastered the ability to point with his eyebrow, Filipino style. Sam was signaling they should go outside into the hall.

"Yeah, it's government issue gear. And anyone in telecom would recognize the prefix as belonging to someone in law enforcement." He nodded yes to Sam. "Why don't we grab a bite in the cafeteria?"

"I saw a street vendor with some kind of grilled something that smelled good. Let's try that."

Now Bogie was certain something was up.

Outdoors it was raining hard, but it was so hot that the rain vaporized as it hit the asphalt. Bogie and Sam brushed along the building, trying to stay dry. They came to a one-legged RP veteran selling grilled chicken, and they huddled under his umbrella, rain beating on the fabric, making it hard to talk. Sam decided to let Bogie buy him lunch, to make up for the dirty ice cream.

Bogie ditched his wet cigarette and lit a fresh one, signaling for two skewers of chicken. He handed one to Sam. "Where did you find out about that eyebrow business?"

"I read it in a businessman's guide to Filipino etiquette. I practiced in the mirror until I could move them one at a time. Had the chamber maid laughing so hard she wet herself." Sam slid a chunk off the skewer and nibbled it. Satisfied with the taste, he pulled another into his mouth and chewed happily.

Bogie was impatient. "So why are we out here on the street?"

Sam slowed down, choosing his words. "I think that some-one is watching you—or maybe just listening. Or perhaps inter-cepting your calls and alpha pages. It's just a feeling, but I—"

"Are simultaneous pages all you have to base this feel-ing on?"

"No, not exactly. But I don't understand the politics here. Saddul said—"

"You been listening to Garcia and Saddul run their mouths? They may want my job, but they aren't spying on me."

"I thought they were your partners."

"Right," said Bogie. "So what the hell are you talking about?"

"Local politics." Sam pulled a photo from his pocket. "The fiscal told me to print out a frame from some newsman's videotape. Had her driver wait so I could send it back to her.

She didn't want me asking around about who the man in the photo might be." Sam felt a pang of betrayal as he handed the picture over to Bogie. "She said she didn't want you to see this until she had a chance to look at it."

Well, I'm sure she's seen it by now, he thought to himself.

Bogie didn't look at the photo, waited for Sam to go on.

"This whole case is getting squirrelly," said Sam. "If the prosecutor doesn't want me to show information to my partner on the case, what is this really about?"

Bogie looked down at the photo, seemed to dismiss it, looked again.

"The guy getting out of the truck cab at the riots—" began Sam.

Bogie motioned him to silence. He put the picture in his pocket and motioned for Sam to walk with him. When they were out of sight of the grill vendor, he ducked into a doorway out of the rain. Sam followed him and they stood close together, rain dripping from their clothes, while Bogie spoke in a low voice.

"Guy working the barbecue's a veteran. For sure, he'd know this guy's name if he heard it. Maybe he reports things he overhears—or maybe he doesn't."

"So who is it?"

"Congressman by the name of Sonny Lagos. Up-and-coming politician, just started a grass roots land reform movement. He's making lots of public appearances, published a manifesto for the homeless. He plans to ride it all the way into the mayor's mansion, maybe the governor's. From there, who knows?"

"So why didn't Jennifer want you to know about this picture?" Sam let the question hang between them for about five seconds.

"As soon as you know what women think, let me know." Bogie scowled.

"Did she think you might be working for Lagos?"

"Look, you already know that she and I were an item before. Maybe she thought I'd use this somehow."

"Use it somehow—against her? So things didn't end well with the two of you?"

"It ended. She stopped taking my calls and told security not to let me through the gate to her housing complex."

"Let's put that aside. What does this picture mean?"

"It places the congressman at the scene of the riots. It's a possibility he was orchestrating them. Against the Santos family holdings."

"Won't that make it easy for Jennifer to investigate him?" said Sam.

"It's not that simple. Lagos and Santos are two of the oldest and wealthiest families in the Philippines. Lagos' father lost the majority of the family property due to a Supreme Court ruling about the legality of Spanish colonial deeds. The Santos family acquired most of the Lagos holdings." Bogie waited for Sam to put things together.

"And you told me Jennifer's father was a judge. *The* judge?"

Bogie nodded. "The families hate each other, but they can't afford to attack each other too directly. For one thing, they have intermarried for four hundred years. But they are jealous rivals for power, and if the power structure breaks down, there's no telling who it will destroy."

"You think Jennifer will make use of this evidence—or suppress it?"

"It's not clear. And if Sonny knows it exists, he may try something rash to eliminate it."

Sam wrestled with his conscience. "Jennifer mentioned this guy Sonny before. He came to her privately and wanted the Tucker investigation stopped."

Bogie stared at Sam, took a nervous drag on his cigarette. "What interest could Lagos have?"

"And how is it connected to Tucker?" said Sam. "If Filipino pols are anything like American politicians, they always have a deep need for cash. But I don't see why the Texas Freemen would be sharing funds with Lagos."

"Harvey needed cash, too. That's why he imported the gamecocks." said Bogie. Sam could see the detective was becoming uncomfortable with the direction this was going. "The connection has to be the guns."

"Maybe they both were after the same shipment of weapons."

"Sometimes national regimes change without benefit of an election," said Bogie. "And sometimes even a legitimate election can precipitate violence."

Sam digested this. "Let's go talk to Lagos," said Sam, "shake his tree, see what falls out."

"That's not something I can do." Bogie looked away. "There are people you don't confront in the RP, not unless you have solid evidence of a capital crime. Being present at a civil disturbance doesn't qualify." Bogie stubbed out his smoke. "But you have convinced me to be paranoid about our phones."

Sam stared at him, embarrassed for his friend. He thought for a bit. "What if an obnoxious Yank were to question Congressman Lagos? Any repercussions there?"

Bogie smiled. "Not as many. Sonny enjoys the US Ambassador's support for his land reform ideas, and he doesn't want to lose it. Just don't mention my name. I'd like to retire with my pension intact."

"How do I get to see this guy?"

"Why don't you ask the Embassy to set it up? Keep NBI out of it, make it seem like an ATF idea."

FRENCH INDUSTRIAL ESPIONAGE—

Washington Post: What is the government doing about our allies stealing industrial secrets from US companies?

Mr. Boucher: I've just told you that we take it seriously—that we take appropriate steps. It's our policy to brief American companies when we have information—about possible threats for their security. The Overseas Security Advisory

Council that we use—it's a joint venture. It's done between the Department of State and *a number of American companies with interests abroad.* (Emphasis added.) It was designed to facilitate the sharing of information and guidance regarding security, and it was created in 1985.

> *U.S. Department of State*
> *Daily Press Briefing*
> *Friday, April 30, 1993, 1:07 P.M.*

twenty-three--

Juan Samoa scanned Club de Sex for Gerard, hoping the frog hadn't left yet. His CIA handler had briefed him about the pharmacological research report and approved a twenty thousand dollar budget plus expenses. He had also noted that the frog's survival was optional.

Juan spotted Gerard, elbows on the bar, in front of a pole dancer. The Frenchman had been on a two-day binge and still hadn't changed out of his Hawaiian shirt. The dancer shimmied off the pole and squatted before Gerard, leaned back until her ponytail brushed the bar top and held the pose, pulsing to the music, while he began an amateur gynecological exam.

Juan walked up behind Gerard and spoke into his ear. "Haven't you heard? You can't go home again."

Gerard turned his head slowly. He was high on something, and had to search for the source of the voice. "The hell you talking about? I go home whenever I wish to do so. I already purchased my return ticket, *non*?"

"You never heard of Thomas Wolfe?" said Juan.

"Is he here? S'he my buyer?"

"No, Thomas couldn't make it tonight." Juan already regretted his attempt at literary humor. "I'm here to get something back from you."

"Get back?" Alcohol and a cocktail of drugs made Gerard a little slow following Juan's conversation. "I bought nothing from this Mr. Wolfe."

"Forget Mr. Wolfe. I am acting as an intermediary. I need back the research papers Harvey Tucker sold you."

"*Mon ami*, this is not Wal-Mart. There are no, how you say, refunds."

"I'll return the money Mr. Tucker received."

Gerard's face had the crafty kind of look only drunks or cartoon animals are able to assume. "So. You will return the money. The question is why, is it not? Why does the amiable Mr. Tucker want his trade secret back?"

Juan realized Gerard had been in a drug and alcohol haze for so long, he hadn't heard about Tucker's death. *How does this guy get any business done with a perpetual buzz like that?*

"It always comes down to politics, Gerard," said Juan. "That's all I'm allowed to say."

"But perhaps I have already passed on this information to my friends in Europe?"

"Mr. Tucker—" Juan emphasized the name—"is certain you haven't done so yet. He hears you are still shopping it around—in Asia. And he's willing to give you a premium for all your trouble—let's say an extra ten thousand."

"Ah, but this is not good business," said Gerard. "That is far less than my mark-up when I resell information of this kind. I double or triple my investment."

Juan leaned in close, using his bulk to intimidate the Frenchman. He smiled bleakly into Gerard's boozy gaze. "But all that mark-up can't be spent if you're dead, can it? And that would be bad business."

Gerard blinked owlishly. "Bad business? *Certainement.*"

"Now if this breakthrough should be 'rediscovered' by any of your other clients, we'd know you have been selling the same goods twice. And you'd be dead. And if you refuse to return it, after my reasonable offer, you'd also be dead, because you're in my country."

Gerard did some drunken mental math. "I see now that a profit of ten thousand dollars—no Euros, please—is sufficient."

"I told Mr. Tucker you had a head for business," said Juan. "I have the cash upstairs. Get the documents and bring them back here in an hour."

Gerard wagged a finger in Juan's face. "But I do not think I shall do any more business with Mr. Tucker."

"Hey, that's what capitalism is all about. Freedom of the marketplace."

PORT OF MANILA—4 P.M. THURSDAY

With Bogie and Sam working together full time, Garcia and Saddul had to pick up the slack in new homicide investigations. Saddul knew that Garcia wished he didn't have to spend so much time with a partner who looked like he bought his clothes at a second-hand store. For his own part, Saddul hoped he wasn't picking up any of Garcia's swishy mannerisms.

Saddul motioned Garcia into the shade, trying to find some relief from the intense sunlight along the exposed pier. He pulled a tissue from his coat, blew his nose into it, crammed the damp wad into his suit coat pocket. His alpha-pager beeped and he read the screen, shaking his head.

"This looks bad. The Port Authority is going to break open the seal on the container before we get there," said Saddul. "There's no sound from inside, and they're worried."

"Tell them to wait for our arrival before they let the press start shooting video," said Garcia.

They hurried toward several containers that had been set aside on the loading dock, but the heat made it harder to move any faster than a slow walk. By the time the two detectives had reached the site, their suits were drenched with perspiration.

Saddul and Garcia ducked under a traffic control barrier and made their way to the cargo container being examined. Two Port Authority cops scrutinized the bill of lading, while a third used bolt cutters to remove the heavy-duty locks.

Saddul leaned over the shoulder of one of the Port Authority men and said, "I'm Detective Saddul, NBI. My partner—Detective Garcia—and I will assume control of the scene if there is evidence of anything beyond smuggling."

"There's already evidence." The Port Authority cop scowled at Saddul. "Your beak not working?"

Saddul put a fresh tissue to his nose and nodded.

"What first made this container seem suspicious?"

"Someone reversed the numbers in the manifest. Happens a lot. Then they call and say their container is overdue because of the typo, try to get it through customs in a big hurry to meet some deadline."

Saddul guessed that "big hurry" implied big bribe. "Why didn't it work this time?"

"No one showed for the hurry-hurry inspection," said the Port cop.

"Any particular reason offered why they didn't show up?" said Saddul.

"I can't say. The phone number given is disconnected."

A second lock fell to the ground, and two men pulled the doors of the container open. Garcia and Saddul poked their heads inside the dark interior, jerked them back as the smell hit them.

Garcia pulled a silk handkerchief from the breast pocket of his suit and tied it around his nose and mouth, bandana style. Saddul had a cotton hanky with a plaid border he pulled from his hip pocket, along with a small flask of gin. He saturated the hanky and held it to his face.

One of the Port Authority workers shined a flashlight into the interior. Bodies lay everywhere. Two men, many women, a few children—none moving—all Chinese.

A fifty-gallon drum in the middle had been serving as a makeshift toilet. The lid was off, and that was a major contributor to the horrific odor. It hit them like a physical blow as they walked inside.

A group of seven bodies lay huddled against one another near a small vent at one corner of the container. They had died fighting for a spot where they might get a breath of air.

Garcia pulled a latex glove from his pocket, slipped it on. He knelt and felt for a pulse as he passed each person. His look became more and more grim as he made his way to the rear of the cargo container.

A large waxed cardboard container of rice balls, twenty or so left, starting to go bad. Two drums that had held water, long since dry. Small suitcases that held all each person had been allowed to bring along.

Saddul opened a battered cardboard suitcase. One change of underwear, a clean blouse, a dress intended for a job interview, papers, a small amount of cash. A picture of two small girls. A picture of an old woman.

Saddul looked at the bodies nearby. He realized that the woman who lay a few feet away had left behind her children and mother, hoping to earn enough as a working girl to pay their way out of China later, trying to keep her kids from the misery she was going to face. Saddul doubted if they would survive without her help.

Garcia called Saddul over to the body of a young girl, no more than fourteen. "What do you think?"

"I think her world must have been pretty shitty if this seemed like a good idea."

Saddul squatted next to Garcia and inspected the girl. He saw a small, cheap address book in the pocket of her skirt, and pulled it out. Inside were Chinese ideograms mixed with Arabic numerals. Saddul thumbed through, looking at each page. He stopped, pointed out one set of numbers to Garcia.

"Aren't these phone prefixes for Subic?" said Saddul. "So why did she end up here in Manila?"

Garcia turned it over in his head, but nothing clicked. "Let's turn this in, get it translated," he said, "but photocopy these phone numbers first."

"A couple of these numbers are right here in Metro Manila."

"It will be easy to find out who she knew in town."

"Always the optimist, aren't you?" said Saddul.

A photographer began shooting the bodies, one at a time, working his way from the rear of the container, methodical in his coverage. He stopped near the group of seven bodies, shot several angles, unhappy that he couldn't isolate each of the bodies, since he was paid by the shot.

Almost as an afterthought he photographed the ideograms chalked on the wall.

工作授自由

twenty-four--

Chito scrunched uncomfortably in the passenger seat as American Mike steered the surplus armored personnel carrier though abandoned US housing that defined the edge of the old Clark Air Force Base. No one had bothered boarding up the houses, and some were occupied by squatters. This far from the city—and this close to the jungle—no one cared.

A decade after Mount Pinatubo's self-immolation, the houses still had six to eight inches of volcanic ash atop their roofs. Where the ash had hit the ground it had served as fertilizer, and the local plants were smothering the homes. It looked like an American suburb in an apocalyptic film from the fifties.

Once past the rows of family housing, Mike parked by a chain-link fence that had served as the furthest boundary of the base. He set the hand brake and got out, motioning Chito to follow. Mike pulled back a section of the fence that was just leaning in place, and put it back after Chito passed through.

Chito followed Mike into the forest, stepping along a trail that would be overgrown by next year. Here and there a little clearing showed drifted mounds of ash, now serving as small planters.

They walked for fifteen minutes, sucking their way through a third doobie, passing a forty-ouncer back and forth. Mike stopped and looked about witlessly.

Chito paused, swaying. "I hope you're not lost. I didn't come for the scenery."

"I'm not lost. The entry is hard to see with all this floral shit growing as fast as it does."

Chito laughed with marijuana-induced amiability. "Floral

shit. Flo-ral shee-itt. That's some mighty fine vocabulary you got there, Mikey. You go to school to learn all that?"

American Mike glared at him, turned aside, took a step, and abruptly disappeared.

Chito stood slack-jawed and stared at the spot where Mike had been an instant before. He mechanically brought the roach to his lips, and stopped, staring at the glowing tip.

"Fuckin' A. Gotta stop smoking this shit. I'm seeing things." He paused while he struggled to clarify his THC-addled thoughts. "No, that's not right. I'm *not* seeing things that I *oughta* be seeing."

He pinched out the joint and stashed the remnant in his pocket. After all, it was like his granny always said: "Today you don't know where to put a bit, tomorrow you won't know where to get a bit." He looked around the jungle, befuddled, with just a hint of fear.

"Mike?" he called querulously. "You there, man?" He took a step forward. "Mike?"

"Dave's not here," said the unseen Mike, segueing into an old Cheech and Chong routine.

Chito stepped toward the sound of Mike's voice, and suddenly Mike came into view. He was holding back some vines that hid a narrow entrance into a corridor. *A corridor inside a tree trunk?*

"Come on, Chito. You gotta see this place."

Chito followed him into the tree trunk and reached out to touch the wall of the hallway. Cement. "What the hell?"

"It's in disguise," said Mike. "They got some movie set guys to design this fake tree and vines to hide the entry to this—this—chamber, I guess you call it."

They went down two flights of industrial steel stairs, through a double-entry door and came into a circular room faced in concrete, about thirty feet tall, maybe fifteen in diameter. Sitting in the middle was a missile of some kind, ten feet tall.

Atop a ladder, a narrow-shouldered man was photographing the exposed interior works. Chito thought the person looked like a weasel with his head in a rat hole. The weasel turned around and Chito realized it was Nosaka in the same instant that Nosaka recognized him.

Nosaka paused when he saw Chito, looked inquiringly to Mike.

"Why have you brought Rivera?"

"You met Chito already?" said Mike, apparently fearing that he might lose his commission. "How was I supposed to know?"

Fear sobered Chito up quick. He knew he shouldn't be seeing Nosaka in this setting. They were supposed to know each other through Olivia. Men as rich as Nosaka didn't like outsiders knowing their business.

"He never mentioned your name, or I wouldn't have come," said Chito. "I would not be so disrespectful as to go around our mutual connection."

Nosaka inspected Chito in silence, waiting for an explanation.

"Mike told me he knew somebody in real estate," said Chito, "someone who could also sell me some Chinese immigrants."

Nosaka turned a steely gaze on Mike. "You told him I was in real estate?"

Mike stammered, blurted, "I never told him your name, man." It looked like he thought things were going bad, and going bad fast.

"We will discuss this later, Mike." Nosaka looked back at Chito, appraising his intelligence. He gestured to the partially deconstructed missile. "You know what this is?"

Chito was sweating freely now. "Looks like most of a missile. American."

Nosaka indicated the empty chamber at the top. "No warhead or guidance system. They made sure to retrieve those."

"The *kanos* had nuclear devices here on Luzon?"

Nosaka started down the ladder. "No. That would have

been a major violation of several international arms control treaties. These held other devices, mostly counter-missile measures, to protect Clark, Subic, and points east," said Nosaka. "They were meant to intercept and take out bombers, even intercontinental missiles, if possible. Still, they have quite a range of their own. And they are fast."

"But useless without their warheads?" said Chito.

"I have friends who might be able to re-arm them. That's why I had Olivia retrieve the French plans. It made a package my buyers couldn't resist—I deliver the vehicle, they add the warhead, and BOOM. Instant jihad."

"I don't want to know about this." Chito tried to think of some way out of his situation. He had one piece of information he could use, but it would compromise Olivia. He couldn't give Nosaka that much control over her.

"I don't like people knowing my business. And I especially don't like people who try to take away my little share of the market." Nosaka was off the ladder now. "You have the right to understand—" Nosaka left it hanging in mid-air.

Chito tried to use just a little of his leverage. "Come on. I'm partners with Olivia. How's she gonna react if—?" He realized Nosaka was staring at him, impassive.

American Mike dropped his head in misery. When Chito turned and sprinted for the door, Mike slammed him into the cement wall. Chito was stunned by the impact and slumped to the floor. Mike put Chito face down and kneeled on his back, as Nosaka made his way over.

"I've never understood why Olivia would send a boy to do a man's business."

MAKATI GALLERIA SUITES—5 A.M. FRIDAY

Sam awoke sweating a little after five a.m., the dream still vivid and feverish. In it he had been back at Club de Sex, pushing his way through a mob of pre-pubescent prostitutes. He could see a man he thought he recognized on the far side of the dance floor, but when he tried to get closer, the girls pressed their bodies against him. The more he struggled, the more tightly he was held.

Sam awakened to find that he was cocooned in the bedclothes. He peeled the damp sheet away and sat on the edge of the bed. Four days of tropical heat interrupted by fever dreams and night sweats.

It came to him that Christy hadn't appeared in a dream since that first night in Manila. He hadn't gone this long without dreaming about her since her death two years ago.

As he cooled off, he had that middle-of-the-night sensation that his skin didn't fit properly. He realized he was hungry, but room service had shut down at one a.m. He padded over to his dresser and found a packet of crackers and cheese. He opened the small refrigerator and pulled out a bowl of mango he had saved.

Sam had never cared for the fruit until he tasted those grown in the Philippines. They were sweeter and juicier than the Mexican mangoes he had eaten in Los Angeles, and he knew he would miss them when he left. It would be like eating fresh pineapple in Hawaii, and trying to recreate the experience on the mainland—always a disappointment.

He looked at the clock on the nightstand and counted backward fifteen hours. Just past two p.m. of the previous afternoon in Los Angeles. He threw on slacks, a shirt and flip flops, and took the elevator downstairs to a bank of pay phones off the lobby. He used his ATF credit card to direct dial, hoping his supervisor hadn't left work for the day.

"ATF, Los Angeles, Ricci speaking."

"Hey, Gene. It's Sam."

"This call on the bureau's tab? Why don't you e-mail me instead?"

"It's not that easy, Gene. This is a crowded city, hard to find real privacy. I probably should have brought my government-issue laptop— Oh, that's right. You didn't approve my requisition."

"You think sarcasm at international rates is improving

your prospect for a new laptop? The least you could do is call during off-peak hours."

"I couldn't be any more off-peak. It's five a.m. here."

"Five a.m.? You're not being paid to party all night."

"Yeah, I wish. I'm awake because a fifteen-hour time zone shift is a killer."

Sam didn't expect any sympathy, but he was surprised at the way Gene switched topics. "Did you know the Filipinos did a background check on your credentials? You must be setting international relations back a decade."

"Matter of fact, Bogie did tell me he checked," said Sam. "He also tried to determine if there was any CIA interest in this case. He couldn't find out. I tried our embassy, but they aren't talking. I was hoping you could see if there is an agent by the name of Juan Samoa active on this case."

"Oh yeah, I already got that message. Several times. From the Embassy. From Homeland Security. From C-I-fucking-A. From everybody except you. Thanks for clearing it through me first."

"I tried. You weren't available. I needed answers. This case doesn't feel right, and it keeps pointing back to somebody blocking me—maybe CIA."

"You think CIA is poaching our case?" said Ricci. "Why would they do that?"

"I was hoping you could tell me. If you get any info, leave me a message at my hotel—just a yes or no. Don't call me on the cell phone I'm using from NBI. I don't think it's secure."

"Am I going to have to add paranoia to your psych profile?" said Ricci.

Sam was steaming by now, but he tried to keep his voice light. "Just because I'm paranoid doesn't mean they're not after me."

There was a sound of paper rattling. "Oh yeah. The sister of the deceased is going to look you up. She doesn't think the U.S. Embassy or the RP cops are doing enough, so she flew on her own dime to Manila to see what's up."

"What? And you told her where to find me?"

"No, State Department did. You're gonna love Ms. Tucker."

"Who gave her my name?" said Sam.

"Listen, I gotta go. My boys and I are going fishing at Tahoe. I wanna beat the traffic out of LA. I'll be gone a few days. You have any problems, call Peterson." Ricci hung up.

Why did Ricci brush me off?

Sam listened to the dial tone for a few seconds, wondering if he would hear a second disconnect. He didn't catch anything, so he hung up, went back to his room, and switched on CNN. The news was both depressing and familiar.

After thirty minutes he switched to the fish channel. He took his time to shower and dress, went to the hotel restaurant for a relaxed breakfast, trying to stretch things out until he could go to NBI at eight a.m. His day would be three hours old before he could start working. A sinus headache had already kicked in.

As he left the hotel, the doorman gave him a warm smile. Sam knew he always would, whether he deserved it or not.

MANILA STREETS—8 A.M. FRIDAY

"Mister Juan, Mister Juan." One of the lost boys tugged on Juan Samoa's pant leg.

Juan looked at the ten-year old, thought his face looked familiar, but wasn't sure. It was hard to differentiate the skinny faces perched on stick-thin bodies. All the boys were dirty, and hunger gave their eyes a uniform gleam of desperation.

"You know where to find Chito, sir?" said the boy. "He ain't been round his usual places."

"Why you need Chito?"

"I found something he might want. It's foreign."

Juan put out his hand. "I'll give it to him when I see him at the club."

The boy stayed back just out of reach. "Chito's been payin' for this kinda stuff."

"Then you better get him to pay you."

"I told you, I can't find him." The boy seemed anxious to be away. "I need to be paid. I haven't eaten today, sir."

"How much does he pay?"

Juan watched as calculation, greed, and fear chased each other across the boy's face.

"Just fifty pesos, sir."

"I don't believe you. Here's twenty."

The boy darted forward, grabbed the coin from Juan, jerked a folder from beneath his filthy shirt, and pressed it into Juan's hand. "Thank you, sir," he called over his shoulder as he disappeared into the human maelstrom that overflowed the sidewalk.

Juan looked down at the folder, a plastic report cover with a Fitzler Pharmaceutical Company watermark. "CONFIDEN-TIAL—MAKE NO COPIES" was stamped on it in bold block letters, along with a ten-digit number, which looked like a file reference ID. He flipped the cover open, but there were no papers inside.

A routing slip was glued to the upper left corner, with a typed column of three letter initials. To the right of that were the same initials in the handwriting of those who had read this particular report, as well as the date each had received it. Juan noticed that the most recent date was more than a year ago.

Juan was all too aware of what had been inside the cover, a report on pharmaceutical design done by an independent research group. The report had been bought and suppressed by the drug giant. The work had promised to provide a low-cost alternative to one of its most profitable products.

When Harvey had shown the report to Olivia, Nosaka and Juan, it had not been tucked inside this cover. It made him wonder if any other items had been separated and were now floating about the black market seeking the highest bidder. There was a brisk demand for such high tech information. *How did this get onto the street? Is Olivia working deals without me?*

NBI HEADQUARTERS—8:30 A.M. FRIDAY

Sam went over the notes from Saddul and Garcia, collating them with the information he and Bogie had found, looking for connections. NBI was open around the clock, but at eight a.m. not many of the day shift had arrived, and Sam had the office to himself.

He saw another folder on Saddul's desk and picked it up. When he saw the photos of the bodies in the cargo container, he moved to put it down, realizing it was a different investigation; but since he was at a temporary dead-end, he thumbed through the black and white images.

He came to the photo of the ideograms and stopped.

Why would someone dying of thirst and heat exhaustion write on the wall? And who had brought chalk with them? A pen or pencil he could understand. He flipped back to the photos of the children's bodies. Maybe they had brought chalk along to play games.

If so, where were hopscotch squares or the Chinese equivalents? He couldn't find them in the photos. He read through the report looking for a mention of any such finding. Nothing.

He grabbed the picture of the ideogram and went down the hall, looking for someone to talk with. A secretary was busy word processing, and he startled her as he came from behind.

"I'm sorry, I didn't mean to make you jump," said Sam.

"It's all right. I didn't expect anyone else to be in yet," she said, giving him a tentative smile. "Aren't you working with Detective Lorenzano? Are you looking for him?"

"No. I mean yes, I am working with Bogie, but I'm not looking for him. I was wondering if anyone in the office reads Chinese?"

The secretary gave him a long stare, before replying carefully. "And you asked me because I look Chinese?"

Sam was a little flustered. Had he committed some faux pas? He wasn't sure of the ethnic background of the secretary. It wasn't that the Filipinos all looked alike. Quite the opposite.

There were all these mixtures of Filipino, Spanish, Chinese, Malay, Negrito, not to mention the genetic contributions made by countless generations of sailors and soldiers from around the globe.

"If I have offended you, I'm sorry," said Sam. "It was unintentional. I just need someone to translate these characters for me. I didn't know I was being rude."

Her face lost some of its stiffness. "You wouldn't know. Ethnic Chinese are resented here in the Philippines. They say we own too many businesses, have all the best jobs. People are envious." She reached for the photo, still regarding him with some suspicion. She glanced at it. "Where is this from?"

"It was written on the inside wall of a cargo container." Sam waited as she digested this. "Do you know what it means?"

"Yes. I can read Chinese, though not proficiently. My grandmother was from Singapore," she said, frowning, as if that would make everything clear to Sam.

It didn't. "Can you translate this for me? It may be helpful."

"It says 'Work makes you free' or perhaps 'Work builds freedom' is a little closer. But why would that be written inside a cargo container?" She grimaced, put her hand to her mouth, as it hit her. "The container with the Chinese illegals?"

Sam nodded and took the photo back from her hand.

"Maybe I've intruded where I shouldn't have. I'll ask Detective Saddul to speak with you about this."

She gave him an angry look. "Please don't! The fact that I can read Chinese is not something I spread around, yes?"

She turned away and began rapidly typing at the keyboard.

Sam looked at the ideograms again. *Why would someone translate the Nazi work camp slogan* "Arbeit macht Frei" *into Chinese?* He went back to Saddul's office, put back the photo, and straightened the disorder he had created.

twenty-five--

*JAPAN'S MILITARY TURNS 50 — STILL SUNK IN EXISTEN-
TIAL QUAGMIRE*

Japan's military turns 50 years old with a troop
deployment in Iraq that many say challenges
the constitutional limits of a nation that once
renounced war forever.

But for a nation that decided to "forever renounce
war" and promised not to possess "war poten-
tial" (military power) in its 1946 constitution, the
golden anniversary comes at a crucial time.

Japan's annual military budget of 46 billion dollars is
the world's second-largest after that of the United
States.

July 1, 2004

BALIBAGO, ANGELES CITY—FRIDAY 9 A.M.

Nosaka had awakened a few minutes after dawn and dismissed last night's whore. It was getting harder to find
the ones willing to submit to the scorpion, and even harder to
put up with how much they charged now. He supposed it was
to be expected with the current round of inflation, but still it
made him angry.

As he stripped down for his bath, he thought how the woman's heart-shaped face reminded him of his first Pinoy comfort
woman. It made him stiffen again just thinking about it.

The occupation of the Philippines had been a heady
experience for a seventeen-year-old boy fresh off his parents'
farm on Honshu. His uniform had helped disguise how slope -
shouldered his slender body was. When he and his comrades

strode through the city, the Filipinos had averted their eyes in respect—perhaps it was fear—moving aside to let them pass, their arms swinging wide, the rightful masters of this newly-acquired territory. He had thought this must be a little taste of how the Emperor felt when he walked through the streets.

That first time at the comfort center, he is so timid, so unsure of whether he is a man yet. He lets the others from his platoon go first. They all mock him, pretending that he is overly polite.

He tries to make discreet inquiry of the older soldiers as to the appropriate behavior in this situation. But they laugh coarsely, telling him to follow his nose. "Once you find the monkey's cunt, you'll know what to do all right, oh yes."

It is his turn to enter the small cubicle. A slight-framed Filipina lies naked on a futon, her eyes glazed from the day's horror. He stands gazing down on her for long moments, wondering if she will speak to him, whether she can speak any Japanese at all.

But she says nothing, never looks his way, two fingers of her right hand twirling a lock of her hair endlessly. He feels a stirring of unease in the pit of his stomach, wonders if he has eaten some bad fish.

He is paralyzed. Why won't she acknowledge his presence, his right to be here, her purpose in serving his needs? His stomach roils and he stares at her, willing her to look at him. But though her eyes are open, she seems elsewhere, and he recognizes the feeling in his stomach as anger.

He steps forward tentatively. Still no reaction from her. He stretches out his foot and prods her lightly with the toe of his boot. Nothing. He pushes again, harder this time, and she reflexively spreads her legs, but says nothing, does not look at him.

She must respond.

He draws back his foot and kicks her hard in the thigh. She looks at him, panic in her eyes. Better. Her eyes scan the room to see if others are there and he senses the snake in his belly coiling tight.

He kicks her again, in the side, as hard as he can, eliciting a grunt of pain.

At last, she knows her master has come.

She curls into a fetal ball and bites down on the edge of the futon to keep from crying out while he beats her.

When his arms are tired, he pulls down his pants and completes her subjugation.

She won't forget me, mistake me for the others. Oh, no.

Nosaka smiled. This fragrant memory was his to bring out and examine at leisure any time he desired it. It seldom failed to bring him to the bursting point, when he would spray his semen around the room and dream his dreams of Japanese dominion over the Pacific. *Our sea. Our territory. Our property. Our subjects. Our destiny.*

He folded his futon, kneeled on his *tatami* mat, and ate a rice ball he had prepared the night before. The morning was already warm, so he remained in his loincloth while he cleaned his room.

NBI—BOGIE'S OFFICE—9:30 A.M. FRIDAY

Back at Bogie's desk, Sam tried to make sense of it all, feeling that it must be connected, but not seeing how it could be. Bogie arrived half an hour later, and the two of them methodically reviewed the evidence on hand, but it turned out two brains weren't much better than one.

"Tucker buys a cargo container-full of Chinese guns, maybe makes arrangements to pay for them as they pass through Manila. It's probable that he needed some of the money from the bird sales to pay for the guns. But Tucker gets killed," said Sam. "A mysterious cargo container shows up, only it's not full of guns, it's full of dead Chinese illegal immigrants, probably headed for employment in the sex industry."

"We know Tucker sold birds to that cockfight arena, and that it probably was also him who left something there for safekeeping," said Bogie. "We also know he had hired Olivia for an S&M session. Tucker's body turns up in the dumpster behind her sex club, naked."

"That reminds me," said Sam. "Did you ever find his clothes?"

"Homeless folks would have pinched those five minutes after they hit the dumpster. Easy to resell," said Bogie. "The pictures of him and Olivia may have been in the pockets. They were found about a block away."

"If he was killed in the club, it seems too obvious—in fact, outright stupid—to put his corpse in the club dumpster," said Sam.

"Not if they thought the body would be collected and dumped at sea the next morning."

"So what happened?"

"City Sanitation Worker slowdown. It never became a full-blown strike, so it didn't make the news," said Bogie. "Perhaps the killers didn't know the body was still behind the club."

Sam thought that over, and went on. "We also know Olivia made a stop at a bank and the cockfight arena, perhaps dropped off something. In the arena manager's office, we found a folder of French documents with handwritten notes on the cover in French and Arabic."

"Is that what Olivia dropped off?" said Bogie. "Or was it something else?"

Sam paused to wince at the next memory. "I managed to lose said folder, I believe to the pedicab driver who ended up dead later that same night."

"And Juan Samoa tells you he is a CIA agent, but I know that Juan owns part of Olivia's business," said Bogie. "Congressman Lagos tells the prosecutor to drop the Tucker case. You see a photo of Lagos at a riot that took place at a new apartment complex owned by the prosecutor's parents." Bogie stubbed out his eighth cigarette. "Yeah, it's all clear now."

"I feel like I'm in quicksand, sinking fast," said Sam.

"Get used to it," said Bogie. "I feel that way at least twice a week. Crimes layered on top of other crimes, intersections between different criminal gangs. I think it's because the city is so crowded, something like ten thousand people per square kilometer."

Sam looked at Bogie, his eyes focused on something in the far distance, and blinked. "That can't be right. Twenty-five thousand people per square mile?"

"How'd you do that?"

"What?"

"Convert population density from square kilometers to square miles."

"It's just a knack. I know a kilometer is about five-eighths of a mile, so a square kilometer is about twenty-five sixty-fourths of a square mile." Sam made a hand motion as if he were turning something upside down. "Twenty-five goes into sixty-four about two and half times, and two and half times ten thousand is twenty-five thousand."

Bogie stared at Sam as if he were a cat with three tails. "In your head? Why?"

"I don't try to do it. It just happens, and I can watch it in my head, then tell you the answer."

"I'm guessing you didn't have any problems passing math classes."

"Sometimes they thought I was cheating, but I wasn't." Sam gave a wry smile. "I do my own income tax returns, too."

"You could be teaching high school or college, getting ready for a fat pension, instead of chasing scum." Bogie's tone was almost accusatory. "You could be an accountant."

"Yeah, but accountants don't get to carry a gun and shoot bad guys," Sam deadpanned.

They heard voices in the hallway and the clatter of high heels on the institutional linoleum, coming closer. The voices stopped just outside their office door, and a petite secretary poked her head inside.

"You have an American visitor," she said, not bothering to clarify whether the visitor was for Bogie or Sam. Distaste was evident in her expression as she withdrew her head.

A large bosom entered the room half a second before its owner. The woman who entered under full sail was clearly American, clearly a visitor, and clearly not used to being escorted by toy-sized secretaries. She stood just inside the doorway and glowered at Bogie and Sam.

Sam and Bogie stared back. About five foot ten in her stocking feet (size eleven extra wide), she was a woman of a certain age. It was apparent that she believed decades spent baking in the sun by the pool had added to her charm.

Perhaps it had. Sam imagined komodo dragons finding themselves greatly attracted to her reptilian epidermis. Her bottle-auburn hair was pulled back into a messy French roll. She wore blue jeans and a denim work shirt, unbuttoned to a level that threatened to release the beasts if she raised either arm above her head.

To Sam's alarm she had a single eyebrow. Fortunately for her, it covered both eyes, providing a protective screen from the sun and rain.

"The Ambassador sent a note asking you to assist Ms. Tucker," squeaked the secretary. She darted through the door, dropped several documents with official stamps on Bogie's desk, skirted the foothills of the woman, and scurried away.

"This where I pick up his goods?" The woman addressed both men, but when Bogie didn't respond, she fixed a laser-like glare on Sam. "He don't speak English?" she asked, indicating Bogie.

Bogie looked up from the US Embassy letter he was reading and handed it to Sam. Sam glanced at it and said, "Ms. Tucker? Sonja Tucker?"

Ms. Tucker swelled in a threatening manner. "Did that so-called public servant at the Embassy spell my name wrong? It's Sone-juhh, with a J, not a Y. That doofus couldn't find his wang with both hands in broad daylight, if you'll pardon my French."

Bogie flicked a quick look at Sam, as if wondering whether he had heard right.

"I'm not sure why you have come here, Ms. Tucker. This

isn't the lost and found," said Sam. "NBI is the equivalent of our FBI back in the States."

"I know where I am. I paid the frigging cabbie to get me here, didn't I? And nearly got robbed in the process." She turned an alarming shade of reddish-brown as memory rekindled her anger. "Little dip wanted a hunnerd Filipino dollars for a fifteen-minute ride, and I knew it wasn't worth more than four, five dollars. I clocked him and dropped a five-spot in the front seat. Teach that sorry son of a bachelor not to try takin' advantage of no American woman."

"You can't assault innocent cabbies, Ms. Tucker," said Bogie.

Ms. Tucker swiveled to look at Bogie. "So. It speaks. And English, too." She appeared to disapprove of Bogie's bilingual skills. "Is either of you two brain surgeons gonna tell me where I can find my brother's goods?"

It was clear to Sam why the Ambassador had scrawled the handwritten note for Sonja. Now she was the NBI's problem—and by extension, his.

Bogie rose from his chair and addressed Ms. Tucker formally. "I am sorry for the loss of your brother. You have our sympathy." He waited to see if she would respond. "We are in the middle of an investigation of his death. We cannot release his personal belongings—"

"I didn't fly ten thousand miles crammed into a seat built for a midget to listen to your horsehockey, buster," Sonja interrupted. "I know my brother's dead, and I'll probably miss the sumbitch after a while. Right now I'm trying to find some goods he filched from my office, put 'em back in place before I get canned."

Bogie's face was a mask of politeness as he pulled a list from a folder and passed it over to Sonja.

"These are the items found on his body and in his hotel room."

Sonja worked her way through the lists, lips working as she read to herself. "It's not there." She thrust the pages back at Bogie. "Anyways, Harv wouldn't have left this particular stuff just lyin' around. Did you check the hotel safe? Or maybe he had a room safe?"

"His hotel had individual safe deposit boxes. We just received the death certificate, which the hotel requires for us to open his box."

She cocked her eyebrow at Bogie contemptuously. "Oh, you hadn't got around to that as yet? Was it gonna happen in the next decade, or what?" She gave Sam a withering look. "You're s'posed to be an American cop. Don't you know your business, either? I'm beginning to see why the Embassy was so wishy-washy about telling me jack."

"Ms. Tucker, you are a guest in a foreign country," said Sam. "You just deliberately insulted the lead investigator looking into your brother's death—"

"Hey, you morons can't take a little honest criticism without gettin' your thong in a twist, you ought to get the hell outta the kitchen." She grabbed the investigation folder from Bogie's desk and turned to go.

Bogie and Sam leapt after her, Sam pulling the folder from her hand. "You can't take that out of here." He tried to keep hold of her arm, and found that she had massive biceps. She shrugged him off without discernible effort.

"How about you two geniuses bring it along—as well as the death certificate, if I heard you right—so we can check out that safe deposit box?"

"Finding your brother's killer is my primary task, Ms. Tucker. And I also want to fulfill the Ambassador's request," said Bogie. "But we *will* follow police procedure."

Sonja snorted and steamed out of the room, Bogie and Sam following in her wake. Sam realized that if they didn't accompany Sonja, she would disrupt the chain of evidence at the hotel. He looked over to Bogie and could see he had come to a similar conclusion.

Bogie pulled out his car keys and jogged ahead of Sonja.

"We can take my car, Ms. Tucker."

"Well, ain't you the gentleman." She gave Sam an appraising look and shook her head.

OTTO'S BAR—10 A.M. FRIDAY

Juan looked around the bar, checking for any familiar faces present. He didn't care about the B-girls, but some of the expats knew him, and they tended to talk too much when they drank—which was all the time. They might mention to friends they had seen him at Working Late at the Office. Maybe it was time to change his hideaway.

Juan leaned on the polished mahogany bar and handed Otto a twenty and a C-note. "Here's a hundred for this month's rent. I need to use my office. And the twenty's for a bottle of whisky, OK?"

An eighty-five pound B-girl in a Lycra tube skirt and tank top sidled up to Juan, pushing her breast against his arm. She was eighteen going on sixty, deep lines etched around her eyes and mouth.

"You wan' some comp'ny in yo' office, big boy? I got sex-etarial skills, you know?" Her pupils were ricocheting like pinballs from a recent hit of speed.

"He don't want your tired *kiki* right now," said Otto. "Back off, Bree."

Juan stared Bree down until she retreated to a booth, muttering dark imprecations about oversized faggots.

Otto pulled a key from his ring, hesitating before he passed it to Juan. "Is this gonna be quick? My helper didn't show up today, and I got a 'pointment pretty soon. Gonna close shop for awhile."

"I'll need about an hour. Lock me in if you like. I'll let myself out the back way."

Otto gave a reluctant nod. "Just make sure Bree's not hiding somewhere. She'd try to drink the place dry before I got back."

Juan's CIA handler had told him he needed a spot where he could work without being observed, a place that wasn't in his home or at the club. If he came under suspicion, those two places were sure to be searched. The handler said it was better to change the location every so often, not establish too steady a pattern.

In Juan's "office"—formerly a supply closet—there was barely room for a student desk and a chair. He had installed a small shelf, stacked a file cube on that, and stashed his laptop inside it like a ledger.

Juan pulled the chain on the bare bulb that hung overhead and latched the door behind him. He scooted the desk against the door and pried up a loose board, pulling out a small fireproof safe big enough to contain a few documents. He put the disc from the copy shop inside, next to two bundles of hundred dollar bills. He had a little over forty thousand now, and he thought that should be enough to get him started in the States.

He knew that there was a large Samoan community in Carson, California. He figured if he could get his US entry visa and a clean birth certificate, he'd make out just fine there. Find some women his own size. He was always half afraid he'd crush these Filipinas.

His handler had said the Ambassador would intervene to have his birth documents revised to remove "UNKNOWN" from the space for father and list the name of the US service-man who had sired him. That bastard had died about a year ago and wouldn't be able to block the change any longer.

But Juan was worried that a year had already gone by since that promise had been made. CIA always had one more little task to do that no one but Juan could handle. Didn't he want to be a freedom fighter for his country?

Of late there had been hints that CIA knew about his other illegal sources of income, things that might present a problem for an entry visa. The US didn't want to import any more crimi-nals; they had plenty of their own.

Juan thought about it, wondering what leverage he could bring to bear. He couldn't threaten to expose his handler or the operations in which he'd been involved. That would be immediate suicide.

Maybe he needed to show his fidelity to a greater degree, earn the reward. What if he were shown to be behind a major move, something so big it couldn't be covered up? The publicity might move the Ambassador to approve his paperwork, out of gratitude.

But how could he bring down the players he knew about without destroying his friends along the way? Olivia and Chito had both crossed the line of legality long ago. The RP government could make a case against them for providing help to elements conspiring to overthrow the government—maybe even treason.

Juan retrieved the disc, booted up his laptop, and jacked the modem connection into his cell phone. He dialed a stateside number and began sending the disc contents.

Chito and Olivia had made those deals themselves. They'd have to live with the consequences. His number one client—and number one loyalty—always had to be the CIA.

twenty-six--

During the drive across town, Sam came to believe in the afterlife—or at least the part about Hell. Sonja had taken the front passenger seat because she needed the legroom after "that fuckin' flight for dwarfs." She complained that the car's seat belt was too small and cut off blood circulation below her waist, and she sure as shit didn't want nothing down there going numb.

She offered a running diatribe on Bogie's driving ability, the dirtiness of Manila and its citizens, the bizarrely high price tags on goods she could see for sale—she appeared to be unaware of the conversion rate of pesos to dollars—the stink in the air from vehicles without emission controls, the funny-looking money the Filipinos used, and the state of her bowels after the crap she ate on the plane.

She made them stop so she could find a ladies' room, then stop again ten minutes later so she could purchase a pack of Marlboros, which she chain-smoked inside the car.

Sam found himself in the role of apologist for Manila. For his part, Bogie looked sidelong at Sonja and said nothing. Sam entertained fantasies of putting his service revolver to her head and reenacting the "accidental" shooting scene from *Pulp Fiction.*

When they got to the hotel, Sonja got coy, waiting for Bogie to open her door. Sam figured that Bogie's pheromonal charms had done their trick and wondered what Bogie would do with yet another admirer.

Fortune smiled on them all: a doorman hurried to Sonja's side of the car and levered her out of the compact NBI vehicle.

Sam popped out of the back seat and stood near Bogie. He looked at his watch. Fifty-eight minutes in close quarters with that woman. He caught Bogie glancing at his own watch. "That only took thirty-four hundred and eighty seconds," said Sam.

"She brings new depth to the phrase 'ugly American'," said Bogie. "You surprised me, too. I didn't realize how much you had absorbed about the Philippines." Bogie watched as Sonja gave the doorman a hearty pat on the back, which nearly knocked him off his feet. "Let's be careful. She's putting on quite an act."

B ogie had to show his NBI credentials, as well as the death certificate, to the hotel manager before she would allow the safety deposit box to be opened. Sam and Sonja sat on one side of a desk in the lobby while Bogie unlocked the box and flipped back the lid.

The box held Harvey's passport, a return airline ticket that was scheduled for a week after his death, a wad of cash, and some slips of paper. Bogie methodically inspected the items. Sonja took a short cut, dumped the contents, and began sorting through them brusquely. Sam watched as she brushed aside Harvey's passport, and glanced at the cash.

"Shee-it. It's not here," said Sonja. "This is gonna cost me my job, maybe my retirement."

"Exactly what are you looking for, Ms. Tucker?" said Sam.

"He took a folder of research reports from my office the day before he flew over here."

"And why is that such a problem?" said Bogie.

"These were confidential papers, not to be copied—or even looked at—by anyone. Since he couldn't copy them, he snaked 'em right outta the safe."

"They were locked in a safe?" said Sam. "Did your brother know how to crack locks?"

Sonja looked uncomfortable and shifted a bit in her chair. Sam remembered her comment about the airline food and hoped this didn't signal some onslaught of Magellan's Revenge.

"He mighta could, but he didn't have to. The safe was already open."

Sam and Bogie waited while Sonja apparently wrestled with her conscience. *Or perhaps it's just gas*, thought Sam.

"I've got to tell you something in confidence. Will this be off the record?"

"If it doesn't involve illegal trafficking in arms, it's outside my jurisdiction," said Sam. Sam saw Sonja's eyes shift when he mentioned illegal arms, as if she were surprised that he knew about that.

Bogie looked at Sonja. "You may proceed, Ms. Tucker."

Sonja looked at Bogie with mistrust. "You're a witness to what he said, Sam. A 'Merican witness." She settled herself and went on. "My brother and I had been looking at these papers, putting our heads together, tryin' to see if there was any way we could turn a profit. I heard my supervisor comin' back early from lunch, so I told Harv to put em back and lock up while I let my boss into the outer office. But my sumbitch brother just put the lot under his shirt and snuck out. Never said a word to me." She paused to wipe away an invisible tear. Sam couldn't tell if it was the memory of her dead brother or the loss of a quick score that was the cause. "Couple days ago I realized they was gone."

"What's in the documents?" said Bogie.

"Let's just say certain drug companies might find the results pretty interesting."

"Pharmaceutical research? That's the kind of company you work for?" said Sam.

"I'm in plant security. Twenty years in the Marine Corps got me connections worth a lot more than my friggin' gumment pension."

Sam was appalled at how easily security safeguards had been circumvented. *Small wonder that industrial espionage is a thriving international business.*

Bogie had finished counting the money. "There's five thousand dollars here. Seems like a lot of cash for a short pleasure trip."

"It's probably for them birds."

"Birds?"

Sonja gave them a funny look. "For poe-lice professionals you hain't found out all that much, have you? Harvey raised fighting cocks in Oklahoma, had hisself an export license to sell 'em in a buncha God-awful places. He came over two, three times a year. Made a couple of other trips to Thailand and Cambodia, but this here was his biggest market."

Bogie sorted through the slips of paper in the bottom of the stack, saw that each had an address, name, phone number, and date. Some had dollar amounts annotated. He passed one over to Sam. "This address looks familiar. Is that the arena we visited?"

"Yeah. The amount says 5K, and that's the amount in the bankroll," said Sam. "Where's the rest of the cash, assuming these other notes also stand for money collected?"

Bogie looked surprised that Sam would ask such a revealing question in front of Sonja. Something flared behind Sonja's eyes, and when she joined the discussion Bogie saw that Sam had read her better than he had.

"How much money we talking about?" said Sonja. "Harv usually came back with about ten grand from selling them birds."

Bogie handed the slips to Sam. "Here you go, math boy. What's it total?"

Sam flipped through the slips. "Eighteen thousand and some change. Some are still blank."

Sonja fanned herself with Harvey's passport, like she'd had a hot flash. "So thirteen thousand is missing from the bird sales? And god only knows what he got for my goods." She broke off, waving the passport furiously, her face flushing.

Bogie finished the inventory of items from the box, took it to the manager's desk to get her to sign off. Raven, the pretty clerk who had helped him with the guest registry records three days earlier, gave him a tentative smile. Bogie returned her smile and stayed to talk with her.

Sam looked away from Bogie's flirtation and back to Sonja. "Seems like Bubba may have been skimming from Sissy's part of the pot," said Sam.

"That's the kinda thing I'd expect from some Jew-Yankee, not a southerner." Sonja lapsed into silence, chewing her lip as she worked over this revelation of her brother's character. "That A-hole, stealing from his own baby sister," she said under her breath. She looked over at Bogie flirting with the clerk, and said to Sam, "Is he the one who searched Harv's room, Sam? I'm not sure I trust his competence."

Sam felt his blood pressure rising, but decided Bogie's reputation didn't need him to defend it. "No, that would have been the local police."

"Let's take a look at his room ourselves. I know a coupla tricks my brother had, things these Flips mighta missed."

> **THE ASIAN WARRIOR WAY OF LIFE** is to have a thick face and a black heart. It is the same in business. The thick face masks your intentions and emotions; you can deceive with a smiling face. Making yourself known to your friends—or your enemies—is to give them power over you.
> You cannot make an omelet without breaking eggs. You may have to sacrifice thousands of men to win the war. To pursue your goals with unwavering resolve, even if there are temporary losses, or bad side effects, is to have a black heart.

CLUB DE SEX—10:30 A.M. FRIDAY

This was all getting too close. Olivia didn't think the Tucker killing was going to come back to her doorstep, but neither had she thought they would take Chito in for questioning, either. The boy hadn't even been to the club that night, and the police must have figured that out.

She grimaced as she remembered the session with Tucker, his increasingly outrageous demands. The problem wasn't the pain; no, she could actually get off on that. It was the pig mask, the humiliation he wanted her to experience.

She still wasn't clear what Nosaka had been up to. And he wasn't about to share any of his grandiose secrets with her, though his ego was all too easy to read. She laughed to herself.

The Japanese think they have such poker faces. You want to grow a thick face and a black heart, turn a few thousand tricks.

Olivia looked at the passbook of her Hong Kong bank account. Seventy-one thousand, four hundred twelve dollars. And her share of the club ought to be worth another hundred K. She thought Juan had the cash to buy out her piece, but she was pretty sure Chito was blowing his money as fast as he made it. Plus, Chito hadn't been earning as much or for as long a time as she had.

Maybe she could take Juan's portion, get a down payment from Chito, and let him pay her over a couple of years. The point was, she was already thirty, and her looks were beginning to go. That meant she'd have to do the perv routines more and more.

She had a head for business, but she knew that part of the reason she had done so well was the automatic attraction men felt for her. It made them easy to play.

She didn't want to turn any more tricks, take any more whippings, pimp any more girls fresh from the provinces. She didn't want to breathe any more airborne shit from Manila's foul vehicles, step over any more homeless folk, pay off any more corrupt bureaucrats.

She wanted a straight life with a straight man.

She wanted Bogie.

And she thought that just maybe he wanted her, too. That had been a pretty thorough fuck he'd given her. It hadn't been just opportunity for him. They'd reconnected.

She wondered if he realized it yet, that they'd be getting back together. Thank God that Santos cow was out of the picture for good. The slut was probably spreading her legs for that American cop by now. Bogie wouldn't be going back there any more.

She opened her safe and extracted the video tape of Bogie, trying to decide if she should erase it. Bogie would break things off permanently if he ever found that she had made it. She cued it up in the playback deck and watched, found herself growing sentimental as she saw how tender he was as he touched the scars on her back.

When the tape ended, she hit rewind, and recorded black over the images. *I need to be Mrs. Lorenzano. A spouse's testimony can always be excluded from a courtroom—by either spouse.*

If she was going to start over with Bogie, they both needed new lines of work. She put the erased tape on the desk top, turned on her computer, and surfed the net.

After about fifty minutes she had found several small islands for sale, within financial reach, if Bogie could bring even a small pension income with him. When she did the math, she realized he still had five years to go before the minimum twenty-five he needed to retire.

She couldn't take five more years. She went back on the web. *Okay, let's look for a little bed and breakfast, a small hotel, a fishing boat for tourists, something.*

Another thirty minutes of searching, and she had found the way out.

Now, how do I make Bogie think this is his idea?

MAKATI ARMS—10 A.M. FRIDAY

Upstairs, it turned out Harvey had been renting a nice suite: bedroom, sitting room, small office area off the bathroom. The bathroom had its own phone, a whirlpool bathtub, separate shower and water closet, the whole room tiled in marble. Sam and Bogie watched in amusement as Sonja tapped

Harv's suitcase for a false bottom, looked behind the TV set, lifted the mattress, and checked inside the toilet tank. They weren't so amused when she pulled a vial of pills in a zip-lock bag from the tank.

"Looks like you done a real thorough detectin' job."

Bogie, heat rising in his face, took the bag from Sonja. He looked at the vial through the clear plastic. "Your brother speak Chinese?"

"Not freakin' likely."

"This label is two years old," said Bogie. "It probably was left behind by another patron. But we'll check it for prints." He placed the entire baggie and vial inside a larger plastic bag.

It was obvious that Sonja was incensed that her find drew such mild response. She hunted about some more, then went to the vanity-desk combo built into an alcove near the bathroom and opened the drawer. It was empty, and in a fit of pique she jerked it from the desk.

Taped to the underside of the drawer was a sheaf of documents. She gave a yip of triumph as she ripped the papers from the wooden drawer bottom, before her face fell.

"All that's left is the title page and these footnotes or whatnot."

Bogie took the papers from Sonja, flipped through them, and handed them to Sam. While Sam perused the documents Bogie pulled another evidence bag from his coat pocket. "I have to apologize, Ms. Tucker. It seems that our local police weren't as thorough as they should have been. I'll put in a call for a full NBI forensic squad to work your brother's room."

Bogie pulled out his cell phone and left the room, anger and embarrassment apparent in his posture.

"I was hopin' I could just collect my goods, crate my brother up, and get back home," Sonja said to Sam. "Looks like I'm gonna be here a little longer than I thought."

"The Embassy will help you find a mortuary that can take care of the arrangements. And now that we know what to look for, perhaps the papers will be easier to locate."

"Yeah, sure." She gave Sam a speculative look. "You know,

my brother always looked forward to these trips. He said they had these special nightclubs with great shows. Told me the Filipinos was always ready for some action, know what I mean? And now here I am at loose ends, so to speak."

Sam feared she wanted to dragoon him as her escort and moved to forestall it. "I'm sure the concierge at your hotel can arrange an escort if you would like to see Manila's night life."

"I don't need no escort. Just point me in the right direction. Harvey claimed Flip pussy was primo, and I wanta try me some."

The world seemed to shift by a slight amount, and Sam took a small step while he found his balance. He couldn't stop the next words that came out of his mouth. "There's a great place, Club Peanut. Loaded with hot-looking singers dressed like American divas. I saw a Filipina Marilyn Monroe, a Leann Rimes—even a Cher I think you'd find attractive."

"I knew an American hound dog like yourself woulda sniffed out the good stuff. I'll give that place a try." She smiled as she said to herself. "Cher, huh?"

twenty-seven--

BARRIO SAN JOSE—11 A.M. FRIDAY

Sam had the doorman get him a cab from the hotel to his meeting with Sonny Lagos. He climbed into yet another Japanese compact sedan with a taximeter and gave the driver the address. The cabbie was a painfully thin man with a large wen distorting the right side of his face. They pulled out of the hotel drive into the afternoon traffic, at once becoming ensnarled in a dense, slow-moving river of cars belching blue smoke.

Sam and Bogie had decided to split up, Sam to interview Lagos about his connection to the riots and his attempt to halt the Tucker investigation. Bogie was going to stay behind at the hotel to oversee the forensic squad and ride herd on Sonja, who wasn't about to miss the opportunity to offer the Filipinos her expert opinions.

"This is a business meeting, sir?" said the cabbie. "That address is in a—residential—area."

"When I called Mr. Lagos on the phone, he asked me

to meet him at that address. Perhaps it's his home."

"Mr. Lagos, the politician, sir?"

Sam nodded, but something was bothering the cabbie.

"That is a poor neighborhood, sir. Congressman Lagos cannot possibly be living there."

"Perhaps I heard it wrong." Sam pulled out the NBI cell phone, but thought better of it. He had to assume that all calls he made from the NBI cell phone were monitored. "Can you pull over to let me use a pay phone?"

The cabbie pulled out his own cell phone, thinking that Sam's was dead. "I hate it when the phone battery goes down." The cabbie smiled, but the wen stretched it into a grimace. "You can use my phone, sir. It will save time not to leave the road and have to re-enter the traffic."

Sam took the phone and tried not to think about it having been pressed to the growth on the cabbie's face. He punched in the numbers and pressed send. A young woman answered the phone and confirmed Mr. Lagos' appointment with Sam at the address he had written down. Something in the secretary's voice indicated that she also had some misgivings.

"It's the correct address," Sam said to the cabbie, handing him back his phone.

The cabbie shrugged uneasily and drove without further comment. Opening his briefcase on his lap to shield the contents from the cabbie's view, Sam retrieved his pistol in its clip-on holster and tucked it into the back of his pants, beneath his suit coat.

He wondered if he should call Saddul or Garcia for backup but decided against it. If the place looked too chancy when he got there, he could just have the cabbie drive on.

"How long a drive is this?"

"Perhaps forty-five minutes, sir," said the cabbie.

"What kind of place is it?"

"It is near the old colonial part of the city."

Sam saw the cabbie's expression change as he looked at Sam in the mirror. By now Sam could recognize the signs when a Filipino wanted to talk politics.

"Most of it was leveled at the end of World War II—when the Allies retook Manila. The fighting was house to house," said the cabbie. "The city was ninety per cent destroyed."

"Ninety per cent? More than Berlin? Or Tokyo?" asked Sam.

"Yes," said the cabbie. "And we were on the same side."

"I know. My grandfather was killed here in the Philippines."

"*Totoó?*" said the cabbie, startled into Tagalog. "Sorry. For true? In the battle of Manila?"

"No. Bataan. The march."

"Aieee," breathed the cabbie. "Fucking Japanese." The cabbie colored, embarrassed by having revealed so much. With a rueful smile, he slapped the dashboard. "I wish they didn't make such good cars."

They drove in silence the remainder of the trip.

The cab pulled through an archway that spanned the road into the *baranggáy*. He drove at ten miles per hour, looking for the address. The streets and sidewalks were packed with ragged peasants, people who had no land or expectations.

The cabbie rolled down the window and asked for help in Tagalog. A pregnant woman nursing a tiny mewling infant arched her eyebrow in the right direction, and the cabbie drove on.

The paved road became packed dirt, with a stream down the middle that carried sewage from the tin roof shanties that stood shoulder to shoulder. Children sailed banana leaf boats down the stream. Here the cardboard shacks stood on stilts above the hillside and had bamboo floors.

As the road descended the slight slope, it branched into a number of muddy paths, and the cabbie stopped the car. He asked once again for directions, but the crowd that now gathered around the cab meant they were going no further. A man wearing pants that had split along the rear seam, leaving his buttocks exposed, pointed to a somewhat larger shanty on stilts.

Sam saw that there was a cross on top, and *"Lagos Pagka-Iná Pagamutan"* was whitewashed above the entry.

"This seems to be the address, sir," said the cabbie. He pointed at the meter.

Sam pulled out ten dollars American and gave it to the cabbie, who thanked him effusively. "Wait for me until my meeting is finished, OK?"

The cabbie killed the engine and pulled out his cell phone. Sam turned and walked toward the building with the cross. As soon as Sam was up the steps he heard the cabbie start up and drive away. Sam was angered but thought, *It's OK. I'll be fine.*

Sam found that he believed that. He felt no sense of threat from the Filipinos he met. Even when they argued politics, it felt like arguing with family members. Once the discussion was over, they still were bound by familial ties.

He wondered if he had let his guard down too much over the last four days. He knew that Americans were kidnapped here, held for ransom, sometimes killed. So why did he feel safe? Maybe it was the disarming politeness. Maybe the ready smiles, the willingness to speak English. Maybe the weather just made it too tiring to be afraid.

And, of course, I do have a gun.

He climbed a set of flimsy stairs that swayed under the unaccustomed weight of an American. When he entered the building he had taken to be a church, he saw that he was mistaken. A woman in a nurse's uniform sat behind a desk, writing in a journal. She looked up and smiled at Sam.

"Mr. Haine? We have been expecting you. I am Nurse Isolde. Please let me show you around our maternity clinic."

Sam was caught off guard. "Perhaps there has been some mistake. I am here to see Congressman Lagos."

"The Congressman will be here presently," said the nurse, reverence in her voice. "He asked if I would escort you." She rose and extended her hand, pointing down a short corridor. "Please."

Sam decided to go along with the program. They passed through a small waiting room full of pregnant women. Nurse

Isolde showed him into a small room with woven-frond partitions. Inside every partitioned area a woman in labor lay on a thin reed mat atop a futon on the floor.

Sam walked along, wide-eyed, surrounded by cries of pain, the recurrent squalls of newborn infants, and smells of disinfectant and amniotic fluid. The floor was made of salvaged one-inch planks, and he could see through the gaps to the ground. The nurse was telling him about their ministry to poor mothers, but Sam was in sensory overload, unable to follow anything she was saying.

As they passed one partition, Sam saw a midwife attending a young woman whose face was battered, her nose broken and flattened, her eyes swollen shut. He could almost feel the contractions, as he watched her belly tighten. Unable to stop himself from looking, Sam felt like a gawker at a freeway accident. Yellowish bruises of fingerprints circled the throat of the woman.

"What happened?" he asked, and at once felt stupid. It was all too obvious.

The woman opened her eyes. Her face lit up, as if she recognized Sam, and she grabbed his ankle, babbling in some Filipino dialect, not Tagalog, gasping out the words between contractions.

Sam froze. He crouched beside the woman, reminded of Christy's face, seeing again her frantic need when the pain of her illness had become too much for her, had transformed her into someone else, had drained away the woman he had married. The memory was so overwhelming, tears ran down his cheeks.

Nurse Isolde knelt beside Sam. With some difficulty she unwrapped the young woman's fingers from Sam's ankle. She looked at him not unkindly. "You are an empathetic man, Mr. Haine. But we are in the way here. She must follow the midwife's instructions."

Sam stood up and walked down the corridor away from the girl. She called out "Mike, Mike!" after him and he looked over his shoulder. But it was Christy's face that floated before him, and he felt a cold wave course through his body.

"What did she say, Nurse?" said Sam, really wanting to ask *Why did she grab me?* By now he knew that such a direct question would make the Filipina uncomfortable.

Nurse Isolde took a long moment before she replied. "Perhaps you remind her of a—boyfriend."

Sam looked at her, not understanding.

"She used to work near the docks," said Nurse, waggling her hand at the euphemism. "Maybe she demanded too much." She shrugged, indicating she was not sure. "Maybe she was no longer convenient for him." She fluttered her hand in apology.

He got it and he didn't like it. "Maybe he was a white sailor." He felt ashamed for her abuse.

The nurse looked at Sam. "You look quite pale, Mr. Haine. Perhaps we should step outside."

Sam followed her onto a small deck at the rear of the building. The sun beat on him unmercifully, bleaching the sea of shanty roofs until his vision adjusted. He saw that all the shanties in this area were on stilts, perhaps four or five feet off the ground. Elevated bamboo paths connected adjacent shacks. Every square foot of shade was occupied by someone, and Sam thought he saw three children dash beneath one of the makeshift homes.

"It doesn't look like this area would flood," said Sam. "Why the stilts?"

"It is not allowed to make foundations here." The nurse gave him a look that said it should be obvious, even to an American.

But Sam didn't understand. "Is that a building code?"

The nurse led him down a short flight of steps and pointed to the space beneath the maternity ward. "This land belonged to the Spanish, but they lost their claim when America defeated them. After Marcos, land without owners became free to be used by the poor people." She pointed to white marble stonework beneath the shanty. "Still, it would be sacrilege to dig these up, so the houses are built on stilts." She ducked her head and motioned Sam to follow her beneath the building.

Sam recognized stone crosses. "You mean this was a colonial graveyard? And now there is a town a meter and a half above it?"

"Yes, that is correct. The town is above."

Sam saw a folded blanket lying across the top of a long stone vault. She followed his glance.

"Only the poorest live down below."

He realized someone used the grave site as a bed. Smoke had blackened a headstone nearby, and a small metal cook pot was hidden behind it.

Nurse Isolde clucked in annoyance when she saw the sooty marks. "I keep telling them not to build fires down here. If this building catches fire, there is no way to put it out. There is no running water in this *baranggáy*." She grabbed the pot, and they went back into the sunlight.

"You have no running water? How many people live here?"

"It's hard to say. Maybe four thousand. But people come and go." She smiled. "Babies are born."

Sam watched as a Mercedes van pulled to a stop next to the building. A solid, no-nonsense Filipino bodyguard got out of the front passenger seat. He scanned the area, decided it was safe, and slid open the rear door for Sonny Lagos.

Sonny was shorter than Sam had judged from the videotape, and he was impeccably groomed. The congressman wore an expensive, tailored *barong*, the embroidered, loose-fitting shirt that was replacing western suits among Filipino pols. Since they were designed not to be tucked into pants, *barongs* had the advantage of being lightweight and breezy. Given the temperature, Sam wished he could wear one without feeling foolish.

Nurse Isolde bowed to Congressman Lagos and indicated Sam.

"It is good to see you, sir. I have been showing Mr. Haine about the facility."

"And it was an interesting tour," said Sam, smiling at the nurse. He was impatient to question Lagos, but knew the amenities would have to be observed. "Thank you for seeing me, sir. Since we haven't met before, perhaps you would like to see my identification." Sam reached for his badge and saw the bodyguard tense up. He slowed his hand motion and folded back his coat to extract the case holding his badge.

Sonny waved his hand. "It won't be necessary, Mr. Haine." He nodded to the bodyguard. "Colonel Pico called the Embassy and checked." He gave Nurse Isolde a glance. "Thank you for your help, Nurse. Mr. Haine and I need to confer in private." Nurse Isolde bowed in apology and disappeared up the stairs into the maternity ward. Sonny turned and led the way.

As they walked among the thicket of stilts, faces peered from the open doorways, occupants smiling shyly. Sam, being a foot taller than the congressman, found that his eye level had him looking across the thresholds into the dark huts. They were bare of furnishings, save for a few sleeping blankets, cooking utensils, and a fire ring made of brick.

They walked in silence for a couple of minutes. Sometimes a peasant would come forward and bow his thanks to Sonny. Sometimes a mother, always in the thinnest, most shapeless of housedresses, would proffer an infant to Sonny. Sam watched as Sonny would place his hand on the infant's head or shoulder, almost as if his touch were beneficence enough.

"What do you make of our little community?" said Sonny. He waited while Sam tried to think of some way to respond. "You have never seen such poverty before, have you, Mr. Haine?"

Sam hesitated. "Actually, I have, on some of my other trips. And there are parts of Appalachia which come close, though never with this many people so close together." He tried to find some way into the topic he wanted to discuss. "It is kind and generous of you to support the medical ward, Congressman. They see you as their benefactor—"

"Not benefactor—defender, Mr. Haine. They need someone to assert their rights, to fight for their homes."

"And that's you?"

"I do what I can. But my children," he gestured to include all the peasants in the shanties, "they are just learning to read, to write—to vote. And there are a thousand *baranggáys* like this. My efforts are never enough." He pointed beneath the shanties, and Sam ducked his head to look. "Who would have foreseen squatter's rights in a graveyard? What legal precedents can we use to defend them, when the government seeks to dispossess them?"

Sam had lost the initiative in this meeting, bludgeoned by the poverty he was being exposed to. He tried to redirect the conversation. "Is that why you were orchestrating the demonstration at the Santos Apartment complex? To establish legal precedents?"

Sonny's face tightened. "That is quite an accusation to make." He turned and began walking back toward his van. "I am creating a new political movement, one dedicated to bringing justice to the landless and homeless."

Sam kept pace with him. "And you can't make an omelet without breaking eggs, is that it? Look, the whole thing's on videotape. You, the truck, your bodyguard acting as driver."

Sonny pulled back. "So what if I was a witness to that spectacle the Santos' family was staging? It's a free country, I can go where I want."

With Sonny off balance and no longer controlling the interview, Sam took the opening. "And interfering with an NBI murder investigation, telling Fiscal Santos to drop the case—you're free to do that, too? Why would you want to obstruct justice, especially when it involves an American, a gun smuggler?"

They were back to the van, and the bodyguard opened the door for Sonny. Sonny stepped in and regained his composure.

"I'd offer you a ride, Mr. Haine, but I have another appointment, and I'm running late." He gave a predatory smirk. "You must be careful as you return to NBI. The streets around here are well-known for muggings. And a wealthy American such as yourself—" He paused. "Well, be safe," he added insincerely. He pulled the van door shut, and the driver put the van into motion.

Sam watched the van thread its way toward the street. He

walked back to the maternity ward, climbed the stairs, and went inside. Nurse Isolde looked up, surprised to see him again.

"Is the Congressman still here?"

"He had another appointment," said Sam. He took out his wallet and withdrew a hundred dollars. "I can see what wonderful things you are doing. I want to help support your work here. Can you take care of this donation?"

Nurse Isolde's eyes widened as Sam handed her the cash. She took the money and put it into a small cash box in a drawer of her desk, which she locked. She looked at Sam, distrust in her eye. "Thank you, Mr. Haine. It will do much good."

Sam knew that his gift had created an obligation. He could see that the nurse was worried, because she was not yet sure what he would want of her.

"Would you please call for a taxi to pick me up?"

Nurse Isolde smiled with relief and pulled a cell phone from her purse.

"And while we wait for the cab, perhaps you can look at these photos with me," said Sam. He pulled a stack of pictures from his suit pocket.

twenty-eight--

It took until mid-afternoon for the forensic team to complete the sweep of Harv Tucker's room. Bogie had faxed the list of addresses, dates, and dollar amounts to Saddul and Garcia, so they could confirm whether Tucker had made sales to all the cockfighting arenas listed on the slips of paper in his lock box. Garcia would get in touch if anything turned up.

By now Bogie was thoroughly sick of Sonja, tired of trying to keep her from grabbing bits of evidence out of the hands of the investigators. It was clear to him that she was hoping to find something else, something other than the pharmaceutical research report.

He kept leading the conversation back to her relationship with her brother, pressing how difficult it must be to have a brother who was cheating you in a business deal. Uncouth as Sonja might be, she wasn't dumb, nor could Bogie goad her into an angry lapse of judgment.

The team finished bagging their collection of evidence—which consisted of hairs, fingernail clippings, a used condom, miscellaneous receipts, phone memos from the front desk message pad, and swabs for explosive residue taken from the interior of Harv's suitcase.

Bogie decided to take one last shot and offered to buy Sonja a drink in the hotel bar. She looked at him with amusement.

"Sure, pardner. A lady never turns down a free drink. At least this lady don't."

"I know it's been difficult for you, watching them go through your brother's room," said Bogie.

"Yeah," she said dryly.

In the bar, Sonja knocked back two bourbons in less than a minute, and Bogie harbored some hope that it would loosen her tongue. He sipped his own whisky and signaled for the bartender to bring Sonja another drink.

Sonja hoisted her glass and smiled at Bogie over the rim.

"I just want you to know up front that I don't put out on the first date," she said.

Bogie fought the urge to choke on his drink. He put his glass down with care.

"This isn't a date, Ms. Tucker. I thought I could help you deal with your loss."

Sonja tossed back her bourbon and laughed immoderately. "Yeah, right."

She reached across the bar and pulled a bowl of pork rinds over. As she pushed a large handful into her mouth, Bogie got a good chance to see just how strong her teeth were.

"I know how this one works," said Sonja. "I watched at my daddy's funeral when all his good buddies started putting the moves on my mother—right at the service and all. Thought they could get in her pants 'cuz she didn't have a man around. Buncha effin' losers. They learned the hard way to watch their backs whenever my brother Harvey was around. He was just sixteen, but he was near full growed. He kicked some A, I can tell ya."

"It must have been hard for the two of you, not having a father during adolescence."

"It sure as shit made Harv toughen up. An' I wasn't nothin' to laugh at neither, though I was twelve at the time. My tits had come in and I was starting to get my height. I had to teach a few of them junior high pimples a lesson or two." Sonja paused to let out a sonorous belch, followed by a loud laugh, drawing stares from a table full of Japanese businessmen next to her.

Nearby the barkeep shuffled nervously and looked at Bogie.

Sonja noticed the bartender and pulled out her purse. She

slapped a twenty on the bar and shouted, "Give this man a drink!" pointing at Bogie. She thumped her chest, causing a seismic wave to pulse through her bosom. "And one more for the little lady!"

The bartender made the twenty disappear and set up the drinks.

Sonja turned and gave Bogie a lascivious wink. "Maybe *I'll* find out whether *you* put out on the first date."

"I thought you had other—preferences."

Sonja scowled at Bogie ferociously. "Are you sayin' what I think you're sayin'? Think again. I ain't no lesbo."

"Of course not. I didn't mean to—"

"Hell, no!" brayed Sonja, getting the attention of the entire bar. "I'm a tri-sexual!"

"A—uhhh—tri?" gargled Bogie.

"If it's sexual, I'll try it!"

She laughed throatily at her own wit, ending in a phlegmy cough. The Japanese businessmen looked away from her in embarrassment. She pinned them with a belligerent stare.

"You Nips got a problem?"

The men looked down. That wasn't enough to deter Sonja.

"My daddy fought you rice-eaters in WW two. We kicked your butts way back when and maybe you need a little reminding about that. Arrogant sons-a-bitches. You never seen a lady could outdrink ya before?" She peered owlishly at the closest Japanese man. "I'm twice the man any of you little turds ever thought a bein'. An' I'm a woman!" She turned when Bogie tapped her arm. "Don't you go touchin' me."

"Let me take you back to your hotel, Ms. Tucker," said Bogie.

"You tryin' to take ad-vana-tage of a lady, mister?"

"No. I'm attempting to assist you back to your hotel. I know this has been a trying day for you."

Sonja sat blinking for a few seconds, then ponderously got off her stool.

"S'a good idea."

As she got up, she staggered, knocking into the table, upsetting all the drinks of the Japanese.

The men looked up. Sonja leaned over their table menacingly, smiling at the way they shrank back.

Once Bogie got her outside to the taxi queue, Sonja turned to him. All traces of the effects of alcohol were gone, and her eyes positively sparkled.

"Damn, that was fun, Bogie. You wanna go to another hotel and do it again?"

Bogie goggled at her.

"Come on, Bogie. Don't be a pussy." She eyed him speculatively, eyes coming to rest on his crotch. "If you show a good-time gal enough fun like that, she loosens up. Maybe you'll even get lucky."

BARYO SAN JOSE—2 P.M. FRIDAY

Sam used Isolde's cell phone to reach Jennifer's office but got her secretary. She told him Jennifer had already left for the day, but she would be glad to relay a message. Sam thanked her and tried Jennifer at the cell phone number she had given him.

Several rings later, he was about to give up when the line clicked open. "Jennifer?"

"Sam? Is that you? I wasn't expecting a call, so the phone was buried in my briefcase."

"I was hoping I could meet with you and talk about the videotape," said Sam. "Perhaps over dinner."

"I don't see how I can do that. I have an engagement later this evening."

"This bears on the case I'm investigating. I won't take much of your time."

Sam waited while Jennifer thought out her schedule.

"OK," she said with a sigh. "I'll give you my home address. We can talk there before I go out."

The cab took Sam through a barred entry, past a security post, into a wealthy enclave. Though the streets were narrow, each home was palatial, backing onto the golf course.

Most of the homes were Spanish colonial style, with stout entry gates. Many of the houses had their own small guard booths at the driveway entries, from which armed private security officers watched the street.

Having watched the videotape of the riot, Sam could see why the plutocrats might have some security concerns. He asked the driver if another cab would be able to pick him up inside the gated neighborhood. The cabbie said the main gate would send a golf cart for him, while the cab remained waiting outside.

A short, stout maid let Sam into Jennifer's home. She led him through an interior courtyard with an Italianate fountain and left him sitting in a spacious room overlooking the tenth green of the golf course. Four antique European settees and a Steinway grand piano did not overfill the room. The fireplace was large enough to roast a water buffalo whole.

Through the French doors, Sam watched a golf foursome stroll up to the eighth green and putt out. As much as he enjoyed the air conditioning and the sense of serenity, the contrast with his recent experience at the *baranggáy* was dreamlike.

The maid returned and asked if he preferred iced tea, beer, or a Coke. A minute later he took his iced tea and went to inspect the fireplace. He wasn't positive, but he thought he had seen it before, either on a trip to Europe or in the movie *Citizen Kane*.

"Surely you don't want a fire in this weather."

Sam turned at the sound of Jennifer's voice, and his drink almost slipped from his hand. Jennifer was wearing a stunning floor-length evening gown of midnight green silk. It was sleeveless, strapless, backless, and tailored to the millimeter. Sam was unaware that his jaw had dropped.

Jennifer laughed lightly. "Oh, good. I guess the dress works the way it's supposed to."

Sam blushed. "I didn't realize technology had come so far."

Jennifer frowned, puzzled. "What?"

"There's an anti-gravity device concealed somewhere. I mean something has to keep that dress up," said Sam. "Where are you going that people will be so lucky?"

"Lucky?"

"To watch you enter the room."

Now it was Jennifer's turn to blush, but she also dimpled at the compliment. "It's a formal dinner with my parents. James is receiving a civic award."

"James?" said Sam. Though it was entirely unreasonable, he still felt a stab of jealousy, and it caught him off guard.

"He's a senator—and my brother." She laughed again, and Sam liked listening to it. "Oh, Sam. You're so transparent. No date is going to show up and take me to the ball. I'm attending with my family."

"It defies belief that you do not have a date."

Jennifer's smile became a trifle brittle. "You sound like my parents."

Mine, too. Sam had long since stopped listening to his folks' advice to begin dating again, never even considered it. It was too painful to think of someone taking the place of Christy. But now he was glad that Jennifer had broken through his isolation. He felt more alive than he had in three years.

It was disconcerting to think that his parents might have been right.

"Did I lose you there, Sam?"

Sam gave himself a mental shake. He pulled a small stack of photos from his inside coat pocket.

"I just came from a medical ward in a *baranggáy*," he said. "I showed these pictures to the nurse there, to see if she recognized any faces."

He handed her the photos—Harv's passport picture, and surveillance shots of Chito, Olivia, and Juan Samoa. Jennifer looked at them and shook her head.

"Other than Harvey Tucker, these are new to me. What did the nurse say?"

"She knew them all." Sam handed her one last picture:

Sonny Lagos sitting in the truck at the Santos Apartments. "This guy, too."

Jennifer froze for a fraction of a second. "And?"

"Since Lagos funds this maternity clinic, they aren't going to object if he uses their facility for an occasional meeting."

"And how are all these people connected?"

"I was hoping you could tell me."

"I am a prosecutor, not an investigator" said Jennifer, stiffly. "The police bring me the evidence they have found, and I build a case." She gave him a hard-edged look. "Why are you showing these to me?"

"Because NBI may not be looking as deep as they should. I wouldn't have thought Bogie was afraid of much, but he wouldn't come along to brace Mr. Lagos." Sam saw something flicker in Jennifer's eyes when she heard Bogie's name.

"You met with Sonny Lagos?" she said.

"The very same guy who turned up in that videotape of the riot at the Santos Apartments. You didn't need to be afraid of Bogie seeing the footage, by the way. Once he knew who it was, he was—reluctant, shall we say?—to ask any questions at all."

Sam felt Jennifer's attitude toward him cooling, as if he had crossed into territory she wanted to reserve for herself, and he felt a pang of loss. *Still,* he thought to himself, *I get a paycheck to investigate crime, not to socialize.*

"You just did it again, Sam. You went someplace else." She laid a hand on his arm. "What's going on?"

"I won't take any more of your time, Jennifer. Just to be clear, the other three photos are active suspects in the murder of Tucker. It's an unlikely coincidence for all of them to have visited *Lagos Pagka-Iná Pagamutan.*"

Something passed behind her eyes when he mentioned the name of the maternity facility. He waited, giving her a chance to speak, but she said nothing, and he gave up. "If you have something you can share with me, I'd be grateful." When she didn't respond, Sam turned to go, setting his glass on a coffee table.

"Sam, could you do me a favor before you leave?"

Sam turned back, a question on his face.

"I haven't picked shoes to go with my dress," she said.

"You think guys know anything about shoes?"

She started up a flight of stairs, beckoning him to follow. "The day we met, you stared at my legs so intently, I thought you'd burn a hole in my stockings." Sam's cheeks burned a little at the memory. Jennifer went on, with a light laugh, "But I could tell you were also checking out my shoes."

"Maybe I just wanted to see how big your feet were?"

Jennifer paused before a door that was ajar. "Perhaps I misjudged you." She pulled the door wide, revealing a large dressing room with an attached walk-in closet. Full-length mirrors made up one wall, while the other three walls were covered floor to ceiling with shoes on store-style shelves. There were so many shoes that they were arranged in columns by color.

Sam halted, a new believer in all the stories about Imelda.

Jennifer caught his look. "Sure, I'll tell you."

Sam glanced at her, perplexed.

"Two thousand, four hundred and eighteen." She pulled a pair of green satin pumps from a shelf and held them against her dress. "Color doesn't quite match, does it?"

"Is this a Filipina thing? Shoes, I mean."

"If you find a style of shoe that you like, it makes sense to get a pair in every color they have."

"I don't know exactly how to say this—but isn't this a lot of money to have tied up in shoes?"

"My family has money," she said. As she talked, she searched the shelves for a better match. "And if we spend it, shoe stores have profits, shoe clerks are employed, importers have orders, longshoremen have jobs. When I buy shoes made in the RP, it employs the craftsmen who design them, the workers who manufacture them. The factories buy leather from local tanneries, who get their hides from local farmers—"

She turned with a pair of slim black velvet stiletto heels in hand. "But I don't need to lecture a capitalist about economics." She held the shoes against the bodice of the dress, increasing her décolletage even more. "Do you think?"

Sam did a little goldfish imitation before he managed, "You—they look great."

She handed the shoes to Sam. "Would you help me? This dress is so tight I don't think I can bend enough to put them on myself."

Sam knelt down as she raised the hem of her dress. This close, he could smell her perfume. She rested her fingertips on his shoulder and extended one foot. When Sam grasped it, heat flashed from his hand to her instep. Sam felt her foot stiffen. "What's wrong?" he said, looking up.

Jennifer's body had flushed. Her skin temperature shot up, and the scent of her pervaded his senses.

"Did you do something to my foot just then?" she asked.

Sam shook his head. "I—was—uh—"

She moved her hand from his shoulder to the top of his head, twining her fingers in his hair. "Come on, do it again."

She pulled his head against her body and Sam could feel the heat through the thin silk. It was clear she wore nothing beneath her clothes, and Sam wondered briefly—ever so briefly—what held up her silk stockings.

He slid his hands up her body as he rose to his feet. Her fingers in his hair pulled his mouth to hers, and they kissed deeply as his hands caught the small of her back, a raw flame against her bare skin. She moaned and then his tongue was in her mouth, and she gave a low-pitched cry from the back of her throat.

Sam moved his lips to her ear, and on to the soft space just below the line of her jaw. She shivered and held onto the back of his neck with both hands as he kissed his way along her throat. With the tip of his tongue he outlined the upper curve of her breast and moved downward.

She arched her back, her body straining upward to meet his kisses. Her breasts pushed free of the strapless bodice, the nipples erect. Sam took them in his mouth one at a time, sucking lightly, biting gently around the swollen tissues of the areola.

Jennifer reached behind her, hands trembling, and tried

to unzip the dress, but with the bodice rolled down the way it was, the zipper wouldn't move. Sam ran his tongue down her torso, pausing at her navel, licking the circumference of the sexy dimple, and Jennifer gasped. She tugged again at the zipper, with no result.

Sam dropped to his knees, cupped her buttocks in his hands, and pressed his lips against the hot silk, kissing through the slick cloth. She cried out as if in pain and tugged once more at the zipper.

This time the thin silk gown tore in her hands, and the dress slithered to the floor. Sam's tongue pressed into her moist flesh.

Jennifer moaned again and again, first rising onto her toes, slightly spreading her legs as both feet settled flat against the floor. Her fingers twisted into his hair, pulling his face deeper, and she wrapped one leg around him, her thigh resting on his shoulder.

The heat of contact between Sam's cheek and her inner thigh made his face slick with sweat. He backed his head away an inch, began kissing softly, bringing her to orgasm, while she wept with pleasure. The tears rolled down her cheeks, a gentle rain on Sam's face.

From the hallway two maids listened to the continuing sounds of lovemaking—the younger with a look of wonder; disgust on the face of the other.

"Aiee," said the maid fresh from the provinces. "The rich are not like you and me."

"No," said the older one, looking sour. "They fuck on the floor. With his nose in her *puki*."

The other maid began to giggle uncontrollably. The two women were in such a hurry to get downstairs before their laughter gave them away, they missed seeing that the new gardener had come inside for a drink of water.

He carried a small camera hidden in the palm of his hand.

NBI—2 P.M. FRIDAY

Garcia sat at one desk, Saddul at the other, working over the notes and addresses taken from Harvey Tucker's hotel lock box. They cross-checked address listings in a reverse phone directory to get the telephone numbers they needed. Garcia had contacted the first four on his list and confirmed that Harv Tucker had sold fighting cocks to each arena, for the exact dollar amounts listed on the slips.

Each of the owners remembered the transaction, since they considered Tucker to be one of the finest gamecock breeders in the world. None of them had found anything unusual, either in the most recent sales or in his behavior. Tucker had been obnoxious every time before, and he had remained true to form.

Saddul took two deep sniffs from a nasal inhaler. He looked up from the reverse directory. "I can't find a phone number for this address on Bulacan."

"Try the address next door, whoever answers can give you the name of the arena, and you can look it up in the regular directory," said Garcia.

Saddul gave Garcia a look that said he had already been there, done that. "I don't think there's any such address. There's a break in the sequence of numbers on that street."

Garcia reached for the slip. He inspected it, handed it back. "Thought maybe you couldn't make out his handwriting, but that's clear."

"How many more calls do you have to make?" said Saddul.

"One left."

"I'm thinking we ought to take a look at this place, see who's living there."

An hour later the two detectives approached an empty lot. It was squeezed between an open-air car repair and the buttressed columns of the elevated train that runs twelve miles through metro Manila. A few homeless folk were trying to make a go of it on the vacant land, and a cardboard lean-to made use of a concrete pillar to serve as one wall of their shelter.

An old man squatted in a corner of the lot, taking a dump *al fresco*. A couple of street urchins shied pebbles at his naked backside, trying for a hole in one. The old man cursed, looked around for a handful of weeds to wipe with, hiked up his pants as he chased after them.

Garcia narrowed his eyes against the tropical light that was frying the hard-packed clay.

"So what do you make of this?" said Garcia.

Even in the shade of the elevated tracks, Saddul was sweating. He hawked up some troublesome phlegm and spat. The exhaust-filled humid air made it feel like they were swimming through a thin soup. Saddul pulled all the slips from his pocket, sorting them by date.

"According to these dates, Tucker made all the sales in four days, then nothing," said Saddul. "There's a five-day gap until this last one."

"Which is two days from now."

"So maybe this one isn't about a bird sale."

"What else could it be?" said Garcia.

"Maybe that's not a street name," said Saddul. "Maybe it's a business. And that number's not an address."

"Could be an invoice number," said Garcia. He thought about it, shook his head. "How about a cargo container ID?"

The more Saddul thought about that, the more he liked the possibilities. "Let's go to the harbor master's office. You call Bogie and let him know what's up. I'll get the car."

twenty-nine--

CLUB DE SEX—2 P.M. FRIDAY

Gerard slumped into the booth across from Juan Samoa. He had been gone for more than a day since he had agreed to get the research papers. Juan didn't look happy to see him.

Gerard's three-day drunk was over. Fear had taken care of that. A new pole dancer came out, her music pounding so loud that Juan had to lean in and speak into Gerard's ear.

"I've got the cash upstairs. Let's get away from this noise."

Gerard pulled away, avoiding Juan's eyes. He signaled to a waitress and mimed drinking a beer. He kept his eyes on the waitress as she went to the bar and brought him a San Mig. He paid the waitress and downed half the bottle in one long gulp, without once looking at Juan.

Juan looked around for the bouncer, caught his eye, and waved him over. When the bouncer was standing behind Gerard, Juan flexed his hand. The bouncer stepped in, grappled Gerard from behind in a bear hug, and lifted him from his seat.

Gerard's struggling became ever more feeble as his face went from an angry flush to a hypoxic magenta. Samoa headed for a back room, and the bouncer followed along, carrying Gerard.

Once in the storage room, the bouncer let Gerard slide from his embrace, but he kept one meaty hand on the Frenchman's shoulder. Gerard doubled over and tried to get his wind back. Juan waited and signed to the bouncer, who grabbed Gerard by the hair and jerked him upright.

"I'm sensing there is a problem," said Juan. "You need to explain—and quickly."

The bouncer hadn't let go of Gerard's hair, and the Frenchman's eyes bulged. "I don't have the papers you want," he sniveled.

"I already offered you a premium. This is not the time to haggle. You *are* going to sell them back to me."

"I can't! I went back to where they were in safekeeping, but the papers were gone. And so was their guardian."

"And who is this guardian?"

"He's the manager at the cockfighting arena."

"Does he have a name, this manager?"

"I don't know his real name. He is called Goldie," said Gerard. He pointed to his mouth. "Because he has the gold teeth in front." Gerard struggled to release his hair from the bouncer's grip. "Maybe Goldie has gone into business for himself."

"Goldie?" Juan smiled grimly. "Those papers were with Goldie all this time? I know him well. He would not take things into his own hands. And you say he is missing?" He nodded to the bouncer, who let go of Gerard's hair.

Gerard came down off his tiptoes. "I couldn't find him. Not at the arena, not at his home. The two men who clean up the place say they have not seen him in three days."

Juan grabbed the front of Gerard's shirt and pulled him close. "If anything you have said is bullshit, you will regret it. Permanently." He released Gerard's shirt and motioned to the bouncer. "He no longer has access to our club."

The bouncer nodded and grabbed the back of Gerard's slacks, jerking them up into the crack of his butt. He pincered Gerard's neck with his other hand and frog-marched him out a rear exit, launching him into a pile of garbage in the alley.

JENNIFER'S BEDROOM—5 P.M. FRIDAY

Jennifer lay on her hip, wrapped in the top sheet, watching Sam. Sam lay spread-eagled on the silk sheet, the sweat on his torso already drying in the breeze from the air conditioner.

She said nothing, waiting, until Sam became a little self-conscious.

"What?" said Sam.

"I won't lie. I needed that. It's been two years since—" She shifted, and the sheet fell away, revealing a breast. "But it seemed like you needed it even more." She waited for his response, hoping he would open up to her.

"I guess it's lucky we found each other before we burst into flame," he said, keeping his tone light. "I'm feeling guilty taking time off from the investigation."

The instant the words were out of his mouth, he recognized the truth behind what he had said: he had been using his job as a substitute for relationships. It was all too easy to lose himself in the work, not think about things he would never have again.

Jennifer made a small moue. "Oh, you're one of those. We can touch, but not talk? I thought better of you, Sam."

"Did you say two years?" Sam raised his eyebrows. "Are the men here all crazy?"

"Don't change the subject."

"I'm not. But you go first."

Jennifer hesitated. "It's difficult for me to date. I have a public image—"

"Because there's never been a female fiscal before?"

Jennifer smiled at that. "You did some homework."

"So, a fiscal is required to be celibate?"

"It's not that. My family is prominent, and I am beyond the age when dutiful daughters get married. My parents expect me to marry well, enhance the family fortunes, and cement alliances."

"How medieval. They want you to be a princess."

"But I don't feel like being wife to someone who sees my primary purpose as being a means for him to gain influence. Every time I date one of these so-called eligible bachelors from the leading families, it starts a storm of rumors and gossip—especially among my mother and aunts."

"And if you date a *kano,* no one is too worried, because you wouldn't possibly—" said Sam, softly. "Therefore, it must be a business meeting."

This accorded so precisely with her father's reasoning that she flinched away from him.

"Please," said Sam. "Jiggle like that again. It looks wonderful on you."

Jennifer colored and Sam watched the flush spread from her face, to her throat, down her breasts. The sheet blocked his further research into how far the effect would radiate.

"God, you're beautiful," said Sam, moving toward her. He grasped the edge of the sheet and flipped it up, catching air, and let it settle across them both.

"You can't possibly be ready to—" She stopped when he covered her mouth with his and cupped his hand between her thighs. She took a deep breath through her nose, inhaling his musk, his sweat, his heat.

Sam's pager went off.

It went off again five minutes later.

And three minutes after that.

On the seventh page, Sam picked it up and read the alpha message from Bogie.

MANILA BAY WATERFRONT—7 P.M. FRIDAY

Manila Bay was a working port, not a resort. From any vantage point a dozen freighters were visible, each waiting its turn to unload cargo. Because the bay was attached to the capital city, policing and customs were more stringently enforced. In practical terms, this meant that of the cargo passing through the bay, perhaps only twenty-five per cent was being smuggled, or avoiding duty, or simply escaping inspection.

Dozens of bars lined the shabby waterfront. Hookers plied their trade along the trash-strewn sidewalks between the bars and the flotsam-edged sand. Rates were low, because these were the hookers whose best earning days lay behind them. They were reduced to servicing drunken sailors and tourists looking for bargains. Most of them were supporting a houseful of international bastard children, as well as the homegrown bastards who were leeching off them.

Just at the high water mark, yellow "CRIME SCENE—DO NOT CROSS" tape was already in place. Several members of the leisure class, of the sort often found holding up buildings, had gathered to offer opinion and color commentary. Though the sun had set, none of them seemed to have urgent errands calling them away. One enterprising soul had brought a flashlight to shine on the corpse.

"Nice shirt. He look like pimp to me, hey?" said Flashlight, standing some twenty feet from the body. Perhaps as a token of his work as a holder-up of structures, he wore oversized pants held in place by a portion of electrical cord.

"No way, man," replied the second, the intellectual of the two. He had studied English in third grade, just before leaving academia. "Got no shoes."

"But he usta. Otherwise why he wearin' socks?"

"I guess you right," said the second. He thought. "Who you think got dem shoes, brotha? I bet dey some fine *sapatos*."

"Fuckin' A. Fine *'patos*."

They spent some time pondering the unfairness of life, which allowed some people to have shoes, while they had none. It was even more unfair that some probably-really-fine shoes had been so near, just for the taking, and once again Lady Luck had hosed two worthy Pinoy.

A uniform made his way over and knocked the flashlight aside. He was going to make more of it, perhaps remove a few teeth, but two aged whores in matching hot pink spandex miniskirts tried to sneak under the tape for a closer look at the body. He hustled after them. He couldn't allow them to contaminate the crime scene.

The first Filipino flipped the flashlight on and off a couple times, saw that the cop's attention was occupied, so he shined it on the body again.

"How dis guy die?" he asked. "I din't hear no gunshots."

"Musta been knife. It be quiet."

"It was no *kutsilyo*, fool. Othawise we be seein' blood aroun' da body."

"If it not gun, and not knife—" The second Pinoy scratched his testicles absently. "Could be a hard attack." A good scratch seemed to stimulate his thinking, so he scratched some more.

"You keep scratchin' like that you be givin' yourself a hard-on attack."

"Hey *baklâ*, you keep lookin' at my hard-on I whip it out and beat you to death with it."

This was so witty that they both started laughing. That led to dual coughing fits harsh enough to make them retire for a nightcap.

S am made his way through the crowd, ignoring the repeated calls of "Hey, Joe! Wanna date?" When he came to the tape he signaled to the uniformed officer and showed his badge. A flash of light indicated that the police photographer was already at work.

"Cause of death?" asked Sam.

"Hard to say, sir."

Bogie ducked under the tape and caught up to Sam. "Who found the body?"

"I did, sir," said the officer.

"So fifty streetwalkers didn't notice a stiff lying face down on their turf?" said Sam. "Sounds like New York."

The cop gave a tight little smile. "People aren't nosy around here, sir."

"Do we know how long the body has been lying here?" asked Bogie.

"I pass this point every two hours, sir."

The two men thanked the beat cop, walked over to the photographer, Jojo. Bogie spoke to him in Tagalog. "Can we take a look, or do you need more shots?"

"I'm finished," he replied in English. "I'll develop these and drop two sets to NBI in the morning."

Chito lay face down in the dirty sand by the water, his right arm stretched over his head. Bogie and Sam squatted near the body, examining it without touching it. Sam swept the beam of a small flashlight across the ground around the corpse. He kept at it for so long that Bogie looked a question at him.

"Just shoe prints, no scuffs," said Sam. "And no footprints of someone wearing only socks."

"Yeah, no signs of a struggle."

"Did you see the marks in the sand by his hand?"

"I couldn't make anything of them," said Bogie. "Maybe they'll be easier to read in the photos."

"Shall we check his pockets?" asked Sam. "Or is that the coroner's job here?"

"Coroner owns the body only after we release it from the crime scene. We go through the victim's effects at the crime scene, bag them for evidence." Bogie pulled a gallon-sized zip-lock from his pocket.

Sam patted down the body. "No coins, no wallet, no chewing gum, no keys."

Bogie pointed to the crowd just beyond the crime scene tape. "They already had two hours to do their own search."

"And they took his shoes, too?"

"Chito always wore expensive shoes. Cost more than any of these guys makes in a couple of months."

Sam patted the front of Chito's pants and heard a crinkling noise. He found the watch pocket and pulled out the photo of Harvey Tucker. He stared at it with some surprise, passed it to Bogie.

Bogie looked at it, bagged it. "Was that left by accident? Or is someone sending a message?"

"If all the local light-fingers missed it, maybe the killer did, too." Sam resumed his inspection of the corpse. "No gunshot wound," he said. "No stabs or cuts. No obvious blunt force trauma to the head. No bruises."

"I'm betting on suffocation as cause of death. See the sand in his mouth?"

Sam leaned forward and shined the flashlight at Chito's mouth. "Missed that." He probed Chito's mouth with a ball-point pen. There was an odd tapping sound. Sam looked perplexed.

Bogie caught the look. "Something wrong?"

"I don't think he died here."

"But the marks he made in the sand?"

"It's from the killer, not Chito. Listen, is there a construction site nearby?" asked Sam.

Bogie looked at him.

"He didn't suffocate on sand," said Sam. "His mouth is stuffed with cement."

Bogie moved beside Sam and tapped the stuff in Chito's mouth with a pencil, felt something solid. He jammed the point of the pencil in and pried out a small bit of the hardened substance. He held it in the beam of Sam's flashlight and worked it till it crumbled between his fingers.

"Not cement. Lahar."

"La-what?" said Sam.

Bogie eyed him, not sure if Sam was putting him on. "It's the same in English as Tagalog. A mixture of sand and volcanic ash. Add water and it sets up like cement."

"Musta been asleep that day in Volcano 101," said Sam.

"And here I thought you knew everything, Detective Haine."

Sam took some of the mineral crumbs from Bogie and rolled them in his hand. "They use this stuff for construction in Manila?"

"It's not structurally sound. In fact, it's a major environmental nuisance. When a monsoon soaks it, the stuff turns slushy and starts flowing like cold lava. Villages get buried. Jungles get mowed down."

"Do I have to play twenty questions?" said Sam. "Where do we find this stuff?"

"We'll go tomorrow. This is what's left of Mount Pinatubo. It's out near Subic Bay, the old US Naval Station."

"Subic?" Sam's face tightened, memories of his father and grandfather crowding into his already overloaded brain. Jennifer. Christy. Burying himself in his work. Maybe CIA trying to take the case away from ATF.

He stood up, stretched his back muscles, and turned to leave. "I need to get back to my hotel. Get some sleep. I'm still jet-lagged."

Bogie brushed his hands and rose to follow Sam as he walked toward the yellow barrier.

"Something wrong?"

Sam shrugged and kept walking. Bogie caught up and matched stride with him.

"Let's share a cab back to your hotel, Sam. I'll buy you a drink—or sleeping pills, if that's what you need."

"No, thanks, I'll get my own cab."

Bogie came to a stop. "Yo! Detective Haine!"

Sam turned around, eyes hooded.

"I'm trying to do you a favor," said Bogie. "You aren't going to get a cab on your own in this part of town."

Sam peered at the dilapidated waterfront, heard the tinny karaoke from the open doors of the bars. For a long bleary moment he watched the flow of Japanese businessmen cruising the strand for Filipinas. *Doesn't this place ever cool down at night?* He already knew he wouldn't sleep this night, either. He turned to face Bogie.

"Yeah, thanks, Bogie. But I'll buy the drinks, OK?" As they walked toward the street, Sam thought to himself. *What time is it in LA? Am I supposed to be eating lunch now?*

And then, *I want to go home.*

thirty--

God is a comedian
playing to an audience
too afraid to laugh.
Voltaire

Parañaque, suburbs of Metro Manila—
8 a.m. Saturday

Gerard pulled his clothes from the dresser and hurled them into a suitcase. In one corner of the bedroom his Filipina mistress wailed. She was a beautiful woman, but her teary grimace had made her ugly, and if there was anything Gerard could not abide, it was an ugly woman.

"But Gee-rard, why can't I go with you?"

"It is too dangerous." *Especially for me if I have to drag you along.* "You will be all right. I have set up an account with the landlord. You can stay here for the rest of the month. He will pay the bills for you, buy you groceries."

She keened over her loss. "You will come back in a month?"

"I did not say that."

"You will send for me in a month, Gee-rard?"

He ignored her and sorted through the clothes in the closet. *I must not weigh myself down. Just one business suit, a coat, two shirts, a tie—*

"Why?" She paused to gulp back sobs, shrieked, "Why are you abandoning me?"

Gerard covered his ears with his hands. *This is the price I pay for going native.* "Do not accuse me. I am not abandoning you. You have a roof over your head. You have food."

"I want *you!*"

"You are still young," he continued. "You will find some-one new." *And if I don't get on that flight, Juan or Chito or Nosaka will catch up to me.*

"What will become of me?" She screamed it, putting her soul into it.

Gerard slammed the suitcase shut. He walked to the door and turned to face her one last time. "I do not know. I do not care. I am done here." He slammed the door behind him, strid-ing briskly down to the main street to catch a cab.

I can start again in Malaysia, perhaps Thailand. There is always a place for an entrepreneur who can supply the right information. He saw a taxi coming along Quirino Avenue and waved it down. *And who stole that Fitzler report? I owe them a death.*

The taxi pulled up, and the Malay driver jumped out, pop-ping open the trunk. "This your lucky day, boss. I get you there super quick."

Gerard put his suitcase and briefcase into the trunk, got into the back seat of the gypsy taxi. "Aquino International Airport. If you make it really super quick I give you five dol-lars extra."

The driver slammed Gerard's door shut and got into the front seat. He smiled at Gerard in the rearview mirror. A thin man with an Uzi rose from his hiding place beneath a blanket on the front floor and pointed the weapon at Gerard.

"And if you are super quick, *I* will win five dollars."

Metro Manila Morgue—9 a.m. Saturday

Doctor Chin noticed that Garcia gagged on his first lungful of morgue air when he and Saddul stepped into the autopsy room. It was forty degrees cooler than the street, maintained at fifty-five degrees Fahrenheit to slow the decomposition of the bodies. It also helped suppress the smell. Somewhat.

The doctor had been busy with Chito's autopsy, and there were stains on his white lab coat. He inspected the policemen as he took Chito's liver from a scale, plopping it back into the body cavity. He stitched together the Y shaped incision, closing Chito's torso. The sutures were large loops of thin wire, spaced every two inches.

"What is so urgent, gentlemen? My preliminary report will be ready this evening." He arched an eyebrow at the corpse. "And he's not going anywhere."

Saddul rolled his eyes at Garcia, as if to say *Coroners and their humor.*

"You have a cause of death yet?" said Garcia.

Chin snorted in condescension. "What? You think someone stuffed his mouth after he was dead? No, he suffocated on the lahar. It was packed solid halfway down his esophagus." He smiled to himself. "Rather creative, that. I don't think I've ever heard of lahar used as the murder weapon." He eyed the detectives. "Is that all? You could have telephoned for that."

"Was there any evidence of torture?" said Saddul. "We're wondering if it ties to the death of that pedicab driver a few days ago."

"There was some trauma to the body, but I am not sure I would characterize it as torture. More like rough persuasion. Bruises to the face and body, consistent with blows from a fist. No punctures, burns, or broken bones. Nothing like that pedicab driver at all."

Garcia and Saddul exchanged a glance. From inside his suit coat Saddul pulled an envelope of eight-by-ten photos from the previous crime scenes.

The first showed the pedicab driver face down near the *baranggáy* entrance. Saddul pointed at the marks near the head of the body.

"These look like Chinese ideograms to us. Do you know what they say?"

Chin's face iced up, and he looked at Saddul with a calculating eye. "If they are Chinese characters, as you suppose, of course I can read them." He took the photo from Saddul and held it close, trying to make out the writing. "This is too indistinct. Is there a closer shot?"

"No. The photographer didn't notice it at the crime scene," said Garcia. "We caught it when we were reviewing the evidence files."

Saddul pulled out a second photo, this time of Chito's body, the ideograms clearly visible in the sand. "How about this one?"

Chin took the photos, glanced at the characters, shook his head. "Let's go to the copier." He led the way to a small office, placed the pedicab driver's death photo on the platen, and dialed in maximum zoom. He made a copy, wasn't happy, made another with increased contrast. He held the photocopy next to Chito's photo, sucking on his teeth as he concentrated.

"These seem to be the same message," said Chin, "but it makes no sense, and the calligraphy is quite stylized."

"So what does it say?" said Saddul.

"Work confers freedom. Or maybe work is freedom." He looked bemused. "What can it mean in this context?"

Saddul pulled out the final photo, the ideogram from inside the cargo container. "Makes more sense in a cargo container full of illegal immigrants."

Chin looked at the two detectives. "What's the connection? Three different locations. Three differing causes of death. It is not probable that either of the other two decedents would have known the illegals."

The euphemism for "Chinese immigrants" hung in the air. Garcia and Saddul stonewalled him.

"May we have the preliminary death certificate?" said Garcia.

Chin pulled a paper from the out-box on his desk. "I used his birth data from the Luzon database to fill in next of kin. I don't believe he was married, so all we have is mother and father."

Saddul looked at the death certificate, did a double take. He pointed out a box to Garcia. Saddul looked back to Chin. "You sure this is accurate?"

Chin was not used to having his work questioned at any level, and certainly not by a mere Filipino cop. "I made no mistake in copying the information. But *your* people—" (and now the "your" meant indigenous Filipino, not NBI) "—entered the data. Maybe garbage in, garbage out."

Saddul did a slow burn at the ethnic insult. "The next of kin is here to accompany the body to the mortuary. You might want to bag the deceased before she comes back here to make the positive ID."

"*Our* people get angry if the body of their loved one is disrespected," said Garcia. He jerked the certificate from Chin's hand. "Detective Lorenzano is out front with the—" Garcia searched for the right word. "The family member. He needs to see this."

US Embassy Gates—9 a.m. Saturday

The Marines kept Sam and his taxi driver standing by the gate to the US Embassy while one of them ran a computer check of Sam's ATFE identification. Two more Marines conducted a sophisticated search of the taxicab. Lipstick-sized video cameras mounted on flexible booms were used to search the car's undercarriage.

A second boom had an electronic sniffer that sought traces of explosive but was able to reject the odors of gasoline, oil, and exhaust. The process took about five minutes and provided the cab driver with great entertainment, while Sam stood in the heat, wondering what was behind the summons to the Embassy.

"Have the driver drop you at the entrance to the Embassy, about two hundred yards up the driveway," said the impeccably uniformed corporal. He looked to be no more than twenty. "You will be met by staff and taken to your meeting, sir."

"Should I have the cab wait?"

"That's not possible, sir. No vehicles may be left standing inside the compound. When you are finished with your meeting, staff will arrange another cab for you."

M r. Ward, the second assistant to the Ambassador, closed the door behind Sam and gestured toward a chair. "My secretary can bring you a soft drink or some bottled water if you wish, Mr. Haine." Ward had a pronounced Harvard accent, and Sam saw that he was wearing a suit, shoes, and tailored silk shirt that must have cost a month's salary. It made him wonder how a second assistant could afford such things.

"Nothing. I'm fine." Sam took a seat in the expensive leather armchair and waited.

The assistant smiled at Sam and opened a folder on his desk. He glanced through several papers before looking at Sam and clearing his throat.

"I want you to know, Mr. Haine, that the Ambassador has been aware of your cooperation with the Philippine National Bureau of Investigation. He asked me to convey his thanks for the good work you have done so far. The reports he received from Captain Velasquez and Detective Lorenzano were quite positive."

He paused to give Sam a smile of approval, which made Sam wonder if such reports were a regular thing.

"You wouldn't believe some of the jerks we get coming over to work with the Filipinos, treating them like our 'little brown brothers'," said Ward. "You have made a favorable impression, and we appreciate it." He waited, beaming.

Sam saw that some response was expected. "Thanks."

"May I speak frankly?" The assistant arranged his face into an expression of worry, tinged with regret.

It was quite a performance, and Sam speculated as to whether they had classes in this kind of thing at Ivy League colleges, maybe secret symposia only offered to people with a future in diplomacy. He wondered whether Ward actually knew something that might be of use.

"I'm a big fan of speaking frankly," said Sam. "What shall we be frank about?"

Ward looked at him askance. "You must understand that I'm just putting two and two together here. No one has given us explicit information. Of necessity, we are not apprised of all activities performed here in the Philippine Republic by various branches of our government. In diplomatic circles that allows us to plausibly deny prior knowledge of certain events."

Sam came upright in the soft leather chair. "Does this mean you are shutting down my investigation? Is that what this is about? On whose orders?"

Ward was calm and reassuring. "Of course not. We are all in this together. We all want to stem the flow of illegal weapons to hate groups in the US." He looked into his folder again and seemed to find the answer he sought. "However, this is a time of extraordinary budgetary constraints. We have a communiqué from the Washington HQ of ATFE that you are funded for just one week of investigation, rather than the original two weeks specified on your visa." The assistant pulled a document from the folder and passed it across to Sam.

Sam skimmed through it once, read it a second time more carefully. He looked at the bureaucrat appraisingly.

"I've never seen a memo like this before. My instructions always come directly from the Los Angeles office. It makes me wonder who in Washington wanted ATFE to back off. Actually, it makes me wonder who has the power to do this. Any ideas, Mr. Ward?"

Ward waited before he replied. "You understand that I am not speaking ex officio? And that no one has told me what to say to you? I am just brainstorming here."

"I get it. You're off the official hook. I never heard this, et cetera, et cetera, and so forth."

"We are officially unaware of any CIA clandestine operations within the borders of one of our staunchest allies in the fight against terror." Ward steepled his fingers together and put on a well-practiced look of wisdom. "But remembering Iran-Contra and the Guatemalans leads me to believe that perhaps the arms shipment you are seeking has been redirected to insurgent groups in the Philippines."

That got Sam's attention. "Are you joking? We don't have a better ally in Southeast Asia. Why would we work against them?"

"You misunderstand. We would be doing this—if indeed we are—to insure the stability of the current government. You see, the various Muslim separatist movements have links to Al Qaeda. Osama bin Laden has a wife and family here. At this point the Muslims might be strong enough to establish an independent clerical state—if they had arms." Ward waited to see if Sam had any response. "You may not remember that when the US withdrew our forces from the RP in '91, the Filipinos changed their constitution to prevent any foreign troops from fighting on their soil."

"I didn't know that, but so what?"

"It's sort of like Iran and Iraq. We give aid to one group of rebels for a while. When they get to be too popular, we infiltrate and promulgate violence to discredit them in the eyes of the general population. Next we fund a second rebel group and let the two insurgent factions fight for dominance, meanwhile killing each other off." He sat back and smiled. "At least that's my uninformed theory."

Sam leaned back in his chair, thinking it over. "And if the insurgents kidnap enough foreigners and cause sufficient trouble, the Filipinos might just invite us back to help clean up the mess. Maybe un-amend the constitution."

"Did you ever read Sherlock Holmes?" said Ward. "He spoke of the 'great game' being played between Russia and England over who would control Afghanistan and dominate Central Asia." He paused significantly. "The games go on, Mr. Haine."

Sam handed the Washington memo back to Ward. "I'll need to confirm this with my LA office."

Ward shrugged as if to say *Do what you must.* "Your funding expires in two days. We have assisted in booking your return flight to Los Angeles." He handed Sam an itinerary with an electronic ticket confirmation number.

Sam gave him a look. Ward gave it back.

"You understand that my analysis of this situation is a guess," said Ward. "I could be wrong."

"And I suppose you could plausibly deny that this conversation ever took place," said Sam.

Ward smiled.

thirty-one--

Bogie came and sat next to Olivia as she sobbed. He put an arm around her, and she buried her face in his shoulder, tears soaking into his jacket.

"Livvie, I'm so sorry."

She tried to reply, but was unable to articulate, so Bogie held her until the shaking stopped. He took tissues from his pocket and let her wipe her eyes and blow her nose.

Bogie sat by her side as Olivia wept, for a long time. Finally, he turned to face her.

"We'll find whoever did this."

She nodded, eyes downcast.

"You are going to need this certificate of death to have his body taken to the mortuary," said Bogie.

She gave him a blank look.

"It's just some paperwork. I'll help you with it."

She still seemed lost.

"Have you called for a funeral home to pick up your brother?"

She nodded yes.

"Can I help you with any of the arrangements?"

"No, I'll do it myself."

Bogie now faced the part he didn't want to pursue. "I read the preliminary death certificate. The mortuary has to receive an official copy before they can take care of Chito." He placed the ornate, engraved document in her hand, and pointed at one of the boxes. "I don't understand why you are listed as his mother."

Olivia stared at the document. Her voice almost inaudible, she replied, "Because he is my son."

"You always called him your brother, Livvie."

"That's how Daddy raised us. If Mama hadn't died when I was little, things might have been different."

Bogie went over it in his head, fitting it together. "You were twelve when he was born?" She inclined her head minutely. "Didn't your father, your uncles go after whoever—"

"No."

Bogie waited for her to go on, but Olivia became still, withdrawing to someplace cold. "Tell me," he said.

"I was nine when Mama died. And I had to become the new mama, because Daddy still wanted a son." She glanced sidelong at Bogie, gauging his understanding. "I didn't want to, but he beat me if I wouldn't come to bed." She stopped talking for a while, lost in the past. "I learned. I found ways to get through it. If I focused on the pain of the beating, I could put away what he did after. During the day I went to school, and the nights disappeared." She smiled involuntarily. "And when Chito was born, I got to be happy again. To watch him at my breast, smiling up at me. Even Daddy was happy. Now he had a son, now he was a man."

Bogie didn't trust himself to look at Olivia. He put his hand to his face as if shielding his eyes from the sun. "You must have other brothers, sisters."

"I was a tiny girl. The birth damaged me. There were no other children, though Daddy still wanted more." Olivia paused for a ragged breath. "Or maybe he just liked beating me into his bed. I'll never know for sure."

Bogie knew there was more, so he just waited.

"When Chito was eight, strong enough to help me, we killed Daddy." Again she smiled without knowing it. She turned to look into Bogie's eyes. "It took him a long time to die. And then we put all the food in the house into Chito's school backpack, and we took the bus to Manila because no one knew us here, and it would be easy to find a job in the big city." She looked at Bogie, her eyes glazed with anguish. "Oh yeah, easy."

"Livvie." Bogie didn't know what else there was to say.

"And now both halves of my secret are gone." Olivia clutched his arm. "I'm free of the past."

Bogie looked at her, trying to imagine the hurt and betrayal that had shaped her life. She had just confessed to a murder almost twenty years old. He had a sworn duty to uphold, but as he turned that possibility over in his mind, he couldn't see himself taking Olivia into custody.

"I am free, but someone is going to have to pay for Chito's death," said Olivia.

Bogie wrestled with the information she had given him. He saw Olivia measuring his reaction, worrying about how he would use what he had just heard.

She attempted a disarming smile.

"Or maybe everything I just said was only a story told by a grief-crazed mother." Every word seemed to come from some frozen part of her soul.

"Leave it to us, Livvie."

But Bogie didn't think she would.

LAND REFORM PARTY OFFICES—10 A.M. SATURDAY

It had taken all the leverage Sonny Lagos could muster to get the Santos brothers to meet with him. He placed the stack of photos on the table. The other two men eyed them without touching them. He pointed to a photo of Jennifer and Sam walking out of Club Peanut arm in arm.

"Your sister is recognizable in this one, Senator Santos. I don't think you can afford to have these pictures in the tabloids. Not during your re-election campaign."

Sonny knew that he was walking close to the edge here. If he angered Jennifer's brothers too much, he would create powerful enemies, so he needed to redirect their anger toward her.

Jennifer's oldest brother was a handsome man in his late forties. His party was grooming him for the presidency, though such things were never certain. Still, he had the looks, the voice, the charisma, and he might pull it off. The senator picked up the photo and dismissed it as he handed it to his brother, the governor.

"I don't see your point, Mr. Lagos. My sister is accompanying an American policeman to a club. So what?"

Sonny offered a second photo, this time to the governor. It showed Jennifer leaning in to speak intimately with Sam, her hand resting possessively on his arm.

"Governor Santos, you don't want these to embarrass your family, cause your parents emotional distress, do you?" said Sonny.

The governor was three years junior to the senator and even more handsome. He was the most capable politician of the family, but he would have to wait his turn for the presidency.

"Our parents are used to it by now. They should never have sent her to Harvard. She picked up a taste for white boys that has brought us nothing but shame. It was one thing when she dated them in the States, but now—here—. Still, my parents will get over it."

Sonny's pulse rate climbed. It was time to play for big stakes. He pulled out a third photo and placed it between the two brothers. In this picture Jennifer lay on her side, nude, Sam's naked body stretched out beside her. Unlike the first two photos, this was one grainy and had what looked like scan lines across it. Sonny had placed post-it notes over her nipples and pubes.

"For modesty's sake," said Sonny.

The two brothers looked sternly at the photo, not trusting themselves to speak. It was obvious that Sonny would tell them soon enough what he wanted.

"I am sorry for the quality of this last picture. It was taken through a screened window. More than sixty exposures. Some of them are quite touching." Sonny pulled the photo back to the pile and buried it in the stack. "It wouldn't take much effort to put them on the Internet."

"How did you come by these?" asked the governor.

Sonny shrugged. "We are political men, men of the world. Trusted helpers are easy to find—or buy."

"I didn't take you for a blackmailer, Sonny," said Senator Santos.

"You mistake my intentions, Senator. This is not about money. I am trying to do you a favor, help keep your campaign from foundering on the reefs of scandal."

Sonny watched as the governor calculated the chances of having him killed and all the photos destroyed without sacrificing his own career. He knew that the governor would come to the conclusion that the odds were not in his favor.

"What is it you want?"

"If I help your campaign, I expect reciprocity," said Sonny. "Each of you will come out in support of my candidacy for the national legislature, with myself as leader of my new party." He paused, letting them get used to the idea. "The Land Reform Party. You might even pick up some votes from my supporters. It could be a synergistic effect, sweeping us all to victory."

The senator had always been a hothead, and his face went pale with fury. He surged to his feet, grabbed the photos, folded them in half, and stuffed them inside his jacket breast pocket. He nodded peremptorily to his brother. "Come on."

Sonny stood, as if he were no more than a polite host, about to see his guests out the door. "You're welcome to the pictures. The originals are in safe hands."

The governor came to his feet, spoke calmly. "We'll be getting back to you, Mr. Lagos. Tomorrow morning at the latest." He touched his brother's arm, and the two men left, the senator slamming the door behind them.

His legs weak, Sonny sat down and let out a nervous breath. Things were in motion.

Terrorist Attacks on Americans: A survey of pre-September 11, 2001, attacks

Planned Explosion of Pacific Airliners—A bomb exploded accidentally in a Manila apartment in January 1995, leading police to discover a major terrorist plot. Associates of Osama bin Laden had planned to blow up 12 planes as they flew from Southeast Asia to the U.S., crash another aircraft into CIA headquarters, and also to kill the Pope while he visited in Manila.

Ramzi Yousef was later arrested in Pakistan and received a life sentence plus 240 years for his role in the plot and for his complicity in the 1993 bombing at the World Trade Center.

US EMBASSY GATES — NOON SATURDAY

Saddul was driving the Mercedes van when the detectives pulled up to the US Embassy gate. Saddul had placed an unopened box of tissues on the dash, which drew hard looks from the Marines on duty.

Bogie got out of the passenger seat, went over, flashed his badge at them, and told them he had received a page from Sam Haine. He told the Marine sergeant that Mr. Haine was just leaving a meeting with Assistant to the Ambassador Ward.

The Marine showed no more emotional response than an automaton, merely looked at the badge and telephoned over to the Embassy. A couple of minutes later Sam came walking down the lengthy drive. He pulled open the van door and climbed into the rear seat of the air-conditioned interior. Saddul threw the van into gear, and they chugged away.

Sam looked around, puzzled. "I didn't expect a party."

Saddul looked in the mirror at Sam. "We're headed for Subic. One of those slips in Tucker's safe deposit box didn't make sense. We think it refers to a cargo container ship, the Bulacan, due to dock tomorrow at Subic."

"That's near where Chito was killed," added Bogie. "Chito had Tucker's picture in his pocket. It all has to be connected somehow. Maybe with four of us looking, we'll get some answers quicker."

Sam settled against the seat cushion. "Let me lay out what we have, make sure we're all on the same page. We're headed for Subic Bay because there's a freighter named Bulacan due to dock there soon. Bulacan was a name on one of the slips in Harvey Tucker's lock box, the one name that didn't correspond to the name of a cockfighting arena. So you figure that maybe the number on the slip is not an amount of money for birds, but the cargo ID for a container full of weapons, right?"

Garcia thought about it. "That about sums it up."

"If all that's true, you'd think ATF would be really happy about the progress of the case, wouldn't you? Instead, I'm being taken off the investigation as of tomorrow," said Sam. "That's why the Embassy called me in. Making sure I'm on the plane tomorrow."

The Filipinos exchanged glances. "Something's not right," said Saddul, pulling his nose out of a soggy tissue.

"Let me go on," said Sam. "Subic is close to the spot where we think Chito was murdered. But we don't know why Chito would have been in Subic in the first place. And when we found his body in Manila Bay, there was a message in Chinese scratched in the dirt, which we know wasn't put there by the deceased, since he died about a hundred kilometers away. So who wrote the message, for whom was it intended, and why was it in Chinese?"

Saddul broke in. "Maybe this means we have a Chinese tong working Manila. It's the same message found by the pedi-cab driver's body and inside the container of dead Chinese illegals."

"But why the pedicab driver?" said Bogie.

"I think he's collateral damage. He just happened to be transporting me when I spotted Chito on the street," said Sam. "Don't forget, Juan Samoa—Chito's compatriot at Club de Sex—was there on the street when I got mugged."

"I'll check with the organized crime task force," said Saddul. "Maybe they can shed some light on this."

They were all silent as the jungle greenery slid by. "In every investigation there are clues that just don't go anywhere," said Bogie. "The case wraps up, and there are still loose ends. Maybe this is one of those."

"We also know that a local politician, Sonny Lagos, asked the fiscal to end the investigation of Tucker's death," said Sam. "But I don't think Lagos cares about Tucker. He just wants to reduce scrutiny of the weapons Tucker was buying."

"That's a big jump, Sam," said Bogie. "Even if it's true, how would that connect to the rivalry between Lagos and the fiscal's family? Or is that something separate?"

"To an outsider—me—it looks as if that particular family rivalry has gone on for a hundred years and will keep going a hundred more," said Sam. "If it's connected at all, I see it as tangential to our investigation."

Saddul stirred in his seat. "Aren't we overlooking something? What about Sonja? How many times has a sister come looking to solve the murder of her brother?" he said. "Especially from eight thousand miles away. And why was she so interested in those slips in his box, but didn't bother writing anything down?"

"Because she's smarter than that," said Bogie. "She recognized the name Bulacan and noted the date. She'll figure she can talk her way around not knowing the ID number. Or maybe she has some other way to verify her claim to the goods." Bogie was silent for a beat. "In fact, I think she stayed behind with me while Harvey's room was being searched just to throw me off, convince me that the slips weren't that important."

"You're giving her too much credit," said Saddul.

"I don't think so. She tricked me with those Japanese businessmen. She got Sam riled up on our ride across town. She has played each of us for a fool at some time or other and laughed out loud about it," said Bogie. "To our faces."

Garcia looked like a man with news, but he hadn't said anything. Instead he was giving Sam the stink-eye.

Sam caught his look and clapped Garcia on the shoulder. "You look like a man who got lucky last night. Redhead about my height?"

Garcia glared at Sam. Saddul looked over his shoulder from driver's seat. "What's this about a redhead? You got a new beau, Garcia?"

Bogie turned around in the front passenger seat, looking with suspicion at Sam. "What did you do, Agent Haine?"

Sam hung his head in mock shame.

Saddul looked over, and said, "You guys been keeping me out of the loop? What's going on? Garcia?"

"I didn't know who it was," said Garcia. "This guy came in. Totally butch, wearing a leather motorcycle hat. Had a mustache, for godsake. And a rocket in his pants the size of an anaconda." He squirmed in his seat, unsettled by some memory. "He even called it his pocket snake. Said it needed its fangs milked."

Saddul found this amusing and sang a line from Garcia's favorite Fred Astaire musical. "Heaven. I'm in heaven. And my heart beats so that I can hardly speak."

"Well, I'll tell you I could hardly speak when I saw the boobs," said Garcia. "I felt like I had been transported to another world. And that was the biggest strap-on I've ever seen."

Bogie had been drinking a soda, and he now shot most of it through his nose, spraying the windshield and Saddul in about equal measure.

"The damn thing had a motor in it."

Sam was now laughing hard but managed to ask, "Sonja was wearing a device?"

"It writhed around like a demented python," said Garcia. "When she pulled off my panties and saw my package she let out a bellowing laugh that about broke my eardrum. She said wasn't that a fucking joke on both of us, and that fucking Sam had a certain fucking sense of humor."

Sam had tears leaking from his eyes. "Hey, come on, Garcia. No hard feelings. Remember how you did me? In the beginning I didn't know you were Cher."

"All's well that ends well," said Bogie, with mock solemnity.

"The bastard stayed the night," said Garcia in icy tones. "I may have suffered permanent damage."

thirty-two--

Nosaka knelt before his family shrine and contemplated the seventy-year-old photograph of his brother. How handsome he looked in his uniform, how correct. How implacable his countenance. The sword held at just the proper angle, poised to take off the head of some Nanking student.

Those were the glory days, when Nippon held dominion over the Chinese half-people, the upstart Korean garlic eaters, the Filipino savages. He tried to look into older brother's eyes in the photo, but they were fixed on the neck of the Chinese prisoner, the path his blade would soon follow.

Oh, Masayoshi, you were fortunate to be spared the experience of defeat by the barbarians.

Why Japan had allied themselves with the barbarian Nazis was beyond reason. The Germans had no true culture to speak of, no history, a crude and unmusical language not suited for poetry.

He chuckled to himself. Still, even in their clumsy language, the motto over the concentration camp entries was almost a koan. Work makes you free. He knew he always got more effort and less resistance when he used it with his Chinese "imports."

He often wondered how China—a country that had been civilized five thousand years ago, that had invented writing when the brutes in Europe were barely out of the caves—how it could have devolved to its present state. Surely, it must be their decadence, turning their faces from the ancestors, affronting the gods by calling their kingdom "celestial."

Still, the mighty Egyptian empire had crumbled after a mere two thousand years, so perhaps he should not be too hard on the Chinese. He turned slightly to regard the picture of his father, in full dress uniform, taken just before he went to fight in World War I. His father had later helped pacify Manchuria, where he earned a reputation as a stern enforcer of the edicts Japan had given the natives.

Finally he made his obeisance to the image of Emperor Akihito, descendant of the sun goddess Amaterasu. Nosaka prayed that the Emperor's vision of "the achievement of complete peace on earth and in the heavens" would come soon. He knew the Emperor could not explain such things openly, but all loyal subjects of the divine one understood this phrase to be code for the Japanese assumption of the reins of world governance.

He closed the doors to the shrine and pulled out his survey map of Luzon Island. He had highlighted his realty holdings, and they were filling in nicely. If he could get hold of the Fitzler research, companies in India would pay him millions in royalties and stock options.

But meanwhile he still needed to maintain his income stream by selling the Chinese weapons and Chinese workers. Diverting the guns from the American buyer to the Filipino politician had placed a large obligation on Lagos.

Nosaka speculated that perhaps the obligation was so large that Lagos would try to have him killed. *No. He still needs my services. I am reliable and safe. He could never trust the Army to supply him. And yet—*

He called Tomo to pick him up in the car.

From Subic to Olongapo—Noon Saturday

Mike met Sonja at Subic Airport. She had come in on the shuttle from Manila, but she was still flying, revved up on something. She wouldn't leave the airport until she had a chance to pee, and after that she needed a beer to relax. After twenty minutes, Mike got her into his personnel carrier.

Driving within the old Subic Navy Base grounds was like driving any place in the US. American traffic standards prevailed: no reckless speeding, no driving on the wrong side of the road, no zipping through stop signs. They had to stop at the manned guard post before they passed through the old perimeter fence.

Within thirty meters of leaving the former US post, standard Philippine road rules applied: constant horns, screeching brakes, erratic lane changes, occasional excursions onto the sidewalk. Sonja rose to the challenge, loving the adrenaline rush of tag team driving, jerking the wheel from Mike's hand now and again to avoid vehicular mayhem. Mike tried to stay calm, toking from a doobie that would have done Winston Churchill proud.

Through it all, Sonja kept up a speed-freak's machine gun chatter, telling Mike about her adventures with some little Flip trannie, recounting the unexpurgated version of her twenty years as a BAM—"That's a broad ass Marine, ya know," she said, giving him a hearty buffet between the shoulder blades and braying a laugh—and generally letting him have a fore-taste of hell.

Mike began to rethink whether he wanted the American forces to return to the RP after all.

They struggled through the midday traffic in Olongapo for half an hour, alternately cursing at other drivers and cringing at near-misses with cargo-laden trucks. After a final dash down the sidewalk, Mike parked the hum-vee next to The American Bar.

With the engine shut off, Sonja began to come down from her crystal high. She reached over and snaked Mike's joint, taking a drag so deep that the tip flared into flame for a few seconds. She held it for a good thirty seconds before exhaling a cloud that filled the interior of the vehicle. Mike could only watch in awe. Sonja took a few cleansing breaths, gave Mike a peculiar look, and opened her door.

Mike led Sonja through the outer bar, back to the meeting

room curtained off at the rear. Mike caught a nod from Nosaka and backed out of the room. He breathed a sigh of relief and went to the bar where he could relieve some of his tension by badgering one of the B-girls.

It was hot enough in the bar so that no one noticed American Mike had added a dark sweat ring to the armpits of his Hawaiian shirt. Mr. Nosaka's presence always made him uneasy, since one never knew when things would turn violent.

He shuddered at the memory of holding down Chito while Nosaka force-fed him a kilo of lahar. He went behind the bar and poured himself a cold one.

Sonja waited at the curtained doorway until her eyes adjusted to the dim light in the room. The baize-covered table and the single bulb with a dealer's conical shade made the place look like an illegal poker room. Mr. Nosaka sat on the far side of the table sipping a Suntory as he looked at her over the rim of his glass.

Sonja saw Nosaka's muscle standing in the shadows against the wall. Looked to her like a Sumo wrestler who'd gone off his feed, weighed no more than two seventy-five now. She scanned for a tell-tale bulge in the bodyguard's coat, didn't spot one. It didn't look like Nosaka was carrying, either, at least not obviously. She smiled to herself, realizing Nosaka thought that fat fuck wrestler of his could take her.

Two friggin' Nips is all? No weapons? I've broken up domestic violence beefs tougher'n this. Yeah, all it's gonna take is a little finesse.

She strode over, pulled a chair up to the table, and leaned in to confront Nosaka.

"You're a hard man to find, Nosaka," said Sonja, dropping the Mister. "Especially since you already have my money, and that shipment of goods is due in tomorrow. I'd a thought it was good business to keep your customer informed and happy."

She took the empty glass on the table, and wagged her finger at Nosaka's bodyguard. "Pour me some of whatever he's drinking, waiter."

Nosaka froze. The bodyguard shifted his weight a tiny bit. Finally Nosaka spoke. "He's not a waiter. But I think you know that. You hoped to provoke him." He gave a tight smile and nodded. "Tomo has other duties."

"Hey, hired help is hired help."

"I don't understand."

"I'll jes bet you don't," smirked Sonja. "Lissen, I know how you Orientals like to do bizniss. But the polite chit chat part is over. Let's get to it, Nosaka. I need signed authorization to take delivery of the goods, in place of my brother."

"That will not be possible. When your brother became deceased—" Nosaka inclined his head about half a degree to show his respect for the dead. "I promised the shipment to another buyer."

"Harvey already had a agreement with you. I'm here to finish my brother's business, so nix that other deal."

"That will not be possible either, Miss Tucker. The new buyer has substantial political power here in the Philippines. His need is greater than yours." Nosaka paused to smile falsely. "And he paid more. So you see, we have no further business. Not now, not in the future."

Sonja swept her glass from the table, and it smashed against the wall. "Let me tell you the way I see it. We have some unfinished business. About three hundred grand worth."

The bodyguard moved away from the wall, but did nothing more.

"I will arrange for a wire transfer of the eighty thousand your brother paid to whatever account you wish, Miss Tucker."

"That's not good enough, jerkoff. I want my guns. They're worth a dam' sight more than eighty K to the militia back home." She half rose, pushing up from the table with one hand. "And I can snap your twiggy little neck before that glorified waiter can cross the room."

Sonja saw Tomo come off the wall. She snatched Nosaka's whisky glass and pegged it into the bodyguard's face. It hit with a satisfying thunk, opening up a nice gash in his forehead from which blood spurted.

Sonja planted on her right foot and launched a roundhouse kick at Tomo. She was surprised to find he was still alert enough to duck out of the way. It was her first hint that this might be harder than she anticipated. She thrust the table hard into Nosaka's chest, pushing him out of the action, and glanced left to see what Tomo was up to.

Which is why she missed seeing American Mike. With a bartender's instinct to head for the sound of breaking glassware, he had come in from behind Sonja, reached around with a Taser and plunged it between her breasts.

Sonja's body arched. She hit the ground kicking and thrashing, and her bladder let loose. Mike danced around trying to avoid being smacked by Sonja and slipped in the spreading puddle of urine. He came down on the base of his spine.

"I think her brother went down easier than that," said Mike, easing himself to a sitting position.

The bodyguard wiped blood out of his eyes and plunged forward, using his knees to pin Sonja's flailing arms to the ground. Tomo looked to Nosaka for instruction. "Shall I?"

Nosaka thought. "There would be a major inquiry if both a sister and a brother were murdered within a week of each other. My political friend would not like that. Mike, you must arrange for her heli transport to Aquino Airport."

Nosaka knelt down and emptied Sonja's purse. Her passport and air tickets were there. He handed them to Mike.

"Put these in an envelope. Tell the pilot that if she awakens, the envelope must not to be given to this woman. Tell him that he will be met at the airport. I'll call the congressman's office now. I'm sure he can arrange that she's on the next flight out of the country. Maybe not a flight home, but to someplace where her—" He paused to smile. "Her *epilepsy* can receive appropriate treatment. Perhaps Singapore."

MacArthur Highway—12:30 p.m. Saturday

After an hour on the road, the detectives stopped at a roadside stand to buy *meryenda*. This time it was a banana leaf bowl filled with rice and grilled chicken strips. Sam kicked at something that looked like a snowdrift made of cement. *So that's what lahar looks like in its native habitat.* He decided to spring for cold sodas for all of them, and they ate as they drove the winding mountain road.

The paved road confirmed which century they were in; otherwise, it felt like they had gone back to a time before the Spanish had arrived. Thatched *nipa* huts, no electricity, no phones, no running water. Sam could hardly believe they were only an hour's drive from Manila.

In a drainage ditch alongside the road an eight-month pregnant woman and her four pre-schoolers were doing the family laundry. A Nike tee shirt didn't quite cover her distended belly. Sam pointed out the pregnant woman to Saddul.

"When her labor begins, will she take a bus to one of those clinics like I saw in the *baranggáy*?"

Saddul shook his head. "Those clinics serve mostly prostitutes or unwed mothers. That would be shameful for her."

"Would a midwife help her deliver the child here?"

Saddul thought it over. "No, the local witch doctor would birth the baby."

"Witch doctor?"

Saddul and Bogie went into a rapid fire Tagalog discussion. Bogie turned to Sam. He seemed embarrassed. "We can't think of a better translation for it. Maybe shaman, medicine man, sorcerer combined."

Sam waited for more, realized it wasn't coming. "I did it again, didn't I?"

"What do you mean?" said Saddul.

"I've asked too much, made you lay out something you'd rather not discuss. I'm sorry. I don't do it on purpose," said Sam. "I'm a fish out of water here in the Philippines, and I don't know which topics to avoid."

"We know," said Bogie. "Deep down we can tell you're a caring kind of guy." He paused, searching for the right words. "That's why we're not offended by your barbarian ways."

The three Filipinos laughed, and Sam joined in. When they settled down, Sam looked over at Garcia.

"OK, Garcia," said Sam. "I can tell you don't like my theory about this case, so what do you think Sonja's involvement is?'

"I'm not sure." Garcia looked perplexed. "But I know she's already checked out of her hotel and hired a car to take her to Clarkton."

"That's about an hour from Subic," said Saddul. "Seems like all the players are headed to the same area."

"Maybe that means something, maybe not, but here's another piece of the puzzle," said Sam. "Juan Samoa approached me when I first arrived, told me he was with the CIA. So he might be the thread that passes through all this. At the Embassy this morning they hinted that perhaps the container of weapons was going to be diverted to one of the separatist groups. They implied that the CIA keeps the different groups picking each other off. They call it low-level conflict management. Never lets any faction get too powerful."

The Filipinos stirred. "I hate hearing that kind of shit," said Garcia. "Why can't you *kanos* let us run our own country?"

"Garcia, you're missing the point," said Saddul. "This changes things." Bogie nodded agreement, looking grim.

Sam said nothing. The three others rode in silence for a couple of minutes. Bogie touched Saddul's shoulder and pointed to a turnoff.

"Let's head for the Subic Free Port. If those arms came ashore, it's certain my father knows about it."

Saddul nodded, making the turn. "Think the military might be involved in this? I mean, we don't have the authorization—or the firepower—to mess with the army."

"That's the reason we need to know for sure who's out there."

thirty-three--

Juan burst into Olivia's office, looking bleak. Olivia put away some papers she was working on, locking them into her desk drawer. He made a mental note of it, but said nothing. He wanted her complete attention.

"Olivia, I found out where Nosaka is."

Olivia looked at him questioningly.

"I have friends who scan the radio frequencies, listening for things I might find of value."

"My, what useful friends," said Olivia

"You don't want to know anything more about them, believe me." Juan sat down across the desk from Olivia. "Nosaka just made an arrangement with Congressman Lagos to have a helicopter pick up someone in Olongapo."

"Olongapo. That's where Chito was going to meet American Mike, check out some new fish." Tears made Olivia's eyes shine. In a whisper she asked, "That's also close to the lahar. Do you think that's where Chito—?"

"I do."

"You sure Nosaka was behind it?"

"The helicopter was called to pick up Sonja Tucker. My friends told me she's Harv's sister." He paused to let that sink in. "And she's unconscious. Taser."

Olivia sat still. "Everything always leads back to him."

"I told you not to do business with him," said Juan. "At least now we can get some payback. Let's sell him to the Abu Sayef. They'll hold him for ransom—and split it with us."

Olivia's eyes shone with something new. "As long as we get some time with him before they pick him up." She went to her wall safe and withdrew something that she dropped into her purse without Juan being able to see what it was.

SUBIC INDUSTRIAL ZONE—2 P.M. SATURDAY

Sam looked on in wonder as they passed dozens of FedEx planes parked next to warehouses the size of Wal-Marts.

"What's this all about, Bogie?"

"The planes? This is the biggest FedEx hub for Asia," said Bogie. "What you're looking at is the largest duty-free port in the world. You can drop ship, warehouse, re-load, and trans-ship, all without duty or customs, as long as the goods aren't destined for the Philippines."

"No customs inspections? No duty? So once you get it inside here—"

"It's one reason this is the smuggling capital of the world. The other reasons are seven thousand islands, an unmeasured amount of shoreline, and four hundred years of tradition. Welcome to free enterprise—at its worst."

"Careful there, buddy. My granddaddy ran bootleg whisky for Joe Kennedy. Brought it down from Canada to Boston during Prohibition," said Sam. "I'm a big believer in free trade."

"And my father still moves an occasional load of cargo without benefit of tax stamps," said Saddul. "He says that's free enterprise—at its best." He scowled at Bogie.

"Like I said, four centuries of tradition," muttered Bogie to no one in particular.

Saddul wasn't going to let it go. "My dad says smuggling's in the eye of the beholder. So government ought to keep its eye shut and its nose out of a trader's business." Saddul looked ready to continue the discussion at any length Bogie desired. Bogie clamped his mouth shut.

Again Sam wondered what he was missing in the interchange. He tried to change the subject. "So—moving on. What does your father do, Bogie?"

Bogie didn't answer, and Saddul snorted as he turned the van's nose into an alley behind a row of light industrial buildings. The van stopped at the roll-up steel door of an shipping bay.

Through the open door Sam could see a collection of

armored personnel carriers in various stages of modification. Twenty men were at work with welding torches, sheet metal, and stacks of Kevlar armor. Sam looked up as a mid-size copter passed low overhead, heading east.

Bogie led them through the shop, explaining to Sam as they walked.

"That's a Bradley. They pull the US engine and replace it with a Jaguar, more horsepower, higher torque. They add a whole new layer of Kevlar armor. It'll stop small arms fire, rocket-propelled grenades, light machine gun rounds."

Bogie stopped and pointed inside one of the vehicles. Sam saw two rows of seats had been placed back to back down the center of the vehicle, snap-in gun mounts installed overhead. There were narrow gun slits that allowed the carrier to be a moving gunship with twenty automatic weapons firing in all directions.

The RP detectives and Sam got to the end of one assembly line. A dried up, sour-looking Filipino in his eighties came out of a small office near a second entry bay. He carried a clipboard that partially concealed a stun gun, but he put it back in his pocket as he walked over to Bogie.

"It's been six months."

"It's good to see you too, Dad," said Bogie, ignoring his father's accusatory tone. He nodded his head in Sam's direction. "You've met my co-workers before, but this is Agent Sam Haine. He's with US Homeland Security."

Sam wondered why Bogie didn't tell his father that he was with ATF. Bogie was wrestling with something, but Sam couldn't figure what. He tried to bridge the awkward pause that was stretching out. He stepped forward and offered his hand.

"It's a pleasure to meet you, Mr. Lorenzano." He glanced into the busy workshop and added, "Or is it Engineer Lorenzano?"

"Just call me Ray." Bogie's father gave a small smile. "I don't need the nonsense with the title." Ray now directed his attention to Sam, excluding Bogie. "I didn't know my boy had any *kano* friends."

Sam heard Bogie sigh. "We're working together on a case. An American murdered in Manila, a Harvey Tucker."

"Never heard of him, can't help you," said Ray. "Still, this makes a nice change. Most of the time when I see police, they are trying to shake me down." There was venom in his voice. "Makes me distrust all cops, you know?"

Saddul and Garcia maintained a safe distance, leaving Sam, Bogie, and Ray some space. "Bogie thought you might know about a cargo container we think is coming into Subic," said Sam. "Tucker was about to take delivery of weapons from China. AK-47s, RPGs, maybe something even bigger."

Something flashed behind Ray's eyes, but all he said was, "Sorry, I can't help you."

"Sam got new information this morning," said Bogie. "He thinks the arms are going to be diverted to a group inside the Philippines. Maybe the Muslims. Or maybe a private security force."

Ray glared at Bogie. "I customize the personnel carriers you see for 'private security' forces. My customers come from all over the world. It's a good business, and a legal one. Put you through college, Mr. Bigshot."

Sam watched Bogie bite his lip, the picture of a man torn between the desire to be respectful to his father and the need for information. Ray didn't let up, just kept the glare going.

"If there had been a business like mine before World War II, the invasion might not have been so easy for the Japanese."

"Let's not have this discussion now, Father," said Bogie.

Garcia apparently decided to see if he could shake things up. "Agent Haine told us the CIA is up to their tricks again. They always have their noses in our affairs—"

Ray swiveled his glare around to scorch Garcia for a while. "You should be damn glad they do."

"Last time I checked my history, we were a sovereign nation," said Garcia. "The US just never wants to let go of us. Sure, they kicked out the Spanish, but then they took us for their own colony."

"Is that how they revise history in public schools these

days?" said Ray. "You should thank God Teddy Roosevelt put the Navy base here. If the US had left us on our own after the Spanish-American War, we'd have been speaking Japanese since nineteen oh two."

The conversation ground to a halt. Sam could tell Bogie and Ray had been down this road before.

"Bogie said you know everything that touches Subic. We don't have much time. The drop is tomorrow, maybe a ship named Bulacan. And I'm being forced off the case as of midnight."

Ray shifted his impassive gaze from Sam to Bogie.

"There's enough weaponry for a small army," said Sam. "We think it might be going to a local politician."

Ray waved his hand in dismissal, but didn't turn away. Sam could see that something he had said had gotten through, so he waited. *Does Ray outfit private armies for local pols?* Still, Ray said nothing. *I wonder if that's what Bogie believes.*

Bogie broke the silence. "Sam has been here before, Dad. To a memorial service. His grandfather served in Subic."

"A lot of sailors did," said Ray. "You can see their abandoned bastards everywhere."

"His grandfather died in Bataan."

Ray looked at Sam, something new—distant and sad—in his eyes.

"You and I will have a drink. I want to hear what you know of your grandfather's story."

thirty-four--

The secretary looked frightened as she opened Jennifer's door. "Fiscal Santos, you have visitors."

Jennifer frowned. "No one is scheduled until–" She broke off as her brothers came into her office. She looked from one to the other, saw nothing good on their faces. "Has something happened to Father?"

Her brother Martin, the governor, looked pointedly at the secretary until she left the room, closing the door behind her. He and his brother Robert pulled up chairs to sit close to Jennifer's desk. Martin leaned forward, speaking low.

"Nothing's wrong with our parents, Jennifer," said Martin.

Her older brother, Robert, spoke with the grave voice he used to such effect when he spoke on the Senate floor. "Not yet, anyway. It depends how much longer you continue your—behavior."

Jennifer felt her face tighten as the anger toward her brothers built up. "I'll thank the two of you to stay out of my personal life." It came out harsher than she intended, and she modulated her voice to be low and confiding. "Or are we here to discuss your mistresses, Martin?"

"The pot calling the kettle black, little sister?" said Martin. "Oh, please."

Jennifer ignored him and rushed on. "Or perhaps your secret second family, Robert?"

Robert drew back as if he had been slapped. "My God, Jennifer. You are supposed to be a role model for decent Filipinas."

Jennifer overrode him. "Although it isn't much of a secret since you bought that house for them. In the same neighbor-

— 269 —

hood where our parents live." White anger spots stood out on Jennifer's cheeks. "You two and your double standards."

Martin pulled a folder from inside his coat and put it on the desk in front of Jennifer. "There are things in here you need to see. I know you are smart enough to do the right thing."

"You need to think about the family's reputation, and not just your own—" began Robert.

Martin took his brother's elbow, motioning him to silence. Robert restrained himself with some difficulty. Both men rose and left the room.

Jennifer threw the folder after them and the photos flew out, scattering across the carpet. It was five minutes before she calmed down enough to retrieve them. After looking at the first two, she wished she had left them lying there.

RAY LORENZANO'S OFFICE—3 P.M. SATURDAY

Sam, Bogie, and Ray sat around three sides of a small desk in Ray's office. It took them half an hour to finish a six-pack of Heinekens that Ray pulled from a small refrigerator in his office. Sam told his grandfather's war history as he knew it, while Ray listened attentively. Saddul and Garcia had long since gone to join the workers for late afternoon *meryenda*.

"You must have heard a lot of stories like this one, Mr. Lorenzano. Maybe we even crossed paths when my dad brought me to the survivors' reunion. I remember a lot of the Filipino veterans were there. They were very kind to my father and us children."

"I have never attended a veterans' reunion, Agent Haine. I chose not to think about those days, remember those things." Ray's voice became pinched. "I am sorry to hear about your grandfather. Sorry for the way he died," he said. "At least he left a son behind back home. My brothers were not so lucky." The words stuck in his throat, and he broke off.

Bogie looked up at this. "What brothers are you talking about? I don't have any uncles."

"All your uncles died before you were born. So did your aunt and your grandparents. Their deaths have been my shame for sixty years. I never spoke of it to you—or anyone else, Bogie. I couldn't tell you. It was my—" He paused to get his breath, steady his voice. "But hearing this story of Bataan—has brought it all back. I think now—maybe I need—no, I must tell this story," said Ray.

Sam saw Bogie's stunned reaction to the news that he had lost an entire family he knew nothing of.

"During the march to Bataan, the Japanese shot anyone who couldn't keep up, anyone who was wounded, anyone who passed out from the heat. The march was three days, part of it through the jungle. Anyone who tried to make a break for it into the bush was shot in the back.

"The Americans didn't try to run for it. They didn't know the jungle, how to live off it, how to find their way.

"As we'd pass through a village, sometimes the Japanese soldiers would rape the women, kill the children, shoot the old people." Ray paused. "We Filipinos who were forced into the march could see what was coming, and we tried to escape whenever there was a chance.

"It got so bad that the Japanese commander sent down an order: 'If someone escapes, find ten of his friends and shoot them in front of everybody.' It was meant to be a lesson, you see."

Ray halted, unable to speak. Tears squeezed from the corners of his eyes, and he pulled a tissue from his pocket and dabbed at them.

"I had just turned fifteen. I was a skinny kid, fast on my feet. I got away.

"I learned the next morning that they shot my three brothers and seven other men from my village." He stopped to wipe his face. "But I was free." He looked as if the words were going to choke him.

"Free to find our parents had already been killed, trying to stop the Japanese from raping my baby sister. She took her own life afterward. Free to hide in the jungle for three years, afraid to show my face." He averted his face, his mouth gaping as he tried to get a full breath. "No, not afraid. Ashamed."

Ray stared at the desktop, tears dropping onto the plastic surface. Sam risked a look at Bogie and saw that he had put his face in his hands, whether from sympathy or shame, he couldn't tell.

Sam spoke to Ray in a low voice. "War does terrible things to us all. But you survived the horror. You began a family. You have a son, and he's a good man."

"But only because–" Ray choked back a sob. "Only because MacArthur returned. It brought my heart back to life."

Bogie raised his face from his hands, his face a frozen mask. "Why did you never tell me this?"

Ray looked at his son. He opened his mouth to speak, but no words came out. He glanced away again.

Sam was afraid to look at either of the two men, fearing he might embarrass them into doing some irreparable harm to each other.

Ray stood up and took the bottles to the trash can, two at a time. "I see now that I should have. You deserved to know the truth about your father."

When Ray finished with the trash he turned to Bogie and Sam.

"The man who is usually behind such arms sales does his business at The American Bar in Olongapo. A Japanese named Nosaka."

thirty-five--

American Mike and Tomo had been gone almost an hour. Nosaka had known it would be no quick task getting the unconscious Sonja to the heli-pad, putting her aboard the chopper, paying the local tower personnel to keep their mouths shut. He had made Mike set him up with two of his B-girls to help pass the time.

Lucy and Pinky were a matched pair, into bondage and humiliation, and they had brought their own gear. Nosaka had Lucy tie Pinky up.

He and Lucy took turns flagellating her with a little whisk made of fishing line that he always carried with him. He had nicknamed it the Scorpion, and he knew from experience that it stung like the devil, bringing blood to the surface at the first blow.

Once Pinky's back was bleeding freely, Nosaka took a mouthful of rum. He swirled it round his mouth, letting the alcohol burn, feeling the fumes seep into his nose, making his eyes water. He sprayed the rum on her back.

As Pinky shrieked, Lucy turned on Nosaka angrily. "This isn't in the deal. The alcohol will make permanent scars—"

Nosaka struck Lucy square across the face with the quirt. "Do you wish to live?" Lucy cowered away from him. "I want you to stop her screams with a passionate kiss. And make me believe it. I don't like whores who merely pretend to feel something, when it is plain that they feel nothing."

The whites were showing around Lucy's irises as she clamped her lips over Pinky's gaping mouth. Nosaka peeled off his clothes as he circled the two women, until he was down to his Speedo underwear. The sweat oozed from his pores, running down his shoulders, making his torso slick.

"I'm not believing you, Lucy." Nosaka shook his head, mock regret on his face. "That doesn't look like a kiss at all. It looks like you're giving her mouth-to-mouth resuscitation."

Pinky was still shrieking, her eyes shut tight against the pain. Nosaka watched Lucy's frantic attempt to keep him in sight out of the corner of her eye, while still muffling Pinky's voice.

"Come on, Lucy. Bite her tongue! Get into it."

He stepped forward and flicked the Scorpion. Twenty more thin angry lines sprang up across Lucy's face. She gasped at the sensation, inhaling one of Pinky's screams. Nosaka's eyes glistened, and he swung the Scorpion, beating a tattoo across their faces and necks, his breath whistling between his teeth as he swung, harder and harder.

A gunshot silenced them all, freezing them in place. Olivia stepped into the pool of light cast by the dealer's lamp. She sucked in a harsh breath, something preternatural in her expression.

Juan Samoa stepped out from behind Olivia and tried to take the gun from her hand, but she sidestepped and pointed the weapon between Juan and Nosaka.

"This is my call, Juan! If I feel like killing this maggot right now—"

Juan backed off. "He's not worth anything to the Abu Sayef if he's dead."

Nosaka started at the mention of the terrorist group. At his motion, Olivia snapped the pistol back to aim at his head.

"Don't be stupid," Olivia said to Nosaka. "You will stay alive just as long as I'm happy." She appraised the two women. "You two, get out of here. This doesn't concern you."

While Lucy struggled with Pinky's bonds, Olivia thought things over and reconsidered. "On second thought, you can take his wallet." She paused again. "But even that doesn't make up for his behavior, so you can each take a swing at him as you go."

Before she could say anything more, Lucy launched an NFL fourth-down kick into Nosaka's crotch, knocking him to the ground. He curled up on the ground like a sautéed shrimp, eyes bulging, gasping for breath.

Pinky walked over and stomped Nosaka repeatedly on the face and neck until Juan pulled her away. His hand on her raw back started her screaming again, and Juan put his other hand over her mouth.

Olivia looked at the B-girls with speculation. "Why don't you two help tie Nosaka-san to the table?"

Juan wrestled Nosaka atop the green baize, while the women buckled restraints onto his wrists and ankles, jerked his arms over his head until he grunted in pain. Juan threaded a loop of rope through the restraints and spread-eagled Nosaka on the tabletop. Pinky popped a rubber ball into his mouth and fastened it in place with a Velcro band.

Olivia walked over to Nosaka. She grabbed a handful of his oily hair, jerked his face toward hers, and whispered, "Do you like sashimi?"

Nosaka's mouth worked, but only a muffled mumble made it through the gag. Olivia put her ear next to the gag and listened. She looked up at the others.

"He says he does. And I love sashimi, myself," said Olivia. "I'm going to make some, but you have to promise you'll share it with me."

Olivia put the pistol back in her purse. She pulled out a long-bladed chef's knife.

"You know what the best sashimi is, don't you?" said Olivia. She slid the gleaming blade from the ornate sheath that protected its scalpel-sharp edge. "Of course you do. Ikezukuri."

Juan looked at Olivia. "What's that?"

Olivia turned toward Juan, a smile stretched too tight across her face.

"You need to start going to better restaurants, Juan-boy," she said. "Ikezukuri means cutting down alive. They nail the living fish to the table top and cut off slices for the diner to eat—fresh, raw, still bleeding."

She whipped the knife down and shaved a slice from Nosaka's flank.

Nosaka tried to scream around the ball. Juan started forward. "Olivia—"

"Don't worry. Abu Sayef will still get their money's worth." She made a second cut. She looked over to Lucy and Pinky and offered each a translucent slice of flesh.

Lucy backed away into the darkness outside the cone of light, turned and ran through the door. Pinky walked up to the table, reached forward hesitantly, took the flesh in her hand, raised it to her mouth, looked like she was going to wolf it, but instead she vomited over Nosaka's torso. Still gagging, she turned and fled the room.

Olivia nodded to Juan, motioning him to stay back, as she sliced through the waistband of Nosaka's underwear. "He won't die, but he'll wish he were dead—yes, he will."

thirty-six--

Saddul parked the van out of sight two blocks away from The American Club. They split their forces for the incursion into the club. Saddul and Garcia walked a block north so they could secure the rear entry, while Bogie and Sam would take the front.

Sam and Bogie waited for three minutes to give the other pair enough time get in place. Sam checked his weapon, made sure the extra magazine was in his pocket. He nodded at Bogie, and they started for the club.

Sam and Bogie were still thirty yards from the building when Bogie pointed out two men nearing the entry from the opposite direction—the bodyguard Tomo and American Mike. "Look at the size of that guy."

They watched as Mike and Tomo hesitated near the entry to the club. Three seconds later two women bolted from the door. Lucy blew past Mike and Tomo. Pinky moved slower, holding her blouse to cover her chest, her back glistening red. Sam watched as Mike made a half-hearted attempt to catch her arm.

Juan Samoa came out of the club entry, spotting Mike and Tomo at once. He quickstepped over to Mike, swung a meaty arm, knocking him flat. He dropped into a wrestler's stance, his eyes on Tomo.

When Sam and Bogie recognized Juan, they broke into a run, but they were slower than Tomo, who rushed Juan and bulldozed him back through the door of the club. Sam got through the door right behind them and saw Tomo slam Juan into the bar.

Juan was bent backward over the mahogany slab, but he jerked his feet up, which flipped Tomo over the bar into the bottles and mirror. They went down together in a shower of glass.

Sam drew his pistol and followed them over the top of the bar. "Freeze!"

They didn't seem to hear him, locked as they were in a titanic bear hug, rolling over broken glass, kicking and bellowing. As Tomo spun on his side trying to break free from Juan, his leg swept Sam's feet out from under him.

Sam went down, hitting his head against the edge of the bar. He was stunned and slowly turned his head, hoping to stop the flashing lights from circling. He inched back from the thrashing men, trying to recover his wits.

B ogie got his piece out and was scanning the bar for other persons when a shot blammed from the room behind the curtain. He got behind the edge of the door, heard shots from the rear of the building. "Sounds like Saddul and Garcia are having trouble," he called to Sam. "I'll check it out."

He took a quick glance around the edge of the door and saw a naked man lying on a table, blood puddling from the gap in his crotch where his genitals used to be. He pulled back, took a deep breath, catching the scent of vomit.

He dashed through the doorway, gun ahead of him. He moved to each corner of the room, realized that whoever had been there had gone out through a dark passageway lined with cases of beer.

He turned back to check the pulse of the man on the table and saw the bullet hole in the center of his forehead. He looked closer and discovered that the man's missing genitals had been stuffed in his mouth. Up close he realized that he had met this man at Club de Sex, days before.

As Bogie straightened up, American Mike came flying through the curtained doorway and tackled him, knocking his gun out of his hand. Mike was bigger than the Filipino detective and manhandled him to the floor, scooting Bogie's body along the ground, trying to get hold of his gun.

Bogie got his forearm up and tried to slam Mike across the windpipe. He didn't connect solidly, which only served to enrage him further. Mike stopped his progress toward the gun and began pummeling Bogie.

Bogie took half a dozen blows to his head and chest, before Mike's head exploded in a burst of red and white, blood and skull fragments flying across the room. Mike's body flopped down onto him, thrashing in its final death spasms.

Saddul reached down and pulled Mike's body off Bogie. Garcia's eyes were round as he looked at the blood covering Bogie's neck and chest, his still-smoking gun hanging by his side.

"You OK?" said Garcia.

Bogie slid from under Mike's corpse and retched onto the floor. "S'not my blood. Help Sam." He pointed through the doorway, where Juan and Tomo could still be heard fighting. Saddul went through the doorway, gun drawn, while Garcia helped Bogie to his feet.

In the other room Sam was back on his feet, approaching Juan and Tomo as they wrestled on the floor. Saddul caught Sam's eye. Sam gestured and grabbed the back of Tomo's neck, trying to pull the men apart, so Saddul followed suit with Juan Samoa. The tactic seemed to have as little effect as fly swatters on angry bulls.

Sam took a step back and pointed his pistol into the air. "I said freeze!" The men on the floor continued to fight. "That's your last warning," and Sam fired his gun into the ceiling.

Tomo looked up, startled. Samoa used the opening to slam a ham-sized fist into Tomo's jaw.

thirty-seven--

The local police arrived about five minutes later, responding to a report of shots fired. Since these two murders occurred in their jurisdiction—and not Metro Manila's—the Olongapo detectives wanted control of the case.

There was prolonged wrangling between the different agencies. After an hour, Bogie's boss at NBI was reached by phone, and a three-way call between Bogie, the Olongapo homicide detective, and Captain Velasquez settled things.

"You *think* this Nosaka was Harvey Tucker's killer?" said Velasquez. "So how are you going to question him now? He's dead. Whoever killed him is a case for Olongapo."

"If we don't follow up here, we won't find out why Tucker was killed," said Bogie. "Or what happened to the—"

Velasquez cut him off. "Don't discuss that on an open phone line."

The Olongapo detective tried to get Bogie's eye, but Bogie avoided him. There was some noise from the NBI side of the call, and it sounded like Velasquez had covered the phone with his hand. After a few seconds, Velasquez came back on.

"I want you back here, Detective. Bring Saddul and Agent Haine with you. Garcia can stay there with the locals, answer questions about his shooting of American Mike. It sounds like a legitimate shoot to me, but that's their job. Garcia can bring back copies of Olongapo's preliminary crime scene reports tomorrow."

"Captain Velasquez, I think that would be a serious mistake—"

"That is an order, Detective Lorenzano. I'll want to see you first thing in the morning," said Velasquez.

"But tomorrow's the—" began Bogie.

Velasquez blew his top. "Yes. It's Sunday. And I'll have to lose my tee time. Don't make it any worse." And he slammed the receiver down, making both Bogie and the Olongapo detective wince.

S addul had given his statement, and gone out to find *meryenda*, saying he'd bring back plates for them. Bogie and Sam sat in a booth, waiting their turn with the Olongapo police, watching as Garcia walked the locals through his actions leading up to shooting American Mike.

Mike had been a popular guy with the local police, making regular contributions to their personal retirement plans, and they weren't happy about his death. They had made Garcia tell his story four times so far, and they seemed to want to hear it again.

Bogie called over to an officer. "Mind if we smoke outside?"

The officer nodded assent, and Bogie motioned Sam to follow him.

Once they were outside, Sam jumped in. "What's going on, Bogie?"

"What's it to you? You're leaving tomorrow."

"I was sent to stop a shipment of guns, try to find out who the supplier is, how they get through customs—"

Bogie cut in. "My guess is that whoever it was that had you recalled a week early is also having me pulled off the case. Someone with a lot of leverage." He paused to light a fresh cigarette. "You placed some calls to Congressman Lagos, didn't you?" Sam nodded, and Bogie pulled a small cell phone from his pocket. "You have the number with you?" They walked over near the crime scene tape, getting away from the patrolman keeping the crowd back.

Sam got out his pocket notebook. "You want me to call him?"

"I don't, but I palmed this phone when I went through Nosaka's pockets. Let's see who he called from here." He flicked open the phone, thumbed buttons as he went through the functions to find the call log. "Here are calls he made today, Sam. Recognize any of the numbers?"

Sam flipped through his pages, comparing numbers. He stopped and looked at Bogie. "Nosaka called that maternity clinic, the same one where I met Lagos." He turned another page. "And he called Lagos' party headquarters." He thought that over. "Time for the obnoxious Yank to phone Lagos?"

Bogie grimaced. "No. I have enough problems." He took a tissue from his pocket and wiped down the phone. "I'll leave it someplace inside, let the Olongapo investigators find it themselves later on."

It was after eleven by the time the local police finished with the crime scene.

Tomo's jaw was broken and, since he was also illiterate, he wouldn't be communicating with anyone for a while.

Juan Samoa was claiming diplomatic immunity, both on the grounds that he was working for the CIA, and also his pending American citizenship. The Olongapo detective in charge looked like he couldn't decide whether to beat the info he wanted out of Juan, or to call the US Embassy on Juan's behalf. He decided he'd try both.

American Mike wasn't going to talk now or ever again. When the locals found the Taser in Mike's pants pocket, a look passed between Sam and Bogie, but they said nothing about Harvey's death.

A patrolman who was doing crowd control made the surprising find of a cell phone that appeared to belong to the dead Japanese. He was all smiles, envisioning the letter of commendation he would receive for finding a crucial piece of evidence that the detectives had missed.

The local police found an open window in the ladies restroom. Whoever had put Nosaka to sleep had gone out that way at the same time Saddul and Garcia were shooting the rear entry lock off.

Since Lucy and Pinky had already left town, there was no one left to say that Olivia or Sonja had ever been there.

It was nearing midnight when Bogie, Saddul, and Sam began the weary drive back to Manila. Traffic crept along the highway, and Saddul pointed to a turnoff.

"I know a shortcut, guys."

"Don't even think of driving on lahar," said Bogie.

Sam slumped back in his seat, sweating. He pulled his cell phone out and dialed Jennifer's number. It was late, but he figured he had good news.

He never got the chance to deliver it. As soon as Jennifer picked up, she filled his ear with fifteen seconds of angry abuse about some revealing photos and hung up. He redialed several times, but there was no answer.

thirty-eight--

B ogie and Saddul dropped Sam at the hotel a few minutes before two a.m. He dragged himself through the entry into the air-conditioned lobby. The woman working night reception caught Sam's eye.

"Sir?" she said. "A FedEx came for you. From Van Nuys, California."

Feeling bone weary, Sam made his way to the counter. "Thanks." He held out his hand for the envelope.

The clerk held on to the envelope an extra moment, smiling at Sam. "It's a small world, sir. My sister and her family live in Van Nuys."

Sam just wanted to get to his room and collapse. Still, he knew the clerk was trying to be friendly. He searched for the right response. "You must miss her. Will you visit her soon?"

Almost at once he recognized that he had put the clerk on the spot. She probably couldn't afford tickets to America, couldn't afford the bribe to get her travel visa. Sam tried to smooth it over.

"Maybe she'll come to see you."

She nodded at Sam, and he made his way to the bank of elevators, opening the FedEx as he walked: airline tickets and a short letter. The note was terse, even for his boss. It told him NOT to miss the flight home, or he would be placed on unpaid leave. It listed the flight number and departure time. Sam groaned when he realized he had to be awake again in three hours in order to pack.

S am card-keyed the door to his room. He didn't bother to turn on the lights, using the tell-tale on his electric shaver to guide himself into the bathroom. He shucked off his pants and shirt, kicked off his shoes and socks, padded barefoot on the cool marble, across the Berber carpet of the sitting area. He flung himself face down on the bed and waited for the phosphors in his eyes to fade.

"You never mentioned a wife," said a voice from a pitch-black corner of the room.

Sam spun sideways, remembered his pistol was in the bathroom, and at last recognized the voice.

"Jennifer?"

"Were you expecting someone else?"

Sam sat up, pulled a pillow across his lap, and switched on the bedside lamp. Jennifer sat in a corner of the room, arms folded across her chest, a folder in one hand.

"I'm glad you're here, after that last phone call. I guess I shouldn't ask how you got into my room."

"A Fiscal's ID can open a lot of doors," said Jennifer.

Sam tried to clarify his thoughts. "You said you weren't going to see me again. In this life or the next, were your exact words."

She threw the folder across to Sam.

Sam opened the envelope. He pulled out a copy of his wedding license.

He felt the color drain from his face, a numbness spreading from his brain throughout his body. There was also a picture of Christy, scanned at low resolution. It looked like her DMV photo.

"Where did—?" His throat constricted. "Why did you do this?"

"My brothers presented those to me. Thought I ought to know more about you."

Sam stared at Christy's picture, the pain renewed and fresh again. He couldn't understand that although nearly three years had passed, just a glimpse of her photo, her smiling face, would bring back that sinking feeling, that pit in his stomach that came when the doctor said she was dead.

Even so, he felt it to be qualitatively different this time. Always before it had contained the emptiness that came from part of his life being gone, irretrievable. Now he recognized that he was losing that sense of imminent collapse into despair. It was what C. S. Lewis called the "second death," the loss of the horrifying sense of loss.

It had been no more than ten seconds, but Jennifer's patience was at an end. "I thought better of you."

Sam looked up from Christy's picture.

"Better than what?"

"My brother wondered if perhaps she would like to know about me." She rose to go. "I told him not to bother."

"I think she already knows." Sam smile was crooked. "My wife died of cancer two years and seven months ago."

Jennifer turned to look at him, the disbelief on her face crumbling. She knelt by the edge of the bed, her face in her hands, a hot blush spreading across her face.

"Oh, Sam. Sam. I'm sorry."

She wept, and the tears felt hot on his leg.

He closed his eyes, not wanting to see either Jennifer or Christy's photo. More than anything, he just wanted to fade away, to lose himself in the darkness. He heard Jennifer get to her feet and switch off the lamp. The door to his room opened, and many heartbeats later it closed.

Sam waited for the throbbing in his carotid artery to subside, lowered his head to the pillow, hoping sleep would come. He lay in the darkness listening to the blood rushing through his eardrums.

And then she slipped into bed beside him, her skin cool where her breasts pressed against his back.

She put an arm over him and rested her hand on his chest over his heart. She kissed the back of his neck, and held onto him as if he were a drowning victim about to slip from her grasp.

"There are no excuses," she murmured into his ear. "I'll offer no platitudes. I'm here."

For the first time in more than three years Sam slept, truly and deeply. And he dreamed.

In his dream he was at the bottom of a dark pool. The water was as thick as syrup, but strangely transparent.

He swam upward, upward, fighting the viscous pull of the past, until he broke though the black surface. He took a deep breath.

It was the future.

~ ~ ~

Provincial Coup Averted—

A cargo container of assault rifles, rocket-propelled grenades, satchel mines, explosives, and detonators was seized yesterday. The action was a joint operation between the RP National Bureau of Investigation and the United States Homeland Security Agency, division of Alcohol, Tobacco, Firearms, and Explosives.

Sources within the government say that the arms had been intended for terrorists within the United States, but rebels within the Philippines had killed Harvey Tucker, the American arms broker who was going to ship the weapons to the US. The armaments were intended for use against the local government in the provinces, in an attempt to establish a second autonomous Muslim region.

Fiscal Jennifer Santos says that the parties responsible for the sale will be found and prosecuted to the fullest extent of the law. US Assistant Ambassador Ward has praised the Philippine government for the joint effort that interdicted "this trafficking in terror."

THE END

Bruce Cook worked in Manila where he researched the material for Philippine Fever. He also has credits on 11 independent features as writer, producer, or director. Currently he teaches Cinema students in Hollywood how to pitch their films. With degrees in Physics, Mathematics, and Communications, Dr. Cook was a laser physicist on the Apollo Project.

He and his wife live in Castaic, California with just enough pets to keep things interesting.

You can reach Bruce through his website at:
www.brucecookonline.com